TALES TIMES TEN

Eligah Boykin

ARPress
45 Dan Road Suite 36
Canton MA 02021

Hotline: 1(800) 220-7660
Fax: 1(855) 752-6001

Ordering Information:
Quantity Sales. Special discounts are available on quantity purchases by corporations, associations, and others. For details, contact the publisher at the address above.

Printed in the United States of America.

ISBN-13   Paperback   979-8-89389-576-6
                         eBook   979-8-89389-577-3

Library of Congress Control Number: 2024920615

CONTENTS

Dedication v

Mister Magic 1
Twinkling Of An Eye 19
The Doctor Clark Files 41
Holy Crossword Dorothy 59
Tactile Understanding 71
Techtown Book Club 89
Land Of A Thousand Cries 125
Sex Education 141
Solving For 'X' 193
Spiritual Signature..237

Dedication

This present volume is the culmination of nearly fifty years of telling my stories to anyone who would listen and laugh and find a thrill in what I was putting down. The stories are varied and are crafted and designed to have an appeal to every taste.

There should be something here to tickle your fancy. Feel free to let me know which ones you liked the most, which ones puzzled you, and which ones left you wanting more. My sole intention is for you to have a good time in the world of my imagination.

At this time, I would like to thank all my English and Creative Writing Instructors for giving me the opportunity and the outlet to express myself as a storyteller and a writer. This has proven to be a more viable endeavor than throwing rocks at Miss King's window with the rest of my ball-playing pals in the parking lot of Hutchinson Elementary during Summer Vacation.

Naturally, I hope to go more in this direction far into the future.

I would also like to thank my High School girl friend Mary Riley for being kind enough to read what short stories I showed her. She gave me much sensitive encouragement and was a better companion to me than I proved to deserve. I also would like to thank Gail Smidthz for taking the time to read my first Science

Fiction short story when I began to venture into that genre while working at Social Services. Finally, I would also like to thank Robert Gover, author of the 'One Hundred Dollar Misunderstanding' for patiently going over sections of both the Chapters of my novels and my short stories in order to help me better improve my sense of craft.

These stories represent the transcendence and overcoming of much rejection, humiliation, degradation and even self-abasement. Much more than I ever bargained for when I first assayed to be the next Ian Fleming or the African American answer to Ernest Hemingway. Now, of course, I am content to be Eligah Boykin, who entered a Pandora's Box in search of riches and renown and found it was a tunnel that led through the dark night of the soul out into the bright sunlight of self realization.

That being said, I hope you enjoy this journey through 'Tales Times Ten' as much as I enjoyed sweating and suffering and exulting through the hard process of mining and panning for these nuggets. There is still a long way to go and I expect you will be game for much more.

—Eligah Boykin

Mister Magic

When Miss Z hurled her thunderbolt our way, she struck straight at the vitals. I never thought I would find myself empathizing with the Prince of Darkness, but I must say a stake through the heart has a horrific pang to it. Zenora insisted that there was nothing we could do to convince her to be part of our Magic act now.

Meechie wouldn't have minded so much except that our lovely assistant chose to give us the news on the eve of our Children's Show at the Cody Library. He sat there sneezing in the middle of a pool of sawdust and grunted ruefully at me. Each time he sneezed a racking cough, the curtains fluttered over the mirrors in the Disappearing Cabinets. He stifled another sneeze into his handkerchief and finished bolting on the doors. The way he clenched his fist round that claw hammer, I thought he was going to choke it to death.

"Bitch," he wheezed resentfully, "that trifling bitch! What type of song and Dance did she give you this time, Maestro? I told you to pass on that heifer. Now she's got us holdin' the pickle. What happened? Bet she got her tits pressed on top uh that pimp Dandy even as we speak! Huh?"

"I don't know. I don't care, 'long as I don't have tuh walk in on that mess. Here man," I grab a mask out of Meechie's tool kit, "put this on before you sneeze yo' life away. Can't say I really blame her, though. Playin' all those children's shows to empty auditoriums must have gotten old to her after awhile. I don't know-" I shrug at him.

"Uh huh. Ain't chu deep! Just go 'head makin' excuses for her like you always do." Meechie drilled in the holes for the removable bolt. "I'll empty her auditorium! An' she bedder not let me catch her out on the streets! The first time we have a sellout crowd and what does she do? She skips on us. Hand me that drill bit," Meechie glared at me while he screwed it into the gun. "-we didn't have to build no cabinets to make Sister Z disappear."

"Aw, shut that stuff up. We'll just have to pick somebody out of the audience to do her part, that's all."

"Uh huh, you got that right." Meechie swung the cabinet doors to and fro to see how they gave and played, then glanced at me suspiciously. "Don't look at me, Maestro. I put on my last wig and dress in Pontiac. You don't get somebody out the audience you outta luck, my brotha."

Zenora wasn't a bad girl when you got down to 'compared to what'. She could be very ladylike when we sawed her in half with the Amazing Laser Eye, or levitated her above the Flaming Grill. The only time she grew mouthy was when we hung her upside down for the Samurai Sword trick. The blood rushing to her head would occasionally give her a migraine, but there was no use pretending she didn't cut a splendid figure in those black tights. The stage lights splashed upon her with those cat ears nestled in her curly black hair, and when the audience marveled at her timed reappearance during the Disappearing Maiden trick, there was no doubt she gave the Act the extra spice it really needed.

That special 'X' factor that is all about glamour and sex appeal.

I adjusted the tie to my tuxedo in the mirror, wondering where I would find another assistant with the beauty pageant glow of Zenora. After all, I was only looking for someone who was a cross between the Supremes' Mary Wilson and Halle Berry. That couldn't be that hard a trick to pull off, could it? I was nearly finished checking my tie, when it seemed to me I could see Miss Z's chuckling face, teasing me in the mirror again. I could hear her taunting voice darting lightly within earshot.

"Ya hah! Whatchu gon' do now, Mister Magic?" I could feel invisible fingers picking lint from the shoulders of my suit. "I done rocked yo' world now, eh, papa? Where you ever gon' get another lady to climb up Heaven's Rope and disappear fo' you snatch it back down?"

When you've been doing this Act as long as I have, you eventually come to realize that good assistants are hard to find.

"Hey, Mister Magic!" Little pixie Cindy stuck her braided head inside my apartment door with an impish grin. "You still want me to do that thang after I get out of class tonight? Hey-hey, Meechie!"

Meechie grunted, still muttering 'bitch' under his breath at the thought of Zenora.

I turned from the mirror and shook my head at Cindy.

"Naw. Better hold tight on that camcorder this time. I don't think this is gonna be one of our better shows."

"How come?" Cindy asked me as she shrugged off a slightly wounded expression. "What happened?"

Cindy Dubose leaned her young, slight frame against the doorjamb and began to bristle with indignation.

"We're just missing an assistant. Don't sweat it." Now the glimmer of an idea flashed into my head. "Say Cindy–" I glanced at her and then at the cabinets nonchalantly as I pressed down my lapels.

"Whut–"

"– why don't you step into one of those cabinets over there so Meechie and I can make sure it doesn't rock"

"Oh, no!" Cindy waves herself back into the hallway. "You not getting me in that thing. For all I know that thing might explode! I know your tricks, Mister Maestro. I'll tell you what, though. Let me go find Mister Jericho; the fool that flunked me in my Multicultural Studies class. You make him disappear for me an' I'll pay you!"

"Right Cindy,"
I wave the lass away as the sound of her voice trails off.
"Let me know how it goes, Mister Magic."
"Right, Cindy,"

When the drum roll sounded and the horns chased the curtains back, all our little problems became history. After pulling doves out of my pockets and mice fleeing cats from my little black bag, I cleared my throat during the squeals from the children and the applause. There was no use dodging it anymore and I was running out of tricks to cover it up.

Now was the time to request an assistant.

Meechie and I looked askance at each other as the spotlight became a searchlight and scoured the audience for the unlikely helper. The drum roll resumed and it seemed I could hear Zenora's ghostly light laugh taunting me with satisfaction.

Our guest assistant stepped onto the stage at the urging of fellow teachers and wild-eyed, giddy students.

The young schoolteacher gushed a warmth and personal magnetism that seemed to produce her very own spotlight. The blue eyes framed by the sun-streaked strands of hair, flashed with self possession and kindly authority. All thoughts of Zenora vanished in the bright collegiate presence of our volunteer. The conservative cut of her grey pinstriped suit dress, rather than play down her generous endowment in the upper stories, molded her figure into sloping planes that spiraled around the swell of her hips and her toned thighs into the draping folds that wrapped her ankles above her neatly laced gym shoes. She parted lips as sweet as the sections of an orange once you have peeled back the rind, and put a finger to them, shushing her students into silence.

Meechie was so thunderstruck all he could do was tug at the collar of his tuxedo. I nudged him with an elbow so he wouldn't forget to pull back the curtains on the disappearing cabinets.

"What's your name, dear?" I asked her, as her hand slipped tremulously into mine.

There was a moment before her response, as she took a deep breath that made her bosom billow like an inflatable vest, when I became aware that she was working magic on me. She was doing her best to conquer her stage fright while our gazes interlocked and we adjusted ourselves to the same public frequency. I started to ask her if I could have this dance, but then, I already knew the answer since this was my show.

A truly lovely assistant is indeed hard to find. Meechie and I do not usually search for them among the educated elite. Zenora was a rare find; a jazz singer who just failed to place at the Miss Fitness competitions. At first, I didn't know quite what to make of our Teacher of the Year. Even the unenlightened would discern at a glance that here was an instructor who could make lifelong bachelors out of young boys who fell under her spell. Such poor unfortunates would wander like nomads through an empty life. Where in their future adventures would they ever find a woman to measure up to the childhood fantasy that shared our stage at this moment in time?

"That's Miss Taylor!" I heard a voice call out of the darkness. "That's our teacher!"

"Quiet, Michael!" The sternness of her expression was betrayed by the boisterous fun in her flashing eyes. "That's my class out there, Mister Magic," She pressed my hand with a spunky 'how-do-you-do'. "I'm Felicity Taylor."

"We're pleased to make acquaintance. I would be honored to have you consent to be our assistant in our next feat of Magic."

"Why thank you, Mister Maestro," I could feel the sweat in her palm as she shook my hand once more with genial resolve. I barely took note of the red bruises that ran along the underside of her forearm. "I would be happy to help you in any way I can."

"Bring our teacher back, Mister Magic!" A voice in the audience warned me amidst the howls and exclamations of our excitable audience.

"Hush Michael!" She sternly frowned at the young man with a soothing voice. "Let's help Mister Magic do his act. He won't hurt me. This is just for fun."

She gave a cheerful wave as she disappeared behind the heavy draped folds of one of the cabinets. A few choice magic words from the man with the magic wand and Miss Taylor's curvaceous form was teleported from one curtained cabinet to the other and back again. After I made her switch places in the cabinets with Meechie, I pulled back the curtain and asked her if she wanted to get a drink of water.

"I wouldn't mind a cup of coffee and a doughnut. I have to grade my tests for tomorrow."

"Alright." She took a bow with me to gasping applause before I deposited her again in the cabinet. I strolled over to Meechie. "Maurice, please escort Miss Taylor down the hallway where the refreshments are."

"Right, Maestro."

I helped Meechie into the other cabinet before he drew the curtains closed.

There was the buildup and the blast of horns from the audio speakers as I pulled back the curtains on both the cabinets. I let the paper doves and confetti flutter out into the audience.

"Wha—?"

"Where'd she go?"

"Hey! Where's our teacher?"

"Yeah! What did you do with her?"

I stood there in the spotlight with my arms folded.

"Where do you think she is now?" I asked the audience with pointed emphasis. "Do you think you can find her? Be sure to check under your seats!"

I love to make them sweat.

"Do you think if we closed the curtains again we might get them to come back?"

The seconds ticked by while everyone looked around for their missing teacher.

"Yeah!" The cry came back from a dumbfounded child here and there. "Do it again, Mister Magic!" The buzz in the audience rose to almost a cheer. "Yeah! Bring them back!"

"Somebody come up here then and help me close the curtains again!" I waved merrily towards anybody that looked like an eager volunteer. "Let's see whether or not we can get them back."

The teachers sent up a couple of their best behaved students. A little Mexican girl and an older simpering boy approached the stage. We closed the curtains again and again. All that ever came out were rabbits, frogs and a couple of snakes we threw out into the audience before it was discovered they were rubber! I saw a stocky adult with a menacing scowl rise up out of the front row in anxious confusion. He looked around at the laughing kids, and turned to me. He started to approach the stage.

"HERE I AM!"

The spotlight found Felicity Taylor up in the balcony in the back of the auditorium, waving with Meechie at her students. The spotlight then winked out and returned to me.

"Let's see if we can't get your teacher to come down from there. Okay?" I suggested.

"Yeah!"

"Come down from there, Miss Taylor!"

The spotlight went back to the balcony, but Felicity Taylor and Meechie were no longer to be found upon their lofty perch.

I turned to the little Mexican girl.

"What's your name, honey?"

"Veronica," she mumbled shyly as she hid one foot.

"Do you think we should bring Miss Taylor back?"

"Yeah," she looked around with an idle smile.

"Help me close the curtains, okay?"

We closed them on the cabinet nearest to us. After that, I went over to the older young man, nearly as tall as myself and asked him his name.

"Rufus-"

"Can you help me get my friend back?"

He looked away in embarrassment and gave me a reluctant nod. So we closed the curtains again on the cabinet further down stage left. I positioned Veronica and Rufus on either side of both cabinets and resumed center stage.

"Now you know what you have to do, boys and girls?" I announced to them seriously. "You have to close your eyes–everybody close their eyes–and when I count to three shout at the top of you lungs, 'COME BACK!', and your teacher and my friend will come back. Ready?"

The drum roll rose to a swell as I slowly counted to three and pointed my wand into the audience as a signal.

"COME BACK!"

The sound of those two words filled the auditorium and on either side of me the curtains to the cabinets fluttered.

"Pull back the curtain, Veronica-" I commanded, "-and you too, Rufus—" Little Veronica and Rufus snatched away the curtains, and when Felicity Taylor came out of Veronica's cabinet, a cheer resounded through the auditorium and the little girl gave her a hug. When Meechie hopped out of the other cabinet he gave Rufus a hearty handshake and a pat on the back. We all took a bow to the roaring approval of the students crowding around the stage. I passed my business card into Felicity's palm as she waved her way back to her seat. Why not? I told you good assistants are hard to find.

Besides, at that time Meechie and I were building a coffin for a Resurrection Act I dreamed up.

Meechie and I looked at each other with relief and gratitude as we took our bows. We had the spotlight trained on Miss Taylor, Veronica and Rufus as the students gave us a wild standing ovation. This was cut short when the class bell rung. We watched as the Librarian, some fearsome and heavyset old woman named Miss Hutchins, ushered them out with glaring admonitions not to race down the halls.

"Man!" Meechie exclaimed with grinning joy. "We should have got Cindy down here this time!"

We watched with pride as our packed house slowly emptied out into the hallways.

"Who was that lady, anyway? Miss Taylor or somebody?" Meechie shook his head at me. "That babe should get PAID!"

"Yeah, but now we got to start all over again and find ourselves another lovely assistant. We were lucky this time, but our luck won't hold out forever."

"You had any sense, you would interview that Taylor lady and mail her a contract, Maestro. She made us look good tonight."

"Yeah, I'll think about it. Come on, help me start taking some of this down. All I know is we'll have settle on some better arrangement soon, because we can't go on like this."

I'm always finding out that I'm righter than I want to be.

When I heard the knock at my apartment door, it was storming outside. I was expecting it would be Zenora, finally responding to the messages I left her, begging me to take her back after hearing about our triumph at the Cody Library. Thanks to that show, we were booked solid up to Halloween. There was nothing that could have prepared me to face a rain drenched Felicity Taylor, shivering in her all weather coat. She looked up at me through water speckled eyelashes, holding my business card between her fingers with a humorous smile. When I saw the bluish-grey discoloration under her right eye I was enraged. She winced away from the touch of my hand and probing fingertips.

"I-I came to return this. May I come in, please?" She asked me, her lip trembling the way it does when a woman can barely hold back the tears. "I-I-I thought—"

"Here! Where are my manners? Come on, I'll take your coat—"

I slipped the coat off her bare shoulders and down her arms. Evidently she was returning from some kind of social affair and the shiner under her eye left me to speculate the rest.

"Is there something I can get you? Come over here and sit down—"

Felicity vigorously shook her head. There was a hint of terror in her eyes as she moved to the window in my living room and looked down through the pelting raindrops. I started to approach her when she held out her hand to halt me. She spoke to the window and I could barely hear what she said.

"We were talking about you and your show at a pool party my girlfriend was having for some friends. I don't recall exactly how your name came up, and I suppose it doesn't really matter anyway, does it?" Felicity glanced my way with a skittish expression. "I don't know–one of my friends teaches Social Science at one of the community colleges near here and she was going on and on about how hard it was to get students motivated to understand their world–and I guess that was when your name came up. I was standing right beside my boyfriend and explaining how you came to our school and got everybody so involved in what you were doing that it was really," Felicity fiercely cast her gaze my way again, "- really, uh, amazing. Anyway, I was telling Theresa–I teach Math myself–you see, that there was probably a way to relate Math and Science in a more playful way to students. I know everything can't be fun all the time," Felicity was waving my card at the window, "but on the other hand, you don't have to make a subject so serious that it ends up becoming a deadly bore." Felicity sighed and turned her back to the window, pressing my card between her closed eyes. "All I said was it would probably be a valuable experience to invite people in the real world into the classroom to talk about how they used the subjects that we teach in their lives and their professions. That was all I said! So I told Theresa and Barb how I was considering inviting you and others into my classroom to talk about the role Math plays in the things that you do. I told her I thought I would start with you because I already had your card and knew how to get in contact with you. That was when Theresa perked up and asked if I had your card on me. I said I think I do, and no sooner do I produce it from my purse then my boyfriend Bobby just goes ballistic!"

Felicity opens her wet eyes now and holds the card out to me.

"Anyway, we had a big fight over this, and I don't want to go into all the details. Here, I'm giving this back to you so as to–so as to avoid anymore trouble."

"That's probably best." I nodded to her soberly as I sat on the arm of my couch. "Alright, I understand."

"I could have sent it back through the mail, but I didn't want you to think it was anything personal I had against you. Personally, I think–you know. I better be going-"

"Right. I'll get your coat—"

I took the card from between her fingers and she followed me back to my closet. I slipped her coat back over her and straightened out her collar. Something about the touch of her skin against my hands and the smell of rain in her hair, the way her body seemed to yield to me as she moved into my receding arms all in a whirling heart aching blur. I found myself holding her, our lips pressed together in the warped temporality of blind, startled ardor. I know you have all heard how the hand is quicker than the eye. What I did not realize until that moment was the heart is even quicker with its emotional sleight of hand. Before I knew what was happening, Felicity was swimming into my embrace. We waded in the moment, until I heard a voice outside my apartment window.

"FELICITY!"

She shrank back from me in distracted anguish, her eyes flitting to the window and then seizing upon me again.

"It's my boyfriend! It's Bobby! I swear to God, I can't believe this! How did he follow me here? Please, you mustn't let him find me here—"

"Your boyfriend?" The stocky fellow that was in the audience comes back to me. I gingerly touched her cheek beneath the bruise. "Is that how you got this?"

Felicity scowled at me and then lowered her head in a shamefaced nod.

"He can't find me here. You don't know him, there's no telling what he'll do—"

Now I notice those fading bruises on her arm again.

"Well, if he treats you like this, I'm not sure I want to get to know him! All right. Okay. You stay here. Let me call Meechie and we'll take care of him, okay?"

The voice kept calling out her name in outrage.

"FELICITY! COME DOWN HERE! NOW!"

She looked at me in terror before pressing her head against my chest. I heard a knock at my door again. It was Cindy.

"Hey, Maestro," Cindy peeks in on a trembling Felicity. "I heard you got down at the Library. Meechie told me I should have been there gettin' it all on tape." Cindy nodded at Felicity as she ran her fingers through her braided hair. "Who is that fool and what's he outside hollerin' about?"

"Please," Felicity pleaded, "let me stay here until he goes away. Please?"

I went over to the rain streaked window. Cindy leans over the window with me.

"Is that him? The fool in that Bugatti?" Cindy asked with pained indignation. "Lord, what a geek!"

"Go 'head, Cindy. Get your camcorder."

"Yo' Maestro."

I pick up the phone from the end table. It isn't long before I have Meechie on the other end.

"Look man," I tell him, "meet me downstairs and bring some heat with you, just in case. Naw, you'll see when you get here. Yeah, I'll see you downstairs. Okay, man."

I hang up the phone with Felicity looking out the window from behind the curtains, over my shoulder. I take her by the shoulders and march her into the bathroom.

"You stay here. I'll go downstairs and talk to him."

"Wha–what are you going to do?"

"I'm going to try and get him to go home. Now you just stay here."

"Be careful. He carries a gun in his glove compartment."

"Okay. Look, you'll be able to see everything out this window. If it looks like I'm gettin' my ass kicked, or you see me raise my hand like this, that means I want you to call the police." I show her the gesture again. "Understand?"

"I think so." She pulls on the sleeves of my shirt.

"Do you have your cell phone handy?"

"It's right here. Look, I was trying to keep all this from happening-"

"I know," I said, as I patted her hand, "I feel you on that one. How were you to know you were dating Mike Hammer? While we're at it, you can call me Nick from here on out."

I glance at her terrified expression in the bathroom mirror when Cindy comes back with the camcorder.

"I've got it, Mister Maestro. Where do you want me to setup?"

"Somewhere you'll be able to get it all on tape. This might make up for us not taking you along to videotape our Magic Show."

"Awww, Mister Magic, you don't have to worry about all that." Cindy blushes shyly. "— but I brought my tripod!"

"There you go. Keep Miss Taylor company until I get back. Here's the phone."

Felicity squeezes my fingertips. I see that self-possession and authority returning to her gaze.

I hustle myself into my jacket.

Outside, I walk up to this red-faced fellow blazing hatred at me. He's got his hand inside his overcoat. This is not a good sign. I'm expecting Meechie to turn the corner any second now, since he lives only a few blocks away.

"What's up?" I begin in a friendly tone. "Where's Felicity?"

"She's with me."

"I want to see her."

"You can't right now. You've got her really frightened. Besides, she just dropped by to help me with a magic trick I've been working on lately."

"That's right. You're the guy! What kind of magic trick are you working on with my girl?"

"Making you disappear."

"You have her come down here now, funny boy."

That hand inside his jacket is making me nervous. I have to admit I feel like a fool standing around waiting for something to go 'click'!

"Who do you think you are, anyway?" The swarthy, black haired fellow demands of me. "This has got nothing to do with you."

"I'm just a friend, Bobby. Ordinarily, I would agree with you, but I can't allow a guest of mine to come to harm in my home. Believe me, you've gotten yourself all upset over nothing. Why don't you go some place where you can cool out and calm down? Once Felicity's convinced there is no reason to be afraid of you, I'm sure she'll give you a call. Right now, however, I think you should go home."

The ugly silence between us expands until it encapsulates us both. "That what you think?" Bobby nods at me with grim determination.

"This is what I think-"

My grip on him slips and he pulls his gun out of his jacket. Uh-oh. I see a nice little thirty-eight. I give Felicity the gesture. I reach for the piece in his fist and our clasped hands tremble above us. I somehow reach out through flexed and strained muscles to cuff him on the chin with the heel of my hand. I bring my foot around behind him and through the enraged expression on his face. I sweep his legs out from under him for the takedown. A shot goes off in the air accompanied by a scream. Meechie tools around the corner in his blue Taurus and stops in the middle of the street with his boys.

"What's goin' on, Maestro? This fool been fuckin' with you?"

"Yeah Meechie," I lift the thirty-eight up from beside the curb. "He wanted to show me what he thought of me—"

Meechie and me hustle our friend against the Blue Taurus.

"That don't make no types a sense." Meechie shakes his head as two linebacker types step quick out of the back seat of the Taurus. "Come on man, git yo' ass up out of duh street."

We turn when we see Felicity making her way out of the apartment vestibule. She makes her way over to my side in a frightened daze.

"Are you all right? Nick?" Felicity asks, gently touching my arm

"Sure, I'm okay. My feelings are just hurt, that's all. Before this little close encounter, I thought I could hold a conversation and exercise due powers of persuasion. You want to file charges against this guy?

"I've already called the police." Felicity bowed her head and looked away from the cursing and spitting, streak of hate that used to be her boyfriend. "They're coming."

"Hey Maestro, look! There they go!" Meechie points at the lighted vehicle coming towards us. "Ain't that something?"

"Yeah. Come on Felicity, I wanna know how you got that shiner—"

"You think you're going to get away with this?" Bobby erupts again, spewing rage. "You take what's mine and I'll put you under. You bastards are going to pay for this! Nobody takes what belongs to me! Nobody-"

Felicity quails before her boyfriend's fuming hate.

"All right. Thanks dudes. Can we all go back inside now?" I put my arm around Felicity.

"Come on, dear, let's go."

"I think your friend Cindy has everything down on video, Mister-I mean Nicholas."

"That would be excellent. Let's go find out."

There is no need to insult your intelligence by suggesting that everything turned out fine and dandy with every issue suitably resolved with its appropriate solution. Real life can get quite messy and this particular event proved to be no exception. The simple truth is that decisions made out of fear, anger and desperation tend not to be very good decisions in the long run. However, whatever questions may be raised at this point are another story for another time. You can take my word for it that any one thing that you take from this story is as good as any other. I would just like to share the one thing I got out of all this.

Good assistants are hard to find and harder to keep.

Twinkling Of An Eye

Nelson approached the withered old man sitting in the park. The grey haired gentleman beckoned him over to his bench with an air of authority. He swept his long coat about his knees as he reached back into the brown paper bag at his side. The pigeons and sparrows gathered about him on the sidewalk. Gently he scattered popcorn and crackers before them as they waddled at his feet. Nelson reluctantly took a seat at the end of the bench. He looked off into the distance and spoke to the fountain in front of them.

"I think she knows, sir."

"No doubt, my boy, no doubt."

"I thought she would be overjoyed at the way things are turning out for us."

The old man turned to Nelson with a twinkle in his eye. "Really? I must say I'm hardly surprised myself."

"I can't understand it. Every aspect of our lives seems enhanced and improved."

"Even certain, uh, physical aspects of the relationship that were causing you some concern, I take it."

"Yes sir. Those issues have resolved themselves to my satisfaction quite nicely."

The old man scattered more popcorn and crushed up crackers before him on the sidewalk. A black raven alighted upon his shoulder as the sparrows picked for crumbs in between the sidewalk grouting. The raven eagerly picked kernels of popcorn from the old man's fingertips as though he were a personal pet.

"A pleasure to hear it, my boy. Where would any of us be without consumer satisfaction? No need to review any of the terms and conditions of the contract then?"

"There's no need on my account," Nelson stated as he looked down and held his doleful face between his fists. "I can't say as much for Danielle. She may prove to be another matter entirely."

The old man looked askance at Nelson before giving him a gesture of dismissal,

"Hmph! Think nothing of it! She'll come around eventually. What do you say we walk a bit and kick it around? Shoo! Shoo!"

The old man waved off the raven perched on his shoulder. The bird flapped away as the reedy gentleman arose and brushed the bird feed out of his lap. But the raven followed at a respectful distance behind as the two of them left their bench and went up the lane.

"The main thing is," the old man stuck his hands deep into the pockets of his long coat, "that you put a stop to her sleeping with those books How's that particular thing going, anyway?"

"The more time we spend together, the less time there is for reading books; I can tell you that."

"Excellent, my boy, excellent."

The old man and the young man walked together in silence. Only the raven and a couple of pigeons seemed to be mute witnesses to their deliberations. They passed by the elm trees and long carpets of grass where couples and families were picnicking. The old man reached forward, searching for the right words.

"You see, I discovered long ago that the disposition of woman is mercurial at best, but malleable to positive suggestion —"

"How's that?"

"Well, it's this way. It has to do with client profile mostly. My personal experience confirmed, by the way, with statistics from our records, has led me to believe that the Man tends to assert his own objectives while the Woman tends to want to work things out so that everybody is happy. Do you follow me?"

Nelson scratched the back of his neck and slowly shook his head.

"No, sir, I can't say I do."

The old man placed a consoling hand on Nelson's shoulder.

"Bear with me, my boy. Let's walk a little bit more…"

The two walked over a hundred yards before the old man broke the silence and started up again.

"Now you remember you came to me because you wanted to put an end to this pattern of unrequited love affairs you were experiencing –"

"Yes, sir. That's right."

"You found this somewhat overweight woman with a somewhat handsome face who might shape up to be a real beauty if you could only get her to stop eating and reading so many books. Right?"

"That's about the size of it."

"This young woman was to prove to be a test case. What you needed was for someone to set up conditions so that the two of you could draw out the best in each other and experience the possibility of long range viability in your relationship."

Nelson carefully regarded the old man and watched as his eyes glistened.

"Naturally, you would have rather figured all this out for yourself as this would have validated your ability to solve your own problems and raised your self esteem. But one unrequited love affair too many broke the camel's back and brought you to your wit's end. This often happens in the adventures of Life. Sometimes it takes a disinterested party to bring a fresh perspective to a situation and help tie all the loose ends together."

Nelson looked over his shoulder and saw the raven still trailing behind them.

"That's when you came to me. You soulfully and intelligently presented all the particulars of your case. I found it a simple matter, really, and drew up the standard contract. We thoroughly went over all terms and conditions and options. One of which was to have the little lady in question attend the signing. But you felt that this might complicate the situation further rather than helping to resolve it. A valid consideration I chose to leave to your discretion. We again reviewed all the clauses, including the escape clause and you were then fully apprised of all your rights. At that time you signed and received a copy for your records. Correct?'

"That's right, sir."

The old man walked with Nelson past the pavilion and then halted with him in front of the gazebo.

"That brings us to our current state of affairs."

"Yes, I would say that is so, sir."

"What you want to do now is to break it to her gently with the least amount of upset. She may not be willing to come into our offices and sign off with you at this stage, but hopefully you will be able to allay her fears so that the two of you can continue to enjoy the advantages and benefits of the contract."

A gentle spring breeze rustled the leaves and made the boughs sway on the trees. Nelson was slow to nod as the old man patted him on the shoulder. He then replaced his hand in the pockets of his long coat and looked off into the distance. Nelson knew he was waiting for an answer.

"I don't exactly know how to do that, sir," Nelson forlornly confessed.

"Take your time, my boy, take your time. Nobody is feeling any pain from this transaction and you have nothing to feel guilty about. Although the spiritual investment has been considerable on your part, she still owes us nothing at this point. You're bearing the full responsibility for the success of this relationship at this time. I would see to it that your partner is made to appreciate this fact."

"I'll do what I can, sir."

"But of course you will. Nelson?"

"Sir?"

"You were right about her, you know."

"How is that, sir?"

"She turned out to be a real beauty under all that adipose tissue, and size does really matter to the lady despite all her protests."

The old man stuck the tip of his tongue into the corner of his mouth with a wry smile. He gave Nelson one more pat on the shoulder.

"Get back to me."

Nelson watched the old man go his way. He was followed by the raven, as the bird eventually flapped to a perch again upon his shoulder. Their silhouettes receded into the horizon.

"What is this?" Danielle demanded querulously as she smacked the open contract with the back of her hand. "Where did this come from?"

Nelson watched her slip into her shower clogs as she sat at her desk. Danielle placed her feet upon a stray pile of books. She tossed the stapled contract against the monitor of her computer in frustration. Nelson carefully picked it up off the bedroom carpet and swiveled just in time to catch the tortured expression on Danielle's face.

"What possessed you, Nelson? Everybody the world over knows better than to do business with HIM!"

But all Nelson could remember was sitting at the edge of the river and wanting to jump in and be done with it all. None of his relationships with women worked out to anything and it was as though he were laboring under some kind of curse. Letters and cards, candy and flowers, all had come to nothing. Even when he called himself lowering his standards he found himself striking out with the opposite sex; and God forbid he consider having a dream girl. No, he felt buried under the weighty mass of all those failed love relations and soon was found looking eagerly into the river for the rest of a watery grave.

That was when he caught sight of the reedy old man. He was dangling his feet on the other side of the iron railing and beckoning to him with a nod and a flinty grin. There were pigeons and sparrows nipping at crumbs on the sidewalk behind him. The line of the rod on his right hand side was quivering taut over the murky water with the promise of a catch on the hook.

Nelson sat wearily on the bed between all the stacks of Danielle's books. He fiddled forlornly with the contract in his hands. He looked up at Danielle hiding her face in her hands. When he lowered his eyes to the floor the strident sound of her voice brought him up again.

"Nelson! Stop playing with that thing for God's sake. You've done us in for sure this time."

"Oh, I don't know," Nelson hesitantly leafed through the pages of the contract again, "– the terms seemed reasonable enough –"

Danielle rose quickly with such a sharp expression on her face Nelson started.

"You can't be serious. That's the nature of his game. He makes it all seem so reasonable and above board, but his 'clients' always end up paying more than they bargained for, you can depend on that. Even a child could see through this. Even someone as mentally challenged as yourself should know –"

Danielle snatched the contract out of Nelson hands with a mocking glance.

"– that this is a prison sentence in Hell! 'Terms'! 'Conditions'! 'Options'!" She turned contemptuously through the pages of the contract. "Oh, and what is this here, Nelson, some kind of laundry list for the Ideal Mate? Item Number One: That she should need me more than I need her. Item Number Two: That I be the dominant one in the relationship and establish the terms and conditions of the relationship. My, my! Isn't that original in these modern times. Item Number Three: That she should always be looking to have sex with me. Typical! Just typical!"

Danielle threw the contract back into Nelson's face. She paced quickly over to the closet knocking down stacks of magazines and paperback novels in her wake. Nelson followed her, gathering the scattered material up. Danielle pulled out hangers for her clothes; her rant against Nelson still ongoing, but becoming no more than a buzz of white noise to him as he noticed how red she was turning in the face.

"Where are you going?"

"'Where are you going?' " Danielle mocked him as she pulled a suitcase out of the closet. "I ought to be catching the first Greyhound out of this town. Where can I go now that you signed us off on the dotted line?"

Danielle clicked open her suitcase and took a deep breath. She glared at Nelson with a tinge of sympathy in spite of herself.

"Maybe becoming God's gift to women was worth becoming contractually obligated to you, but morphing into your idea of a calendar girl isn't exactly motivating me to cosign on this deal. Idiot! How is he doing this? Is it something he's piping through the air vents? Is it in our drinking water? Are we some kind of test subjects for a new kind of Human Growth Hormone? Or did he tell you all that was classified when he handed you the pen for your John Hancock?"

Danielle furiously stuffed her clothes into her suitcase. She shimmied into a blouse and a skirt over her body stocking. Shuffling into her coat, she replaced the clasps on her suitcase.

"Science marches on, right, Nelson?" Danielle taunted Nelson as she flipped open her cell phone. "What? Are you going to bitch slap me and make me stay? I certainly would like to see you try! Oh! When do you start being the 'dominant one'?"

Danielle snatched up her suitcase and regarded Nelson with bristling defiance.

"I'm out of here."

Nelson watched the door slam shut. He sat on the bed with his mouth still half open to reply. The sound of her footsteps echoed down the hallway and now he realized he was in this alone.

Danielle grasped her collar around her throat. There was a slight wind whistling through the street catching at her skirt and the ends of her coat. The suitcase she was carrying to her Ford Focus was getting as heavy as the gray sky above her. She knew her girlfriend would put her up for the night until she could somehow arrange for more permanent accommodations. A light drizzle sprayed her face and ran in drops off her fingertips as she reached for the keypad in her coat pocket.

Even in her despondence she could not help but note that the male passerby kept giving her second and third looks. This irritated her and made her wonder what was out of place about her attire. She could hear singing as she made her way around her apartment building to the gang of burly young men camping about her car.

"Here she is," a tattooed fellow in a sleeveless under shirt announced to his cohorts, "You sure are lookin' good this evening, baby doll. What can we do for you?"

Danielle looked around to see whom they were talking to and realized with a flash that they were talking to her. Incredible! Could this guy actually be coming onto her? She set her suitcase down and just managed to stop herself from opening the door to her car with her keypad. A trio that looked like linebackers killing time in the offseason from the National Football League leered at her behind the tattooed one. They mumbled something between themselves with grins and chuckles, looking Danielle over with impish relish.

"Good evening. I would appreciate it if you would let me get to my car, guys. How about it?"

"Are you in some kind of hurry?" asked the tattooed one.

"Yeah, I sort of am," confessed Danielle as she casually replaced her keypad back into her coat pocket. "Well, it was nice meeting you –"

She picked her suitcase back up and proceeded around to the driver's side of her car. The tattooed one moved quickly to block her path and put consoling hands on both her shoulders. He backed her up a couple of paces. "Whoa – whoa – whoa – don't be in such a hurry, darling – we're just getting to know one another. We know how it is, don't we, brothers?"

A couple of the hulking men took a seat on the hood of Danielle's car.

"Right, Mario," assented one of them while the other fingered Danielle's collar. "See, we're from out of town, sweetheart. We were just discussing how hard it is for healthy young men like us to meet decent well-put-together women like yourself. We were just hoping someone like you would come along who could give us a tour."

There was no mistaking the situation now. Danielle felt a scream welling up from the pit of her stomach and struggled with all her might to stifle it. The face of the tattooed one was so close she could smell his breath.

"How about it? Do you think you could fit us into your schedule? We've got a car. We could be your escort while you show us the sights."

Danielle attempted to take another step back, but her heel bumped into the edge of the wall behind her. The four men huddled around her, their bulky shadowy figures nearly swallowing her up in the darkness. Danielle held the suitcase in front of her as though it were a shield. She could feel the eyes of the men pawing her body and it felt like being trapped inside an X-Ray machine while an invisible noose was being slowly drawn about her. The sound of her breath came out of her in short misty whispers.

"Excuse me!"

A new lone male voice pierced the silence with urgency.

"Now dude," the tattooed one drew his weapon and latched back the safety catch. "Can't you see me and my bro are busy right now–?"

The tattooed one whirled to take aim as his companions slipped out their Glocks and nine millimeters, but found no target in the shadows. The xenon white light and the red lasers skittered around buildings and under the fire escape discovering no one there. Slowly and carefully the gang stepped away from Danielle to assume attack positions.

"Where you at? Huh?" The tattooed one asked and stepped back towards Danielle almost as an afterthought. "Come on out here so we can see you…"

"Stay away from my bitch!"

"Your bitch?" The tattooed one exclaimed as raucous laughter echoed off the walls of the buildings surrounding them. "Come on out! I got your bitch right here – !"

The sound of gunfire seemed to come from all directions at once.

"Mario! I'm hit, man!"

"Uh! My leg! Mario, them bitches got me in mah leg–!"

"I'm gone, man! Damn Mario, you done walked our asses into a damn ambush!"

Danielle looked through the fingers of her hand at the grimaces of her assailants now scattering before her and returning fire at an unknown and unseen enemy even as they made tracks. She could hear their footsteps and their curses receding away. Now she arose from the low crouch she was curled up in when she first started to scream. There was still the sound of something firing like an Uzi submachine gun farther away in the distance with every halted breath she took.

Danielle came to her full height unsteadily and finally swallowed with relief now that the silence was no longer punctuated with the crack of firearms. She took in with heavy-breasted full breaths the utter silence that now gathered its cloak about her gritty surroundings. She made a fist around the keypad in her coat pocket and was on the verge of breaking down into tears when she heard the dim staccato tapping of footsteps heading her way. Nelson emerged out of the shadows from around the corner with a grim determined expression on his face.

"What are you doing here?" Danielle demanded with asperity.

"I've been known to hang out in the best of places. Where are you going?"

"I was thinking of spending the night with my sister Pamela. After that I don't know…"

"Give me the keys."

Danielle complied before she knew what she was doing.

"Get in," Nelson nodded as he opened the door to the driver's side, "I'll take you there."

Danielle let out a sigh of exasperation as Nelson took her suitcase and threw it into the back seat.

"Oh, alright, Nelson."

Once Danielle strapped in her seat belt not another word was spoken between them. The drive passed uneventfully under the elms and streetlights and incandescent billboards until finally Nelson parked the Ford Focus at the curb. They were arrived in front of the house of Danielle's sister now. He handed her the keys and got out.

Danielle regarded Nelson with a mixture of contempt and a pang of sympathy.

"When will I see you again?" Danielle was surprised to hear herself ask him in spite of everything. "Are you planning to see him once more to tie up all the loose ends to your 'contractual obligations'?"

The sound of passing cars and a police siren blaring past in a Doppler effect filled the silence between them.

"I don't know." Nelson confessed with dry reluctance. "I'll give you a call."

Danielle watched as he crossed the street between the whizzing cars into heavy traffic and disappeared from view.

"Everything ironed out between you and Little Miss?" The reedy old man asked Nelson as he fed the raven on his shoulder bacon bits.

"Not hardly, sir. I'm afraid she just hasn't taken much of a liking to you."

"Oh? Is that so? We're registered with the Better Business Bureau and you should have her know I come highly recommended."

Nelson looked away from the park bench and down the path lined with highly manicured lawns and fruit trees. He sighed holding the contract in his hands between his knees. He glanced at the reedy old man who was chuckling at him with a bemused smile.

"Danielle thinks I should have my head examined for doing business with you. She just about said as much to me."

The distinguished grey gentleman patted Nelson on the knee with a gnarled hand.

"Oh, she'll come around, my good man, she'll come around. Take it from me. There is a bond between the two of you now that even Siamese Twins would envy. Why, I'll wager at this very moment there is an ache in her heart for you not unlike that of an amputee with a phantom limb. Have faith and trust the process, my lad. We do good work and nothing will be amiss in the end. You'll see."

Nelson anxiously watched as the old man scattered more bread crumbs and a red cardinal alighted amongst the pigeons milling on the sidewalk. The appearance of this newest feathered friend caused a puzzled frown to appear upon the face of the aged tradesman for the mere space of a brief moment. Nelson uttered once again a forlorn sigh.

"She's moved back in with her sister." Nelson stated with dour resignation.

"A trifle, my boy, a trifle." The old man tossed more crumbs before him on the walk. "Come up to the office in the morning and we'll nail down all the fine details to this matter once and for all. Okay?"

Before Nelson could answer, the old man and the young man turned to the sound of high heels clicking down the walkway towards them. Even through the flaring sunlight of the morning, Nelson recognized Danielle's fragrance and the gait of a shapely silhouette he could just make out to be her. She finally came into full view squinting into the Sun with her hair rippling about her face in the stiff wind.

"Hello, Nelson. I hope you don't mind if I join you. Oh, don't bother rising on my account…"

"Speak of the – my, my, my! You must be the lady in question, aren't you?" The old man creaked to his feet and took Danielle's hand in his own.

Danielle felt a chill of revulsion stab through her heart as the withered gentleman kissed the back of her hand.

"Sit down, Danielle." Nelson ordered her.

"Nelson, I thought…"

"Sit down."

"Yes, Nelson. Of course."

Danielle nodded to the solicitous old man and carefully disengaged her hand. She took a seat on the park bench next to Nelson with a frown.

"I just thought I would stop by and see who you were dealing with." Danielle stated simply as she lowered her gaze.

"A pleasure to have you here, my dear." The grey gentleman said as he took the contract out of Nelson's hands. "We just need your signature and I'll be on my way."

"I'll just bet you do," remarked Danielle, recoiling in fascination, "so you're the one."

"At your service, my lady. I hope our labors on your behalf have met with your satisfaction."

"I'm not sure I understand what you're referring to exactly." Danielle said with a sneer and a blush.

The old man let the black raven peck the last bacon bit out of the palm of his hand. He then lifted the bird off his forefinger and cast Danielle a knowing smile.

"At the risk of being indelicate, let us just say that Nelson contracted with me to help him accomplish certain, uh, improvements in his pair bonding and love life. I hope as his partner you have no complaints to voice. However, should that be the case, I would be happy to discuss modifications to our present arrangement to resolve successfully any issues or concerns you might have. Hmmnn…"

The old man reached for a pen in his breast pocket and narrowed his eyes at the red cardinal enjoying his breadcrumbs. The pigeons and sparrows flapped about and roosted at his feet. He crossed his spindly legs and looked off with deliberation. He waved his pen in the air like a conductor to the silence of the couple before him.

Danielle pressed shoulders with Nelson and took his hand.

"The contract price seems a little high to my mind," Danielle admitted reluctantly.

"Oh spare me the clichés," the withered one chuckled, "if I possessed the coin of the realm for every time someone has told me that 'Beauty is only skin deep; it's really what's inside that matters', or how 'Money can't buy Love' or how 'Size doesn't really matter', or how '– I'm just looking for someone nice who's easy to talk to…', I would retire to the Virgin Islands. Now are we ready to sign off on this, or do we need to talk about this some more?"

"How did you ever get involved with this guy?" Danielle whispered into Nelson's ear.

"He became involved with me in much the same way that all my clients do." The old man followed up quickly. "At some point in his life, Nelson realized out of his desperation that he had simply had enough. He wanted no more of being the skinny, gangly kid from the East Side of Detroit. No more prayers to an uncaring God who obviously wasn't listening anyway. He was ready to do anything to see the condition he was in come to an end. Just as you wanted to stop being the fat, slovenly young woman who just might get a man if she would only fix herself up some. Isn't that how your friends put it to you?"

"What would you know about friends?" Danielle asked in a testy manner. "You have to have values to know anything about that. That's really not part of the package with you, is it?"

The old man whistled as one who had heard it all before.

"A feisty one, Nelson! Does she always go on this way?"

All the while Nelson sat still and silent with his eyes fixed upon the ground. Danielle found it hard now to sense what he was thinking. She rubbed and patted his shoulder, but this did not get him to raise his head.

"These discussions are interesting, but somewhat academic, don't you believe?" The old man observed as he placed the tip of his pen at the corner of his mouth. "Now beauty may or may not be only skin deep, but it never hurts to have a full head of hair and the muscle tone of a gymnast or a bikini girl you may have noticed lately. Money may or may not buy love but it works well for clean sheets and mints on the pillow. Size may or may not matter, but few complain of too much of a good thing in the bedroom. Someone nice and easy to talk to may be a comfort, but it never hurts to stand with a man who can rein you in and is willing and able to take charge."

The old man ticked these items off on his fingers one by one before turning once again to the couple with pen in hand.

"Now. Are there any more clichés we should cover or can we sign off on this thing now?"

Danielle slowly shook her head and looked over to Nelson with an imploring expression on her face. He was impassive and she felt as though she were holding onto stone.

"Why didn't you come to me, Nelson? You should have come to me first." Danielle insisted, furiously holding onto him ever tighter. "We could have talked this out. I would have listened. You could have explained to me how you felt and we could have worked something out. Something better at least than having to go to HIM!"

Danielle hurled the old gentleman a look of bitter hatred and defiance.

He regarded her with a kind of mock pity and clucked his tongue.

"Tsk! Tsk! Tsk!" The old man chided with triumphant relish. "Whoever said 'Two heads are better than one' should be the fly on the wall to this happy turn of events. Looks like another tired old cliché has bit the dust before our very eyes. Now I see that you were right, Nelson. We should have kept this strictly Man Talk just between you and me."

The wind picked up briskly and flared Danielle's coat and teased her tresses about her face. The birds about the old man scattered and alighted again.

"But more to your point, my dear, what would you have our poor Nelson do? Perhaps he should have advised you to see a hairdresser and to lose weight, but I scarcely believe any self-improvement program could have garnered the results you now enjoy. Face it, young lady, you're becoming a spellbinding beauty even as we speak. Perhaps you should have advised Nelson to join his local YMCA and take dancing lessons along with a course in etiquette, but somehow I just don't think that would have put as much pizazz in your relationship as you are currently experiencing. At any rate, no need to thank me right now. We just need your signature below that of Nelson's and you can take your bad boy home to deliver to you that much needed spanking."

Danielle simmered with protest.

"Unbelievable! How can you sit there and be so glib and smug about all this?"

Nelson uttered a sigh of exasperation. "Danielle?"

"Yes? Nelson?"

"Shut up now."

Danielle opened her mouth in outrage and yet nothing came out. At length she bowed her head again with an anguished whisper.

"Yes, Nelson…"

The old man threw up his hands.

"People! People! People! I'm a simple businessman, not a lonely-hearts counselor. Granted there must be myriad ways to handle the trials of life, but I happen to believe I offer a pretty good service when all is said and done. Take a moment to consider all that you have gained and all that there will be to gain once you have taken full advantage of this once in a lifetime opportunity."

Nelson and Danielle studied the concrete sidewalk beneath their feet with an ever growing sense of resignation. Finally, Nelson raised his head with grim resolve. "I think it best you go now, Danielle," he stated to the thin air before him.

Danielle turned to regard Nelson with disbelief etched upon her face. She nervously clasped her collar about her neck with trembling hands.

"What? What did you say? I don't understand, Nelson. Why are you telling me this now?"

"I can see I shouldn't have gotten you involved in this. I apologize. Now go."

"Go? Where should I go, Nelson?" Danielle spat out in a bitter whisper.

Nelson shrugged in a listless apathy without looking at her.

"Back. Back to your sister's until this is over. I enjoyed your companionship, but I can see this is too much to ask even of you. Walk away now and don't look back. The gentleman here knows I was right. This is really a matter just between us."

Danielle smoothed out the wrinkles of her coat on her lap. She looked up at Nelson with glistening eyes but saw no hope.

"Oh. So you're dumping me now? Am I dismissed now?"

"Even I can see this is not for you. You don't need this. I do."

"Oh? So he works his little tricks and you have your fun with me and now that's it. Right? You figure I will be all right now that I have this killer body and should have no problem finding a man. I guess you think you're doing me some kind of a favor, is that it, Mister?"

Nelson looked at her and made fists on his knees.

"Look. You're not committed. You haven't signed anything. You're free to go."

"Right. Now that we've had our little fling, I should shop around. Right? See the world and find out what other fish there are in the sea. Is that it? Just leave you to walk into the furnace with our good friend here."

Danielle stood up. She was having trouble with the top button to her coat just above her thumping heart.

"Alright, Nelson. If that's the way you feel about it."

The reedy old man folded up the contract and put it inside his long coat.

"Come to the office in the morning, Nelson. We can finalize all the details at that time. Alright?"

"Alright," Nelson uttered in a whisper.

Danielle's face turned red with labored breathing. She watched with a bitter scowl as the old man took the pen he was carrying and started to replace it in his inside pocket.

"Damn you, Nelson," Danielle hissed between her teeth, "and damn me too for getting mixed up with the likes of you."

Danielle darted her hand forward with a wincing, pained expression. "Give me that pen."

Nelson and the old man mirrored each other's startled surprise with open mouths.

"C'mon! The contract too!" Danielle demanded with a quivering open palm.

"My dear, I…" The old man began uncertainly as his hand went reluctantly into the folds of his coat. "Are you sure?"

Danielle thrust her hand inside the gentleman's coat and produced the folded contract. She sank to her knees with the pen in her other hand. Nelson watched with stupefaction as she used the old man's lap as a desk to hurriedly scribble her signature underneath his own. Danielle slapped the pen down on the paper before rising to her feet with a trembling sob.

"There! Is that what you wanted? Is everything in order now?"

She staggered back to her place on the bench next to Nelson, wrapping her arms convulsively about his neck and hiding her tear streaked face against his chest.

"I love you, Nelson," Danielle confessed into the crook of his neck. "Better we go to Hell together keeping each other company at least."

"There, there, baby," Nelson consoled her with pats on the back in a kind of frozen dismay, "there, there, now…"

"I just can't let this thing separate us. I can't!"

"Now, now, Danielle, now, now… I'm here, I'm here…" Nelson said feeling a burning, stinging sensation as his own eyes welled up with tears. "We're all in this together now…"

There was a feeling in his heart such as warm air rising that was altogether new to him. He glanced at the reedy old gentleman and brought into the red haze behind his closed eyes the image of someone writhing in consternation and a strange unnamable discontent. Even as his soul filled with Danielle's penitent emotion, he could not help but note that the old man seemed unhappy. But why should that be? The contract bore both their signatures now.

Before long what the two of them felt for each other blotted out everyone and everything else. They were bound ever more tightly within each other's caresses and felt inextricably pressed together as though they were caught up within a tight, soft ball of yarn. Their emotions finally subsided and when they opened their eyes at last the old man sitting before them was gone.

The couple whirled around and looked in all directions. Wherever they peered through the trees or across the wide green lawns where children scattered and ran, the grey old gentleman was nowhere to be found. The birds continued to roost and peck at the breadcrumbs at their feet. Nelson and Danielle held onto each other, watching the red cardinal joining the sparrows and the pigeons hunting up bits of ground up crackers with their beaks. The raven was no longer among them.

Danielle pressed her fingertips to her lips as she went pale.

"Where did he go?"

The old man sat in his office at INFINITEX.INC. He pursed his lips and steepled his fingertips. The beautiful secretary in his employ hitched her glasses back upon the bridge of her nose. She scanned the computer screen before her with a frown.

"What about this contract here, sir?" She asked as she turned to him and tossed back a wing of hair over her shoulder. "What should I do with it now?"

"What contract are we talking about, Mona?"

"This one you drew up for the couple obsessed with Self Improvement. I see the signatures, but what about this asterisk at the top? That usually indicates that the escape clause was activated, but the required documentation is missing. Did you close the sale or not? I don't know whether to file it under APPROVED or VOIDED, sir. Exactly what happened with this one?"

"Print it out for me."

The old man watched with relish as his secretary wiggled her curvy form over to the printout tray and back.

"Here you are, sir."

"Thank you, Mona."

"Here, let me staple it for you."

"Thank you, dear."

The grey gentleman took the contract from her and tossed it into the PENDING basket on his desk. He took a couple of peanuts out of a small dish and fed them to the raven perched on the arm of his chair.

The Doctor Clark Files

"Really? You were given authorization to access and study The Doctor Clark Files? How did you do it?"

"I submitted my proposal and my application. I was rather surprised it was approved."

"That sort of stuff from the 20th Century is privileged, classified information."

"I'm aware of that."

"Aren't you afraid?"

"What should I have to be afraid about?"

"That you might inadvertently find yourself in violation of the codes and statutes concerning the Cultural Welfare. People have been imprisoned for messing around with that 20th Century stuff."

There was an awkward, nervous, glancing and guarded silence between them.

STATUS OF FILE REQUEST

"Are The Doctor Clark Files available?"

"Yes, we have them. Do you have your card with you?'

"I have it here somewhere … Yes! Here you are."

"Thank you. Hmnn, your records appear to be complete."

"Will the transcripts be included?"

"You will be provided with everything. Please be seated and your number will be called when your request has arrived."

STUDENT CONSULTATION

Rachel Horwich stood on the stoop knocking at my front door. She cut a beautiful figure up there and I really could not find fault with her. I drove my Buick LaCrosse up the driveway, taking care not to return her timid wave as I parked my red car in the garage.

I walked under the grapevine and passed the side door, stifling an impulse to unlock it and slip in that way. I really wanted to avoid a public encounter with her. An instructor meeting a student teacher at the place of his private residence was not exactly the height of professional decorum.

"Professor Clark? Hi! I've been waiting for you," Rachel cheerfully called out as she stomped the chill out of her toes.

I nodded silently, unable to complain about the way Rachel dressed up my porch. She was wearing a black all weather coat and heels and her attire gave the impression she was coming to me for a job interview. The only thing wrong with this picture was that she was meeting me at my home rather than my office. It also did not help that she was drop dead gorgeous with large watery blue eyes, full reddish-pink lips and red hair like falling leaves spilling down her shoulders.

"I missed my appointment, Doctor Clark –"

"I gathered as much…" I said to the concrete steps as I ascended. She bit her lip, looking at me expectantly.

"We can reschedule for another time, Rachel. That probably would be best, don't you think?"

"Oh no," she said, looking off in the direction of my neighbor's house, "I was so hoping I could leave my paper with you here so I don't miss the deadline."

I saw the large yellow manila envelope sticking out of her black patent leather purse for the first time. The purse hung from the crook of her elbow like a dead pendulum. I cocked an eyebrow.

"You know, you could have put your paper in my drop box, Miss Horwich."

"I know, I know. It's just that there was so much mail in your slot. I was so afraid that you might never get to me. I thought it would be so much better to personally hand it to you. That way I would know you got it."

Now I looked her straight in the eyes and weighed her earnest expression in my mind. I put out my open hand for the envelope and let out a sigh.

"Alright. I'll accept your paper this time, Miss Horwich."

She reached out with grateful relief to touch my shoulder with her fingertips, but then drew back beneath my forbidding stare.

"Oh, thank you, Doctor Clark, I was so afraid I wouldn't be able –"

She placed the big envelope in my hand.

"Here, Doctor Clark. I'm so glad I caught up with you. Please forgive me, I swear I'll never do anything like this again. I swear –"

"Alright," I chuckled, "I forgive you. But after this, Miss Horwich, I would prefer you submit your work in the usual way like everyone else. Thank you."

I turned to unlock the door to my house, expecting her to skip down the steps with youthful exuberance now that her mission was complete. The fact that she was still standing on my porch when I opened the front door made me curiously nervous. I saw her lips part, but not one word came out of her mouth.

"Is there something else, Miss Horwich?"

"No, I suppose that's everything for now…"

"Where are you parked, Miss Horwich?"

"Oh. I caught the bus over here, Doctor Clark. I was just so worried I would get an incomplete on this paper."

"You caught the bus over here?"

"I'll be alright."

I looked up and scouted the evening clouds.

"You should have come with a friend, Miss Horwich. It's getting dark now –"

"Oh, I'll be alright –"

"No, you better hold tight. I'll put this up and drive you to a Bus Stop. The last thing I want is to see you come up missing on the six o'clock News…"

I should have left her standing there on the porch. I know that now. But the way she stood there shivering, blowing into her gloved hands and stamping her feet got to me.

"Why don't you come in and warm up for a minute?"

Now tell me you would not have done the same.

I threw her manila envelope on top of the others stacked there upon my desk in the study. She stood against the closed door pressing her back against it. She looked up and closed her eyes with an enigmatic smile on her face. At first glance, I thought she was just glad to be out of the cold.

"You've got so many books, Doctor Clark! Is it alright if I have a glass of water?"

I shrugged and went into the kitchen. I was debating with myself whether or not I should wait with her for a bus to come or just drive her home and be done with it. I took some bottled water out of the refrigerator and poured it into a glass for her. I came out of the kitchen certain of only one thing.

"Next time you go out on an adventure like this, Miss Horwich, be sure to bring a friend –"

I entered my living room and she was slipping out of her heels and setting them neatly by the door. Usually a person will take off their shoes at the entrance so as not to track the carpet. What is not so usual is for a person to have their slip, stockings, suit-dress, bra and panties carefully folded on the seat of my sofa chair. I could see her black coat draped over the back end of the chair as she reached out her quivering hands wearing nothing but a humble look on her face.

"I can't help myself, Doctor Clark. I have such a crush on you."

The more I examine that moment the less I can make of it. I have reviewed it many times in my mind and my reaction to Rachel still baffles me. The mystery of that instant in time still defies my attempts to unravel it.

There are all the versions of what you're supposed to do in situations of this kind. First you are supposed to immediately and instantly exhibit a strong moral reaction towards having a student naked in your living room. Moral inspiration should be your guide in matters such as this. You are supposed to set an example of ethical understanding and rectitude to those under your care and instruction. Teachers are expected to uphold the standards of the community with regards to the propriety and dignity of all parties concerned.

All I can say is she looked too much like a painting or a living sculpture. She was a vision of fiery blooming youth clothed in freckled, strawberry milkshake skin of voluptuous proportions. My eyes revealed how my imagination was seized as I regarded her with a worshipful gaze.

She was to me a fount of repressed sexual fantasies coming to life.

None of this occurred to me while I gave Rachel Horwich her glass of water. She sipped from it eyeing me carefully with a quizzical expression. I felt like I was in a daze while she backed towards the door and twisted the knob to make sure it was locked. She twisted around and latched the chain. "Excuse me, sir," said Rachel as she set her half empty glass upon a nearby lampstand, "why don't you sit down right here? I'll move my clothes…"

I was having an erection so intense I could barely walk as Rachel took me by the hand and gently sat me down in my sofa chair. She quickly unbuttoned my coat and noted the bulge in my pants. She placed her hand along my inner thigh and looked up at me with approval swimming in her watery blue eyes. She slowly began to undo the zipper to my pants.

"I know how you feel, Doctor Clark," she explained soothingly as she pulled and worked my zipper open, "I felt like such a fool myself. I woke up one morning with your face exploding like a fire in my heart and your name running like thunder in my ears. I thought I was going out of my mind, Emanuel. The joy was an ache and an agony to me. I felt like I was going to die!"

"Rachel, I don't understand –"

Suddenly she was holding me, licking me, kissing me, sucking me softly and looking up at me with those blue eyes imploring me for approval. My fingers dug into her curls and picked at the strands of her red hair as my mind swirled in the misty whisper of her voice.

"Christ put you into the heart of me, Emanuel. I thought it was all in my mind. I felt like it was some kind of crazy fantasy. I was so sure these feelings were going to ruin me—ruin my life –"

"Rachel, what is this – what is happening –"

"I don't know anything. All I know is I have to have you, and you can't deny me anything! Anything! Christ has written your name across my heart!"

I attempted to raise my voice in protest, but I was swallowed up in the strawberry cream and blush of her beauty and the ecstasy of her scent, the feel of her skin stroking a throbbing fever in my mind.

"I know it's true now. You feel the same way about me as I feel about you. Are you going to push me away now, Doctor Clark? Are you going to make me put my clothes back on and throw me out?

"Rachel I – I never imagined –"

"I took such a chance on you! I was so afraid – I was so afraid – you have no idea how afraid I was –"

"There is nothing to be afraid, Miss Horwich –"

"Oh, I know! I do so know that now –"

"I think – I think there might be some misunderstanding here –"

"I'll take notes, Doctor Clark. Mmmm, I know you'll straighten me out on all the fine points –"

"Perhaps we should take the time to discuss these feelings, Rachel –"

"I found all the best books I could get my hands on, Doctor Clark –"

"I'm sure you did, Rachel. You've always struck me as a quick study – Rachel!"

"Do you really think so? How am I doing now? Am I doing this right? It seems to me I am, Emanuel – I'm just following the diagrams as I remember them. Mmmm, I've never actually practiced fellatio on a man before –"

She looked up at me with such beautiful earnestness.

"You're doing just fine, Rachel –"

"Mmmm, thank you, Doctor Clark."

There is something to be said for the enthusiasm of youth. What Rachel lacked in finesse she more than made up for in dutiful application. There is something heartwarming about looking down into the rosy face and blue eyes of a young lady more than willing to please. Rachel made me feel like a large cone of chocolate ice cream, but in this case, the pleasure seemed to be all mine. She kept looking up at me with every flick of her tongue, carefully eyeing the waxing and waning of my delight as she sat back and leaned forward with engaging puckered lips. I felt her mouth sliding up and down with an almost hypnotic rhythm and saw something like a red fingertip going round and around in a dreamy haze.

"Do you want me to talk dirty to you, sir?" Rachel asked me.

"No, Rachel. Just take your time, you doing just fine! I'm grading on a curve…"

RESULTS OF CONSULTATION

When I stood at the window the Sun was just coming up. I was lost in the thought that my career was ruined in one fell swoop. Somewhere through this swirling fog the sound of her voice brought me abruptly back into the present. There she was a fiery red storm swaddled in my sheets and murmuring my name. The way the Sun fringed her bare form dispensed any doubt that this was all a dream.

"Emanuel? Doctor Clark?"

"Yes, Rachel?"

I sighed wearily.

"What have we done here?"

"I'll have to admit I'm without an explanation at this time."

"Oh. What should we do now?"

I turned to look out the bedroom window once more.

"You say Christ came to you and gave you his approval?"

"Oh yes! I am quite certain of that. I can feel him in my heart even now approving of us being together. Yes, even as we speak."

The authority of my doubt and skepticism paled and wanly evaporated beside the authority of her certainty. I was left standing naked at my bedroom window, unable to hide or deny the sight of my growing passion for her.

"Doesn't it strike you as strange that he did not come to us simultaneously and anoint us with the certitude you now appear to have for me?"

Rachel sat up and placed her fingertips in an attitude of prayer before her lips. There was humor in her watery blue eyes as she peered at me frankly.

"We could pray about it, Doctor Clark. Since our Lord has somehow managed to summon our attention concerning this matter…"

"Yes, I think that would be best about now."

How hollow those words seemed to me even as I uttered them! The truth was obvious to the mature adult as was the throb of my erection now for Rachel. I should have made her put her clothes back on and pulled down the Bible from my bookcase at that point. The time to pray was at the outset when we were still properly engaging our social roles as student and teacher.

That was the time to properly examine whether or not this was indeed a spiritual call or merely an appeal to the carnal mind.

But that opportunity was long gone. All I could do was forlornly sink to my knees now that I was suddenly demoted from Rachel's mentor to her lover.

She consolingly patted my hand before we began to pray.

At least now we were beginning to reflect upon the consequences of what we had done…

STATUS OF FILE REPORT

"Are these the discs you received in their entirety?'

"Yes, I was very careful not to leave them out while studying."

"Do you require any additional materials for your report?"

"No. I believe the data you have provided me with will be quite sufficient."

"Are there any additional concerns that need to be addressed at this time?"

"You can find all the recommendations I have made contained within my paper."

"We look forward to reviewing your report."

WITNESS CONSULTATION

He heard her stumbling in her boots over the snow shovels that he left leaning against the bannister on the porch. There was a light frost on the walkway despite the fact that he only recently finished shoveling it free of snow. He was barely sitting down to enjoy a mug of hot cocoa when he saw her coming up the steps as the street lights came on for the night.

He gave a distracted sigh as he rose up again to unlock the door while the chimes rang. He meditated as to whether to set his mug of cocoa down or simply to hold its steaming contents by the handle. He saw her reddened face peering back at him from behind the latch as he unchained it. There was some reluctance in his manner as he let her inside to stamp the snow off her boots and the cold out of her toes.

"You should have scraped the ice off the steps before I got here," she critically noted with a haughty air, "a body could break their neck or something out there."

"Well, it wouldn't hurt to call before you come knocking, you know."

"Hmph. It wouldn't hurt if you took my coat and offered me some refreshment either."

"Excuse me, Rachel. Let me take your coat. I'll get some more cocoa from the kitchen."

"That's what I like to hear."

She removed her red head warmer and bent down to shake the ice crystals out of her tumbling auburn tresses until her hair almost swept the floor. Rachel was an imposing figure standing before the doorway. When he returned with her cup of cocoa, she was moving about the living room without a stitch on closing the drapes.

Clark would have reproved her for such a gesture, but for the vision of inspiring beauty she presented in performing such a simple act.

"Rachel, this isn't necessary —"

She stood after closing the last drape with her hands clasped before her.

"Please, Doctor Clark, let me speak. I don't want to read any more books or help you win any more awards and prizes, scholastic or otherwise. You don't have to advise and guide me concerning my artwork or my literary ambitions. We don't have to go swimming or dancing or hiking and biking. I'm not interested in whether we make good study or work partners. You don't have to take tennis lessons or learn how to golf to get along better with my friends and family, and I'm not making any special effort to perfect my Free Throw shot or taking bowling lessons to get along better with your buddies."

Rachel took a deep breath and began again to speak. There was the most earnest expression upon her face.

"I'm not looking to be part of any grand vision or scheme for the Future. I just want you to fuck me as hard and as long and as often as love will allow. Should you get me pregnant I would never think of getting an abortion and I'll have your baby whether you marry me or not. I just thought it would be best to get all this out in front now so that you know what is needed and wanted from yours truly."

Rachel took a deep breath, her huge breasts heaving above her swelling lungs. She gazed at Clark with flickers of diffidence that she somehow managed to mask as she resumed an air of self-possession. Something new was entering her life, and she felt her whole being was clothed somehow in a strange kind of sexual authority.

"Now. Are there any questions?" Rachel asked as she lifted her chin to Clark defiantly.

Clark regarded Rachel thoughtfully.

"Here," he held forth the steaming mug to her. "Take your cocoa…"

"Yes sir."

Rachel stepped forward as Clark handed the mug to her by the handle.

"Careful now," he cautioned, "it's hot!"

"Yes sir," Rachel nodded as she gingerly sipped from the mug.

"Now pick up your things."

Rachel looked up at Clark with her watery blue eyes full of expectation.

"There's a hanger in my bedroom down the hallway to your left. You can hang up your things in there."

Rachel looked at Clark as though she was being handed her diploma. She set her cup of cocoa on the mantel above the fireplace.

"Yes sir! Thank you, sir…"

Rachel collected her things off the carpet and headed quickly down the hallway.

"Now once you've put up your things," Clark called after her, "you should see two pairs of slippers in the closet.

"Sir? Oh! I see them, sir!"

"Good. You put on the gold ones and bring the suede-back slippers out to me."

"Okay! Here I come!"

Clark sat down with dutiful weariness and began to unbutton his shirt. Rachel came out in a rush of youthful excitement. The sight of her immediately invigorated him. He pointed to the closet in the living room.

"Look up there and you should find a small cardboard box sealed with blue duct tape."

"Up here?"

"Right. Turn on the light and you'll see better."

"Okay. Yeah, I see it now…"

"Good. Reach up and get it."

"Alright. I've got it now."

"Excellent. Open it up."

Rachel stood there in front of the closet with the box in her hands. She pinched at the duct tape on the box with the white tips of her fingernails.

"Take your time. Get a knife from the kitchen."

Rachel set the box on the arm of a nearby sofa chair. She shuffled and clacked away in the open-toed golden slippers she was now wearing. When she came back Rachel took up the box again and carefully cut away the duct tape from its edges.

"Cut away from your hands, Rachel."

"I am, Emanuel…"

She lifted away the flaps on the cardboard and pulled forth a strange object made out of painted construction paper.

"What is this, Emanuel?"

"Call me Manny, Rachel. How many sides are there to what you've got in your hand?"

Clark watched Rachel's lips move with amusement as she mumbled to herself turning the object around in her hands.

"Eight? No ten! This has something to do with Geometry, doesn't it? I've seen this before. You call it something. Like a cube or a pyramid or something…"

"It's a dodecahedron, Rachel."

"That's right. Something like one of the Platonic Solids…"

"Exactly. Shake it."

"What?"

"I said shake it."

"Oh. Alright…"

Rachel eagerly shook the object in her hands and became aware of something rattling inside. She glanced at Clark with questioning eyes.

"What's that?"

"Open it up and see."

Rachel took up the knife again and picked at the edges of the paper dodecahedron.

"Cut away from your hands, Rachel."

"Okay, I am…"

Rachel slit through one of the sides of the paper object. She carefully extracted a hinged black velvet box from inside the remains of the paper dodecahedron.

"Emanuel?"

"Call me Manny."

Rachel looked at Clark and then at the black velvet box in her hands.

She was all wide-eyed wonder now.

"Why don't you have a seat, Miss Horwich?"

Rachel stepped back numbly and sat down on the blue cushion of a sofa chair. She was staring forward as though lost in space.

"What is this you've given me, Manny?"

"Open it up and see."

Rachel opened up the black velvet box and the small ring glittered nestled upon the silk bed inside. Clark watched as her face turned red and her eyes began to bristle with tears. He continued to take off his shirt and unbuckle the belt on his pants.

"Why don't you try it on for size?" Clark tenderly urged her.

"May I?" Rachel murmured with a whisper.

"I don't see why not."

Rachel delicately removed the ring from its bed and slipped it onto her finger. Clark watched her gulp as she kept her head bowed.

"You know," Clark began, "when people in the Bible have sexual relationships with each other they're described as 'knowing' each other. I've always wondered how we went from 'knowing' to 'fucking'. I was hoping between your studies for your Masters Degree and your Doctorate, we might investigate these matters and come to some useful conclusions. I would appreciate any assistance you could give me."

"I'll help you in any way I can, Doctor Clark."

Clark pulled off the rest of his underwear and placed the articles neatly on top of the shirt and the folded pair of pants draped over his sofa chair. He watched Rachel as she flicked away the tears that were pelting her knees. When she finally raised her bowed head, Clark was startled to note the angelic expression that shone on her face.

"Uh – I know that, Rachel. Take my clothes over there into the bedroom."

"Thank you, Manny, thank you…"

When Rachel returned from the bedroom, she was gratified to find Clark turning off the last of the living room lights with a tremendous erection. Now he was as naked as she was as he handed her the cup of cocoa off the living room mantelpiece. The streetlights cast a pale blue glow on their bodies from the darkness outside.

"I set your clothes on the dresser, Manny," she informed him as she sipped the cocoa from her cup.

"Good. I hope you'll forgive me when I admit I'm not much of an authority on 'the mystery of Christ' or any romantic notions associated with it –"

Clark swept Rachel off her feet and firmly into his arms.

"Whoa! Careful there, sir! I'll spill my cocoa."

"Sorry about that, Rachel."

"No need for concern on your part, sir. Regarding 'the mystery of Christ', I'll have you know I have been duly appointed to assist you with that part of the research."

"Let's get started then, lady. There's no time like the present."

Clark carried Rachel towards the bedroom while she resumed sipping her cocoa.

"How do you sleep in here with all these books?" Rachel exclaimed as she lay across Clark's bed poring through some Chinese volume having to do with love and sex. "I would be like a hermit in here with all this reading matter to hand."

Clark watched her kicking back in her blushing pink nakedness. The sight of her fixing her reading glasses to the bridge of her nose sent a thrill through him while he fixed his tie in the mirror. He silently noted to himself with amusement how her voluptuous presence highlighted his bedroom. Clark reached for his suit coat as he realized how much Rachel seemed like a fugitive from a girlie magazine.

"Now you have your opportunity, Miss Horwich."

"Do you have classes today?"

"Yes."

"When are you coming back?"

"This evening. I should be gone most of the day."

"Should I have dinner ready for you by the time you come back home?"

"Sure. I would be interested to see what you come up with."

"I'll fix you something special, honey."

"Sure. Surprise me. Do you need to get groceries or anything?"

"I'm not sure. I'll have to take a good look at your fridge, Manny."

"Alright. I left you a spare set of keys if you need to get out and about. You might want to spend some time studying for your next class with me…"

"I'll take that under advisement, sir."

Clark regarded her with affection as he shrugged into his overcoat. She stretched out and languidly examined the ring on her finger with an almost haughty sigh He picked up his briefcase and walked over to her as she traced her lower lip with a fingertip. He reached down to plant a goodbye kiss on her and felt her tongue flicking coquettishly inside his mouth.

"Bye…" she murmured as she heard the door close behind him with a final click.

DEPARTURE CONSULTATION

She watched them packing their luggage into the back seats and the trunk. The sight of them made her sigh with disgust. The winter breeze went softly through her curtains as she pulled her shades down. What a pair they made dressed up so properly in all their professional attire. Who did they think they were fooling! They certainly were not fooling her.

The red Buick LaCrosse made its way cruising down the street and disappeared over the horizon. The Sun melted into the gathering darkness of sunset. She reached for her cell phone to make the call.

"Yes, I see them now," she reported scowling. "That indeed could be so. Yes, they were all packed up to go on some kind of trip for all I could tell. No public displays of affection to report. No. He could be sending her off to college with his blessings for all these 'neighbors' of mine would care. Yes, of course … I'll keep you posted…"

She clicked her cell phone off with vindictive satisfaction.

CONFIRMATION OF STATUS

"We're here with our research team."

"Yes, we have your request on file."

"We will need The Doctor Clark Files to verify our current findings."

"Our apologies to you and your team. The Doctor Clark Files cannot be made available to you at this time."

"Oh? Is there some discrepancy with regard to our credentials?"

"That appears to be the case, unfortunately. We have found it necessary to alert the authorities. Please be advised that there will be no violation of your legal rights."

"Our legal rights?"

"Yes, in cases such as these where there may be a possible dispute we suggest the parties involved forego any idea of fleeing or resisting arrest until the pending investigation is concluded to the satisfaction of all concerned."

"Investigation? I'm afraid I don't understand."

"You will be provided with everything. Please be seated and your number will be called when the authorities have arrived."

Holy Crossword
Dorothy

Four across. I should know this. Chango. No, that's not it. I read the thing from cover to cover and I should know all this. Four across. Founder of Hyperspace Mechanics. I don't know. One down. Better try that. A native or inhabitant of Africa. That's an easier one to handle. Better count the squares. Seven. Yeah, I know this. A-F-R-I-C-A-N. That's it, baby, you got it- sister. Now four across again. I ought to refer to the book again, but let me see if I can wing it. Definitely not C-H-A- N-G-O, because the R is where the N should be now. Let me see–C-H-A-R-N-O. Oh, right! Professor Charno, the baldheaded fellow with the blue skin. Should have known something wasn't quite kosher. Five across. Every time I went for coffee, there he would be across the street. Five across. I don't know. Pretending to read the Free Press when he was really just checking me out to see where I was going. Um. The ones down seem easier than the ones across. Let me see. Two down and fun to go.

Ha. A rapier wit, mah lady. Should have told somebody. Two down. A main street in Detroit. Now aren't we keeping it local. Got to be W-O-O-D–that's right–W-A-R-D, that's right, that's it. Six across.

Thought it was just a coincidence the first few times I saw him across the street or behind me in the late afternoon crush to get home. Six across. First name of Randurian conqueror. That's easy too. D-R-U-L-L. Drull Drugor. Eight across. Highly skilled teacher. I-N–no, can't be instructor. D-R–no, can't be that either. Should have told some friends. Professor! Got to be Professor. Yeah, P-R- O-F-E-S-S-O-R. Professor Charno. What was I thinking to let him blithely stalk me like that? Should have left work with friends. Hmph. Three down. A sailor? A seaman-whatever. What else could a sailor or seaman be? I don't know, better try something else. Ten across. Surname of Randurian Tyrant. I know that. I already have Drull down. Let me see-D-R-U-G-O-R. Uh-huh, that will do it. What's next? Eleven across. What I should have done was have Teddy pick me up at work. He could have been my eye witness.

Fourth planet from the Sun. That's not earth, that's for sure. What's the next one. Oh, I know, it's gotta be Mars. Let me check-how many letters? M-A-R-S. Yep, moving right along. Teddy would have known what to do. The only thing is it would have led to other things. Picking me up after work would have given him plenty of opportunity to pressure me for a date. No, I didn't want to go there.; didn't want to go through all that. Margaret worked downtown just up the street. I could have called her and gave her the lowdown.

Um. Seven down now. To serve as a prediction; what's that all about? Can't be OMEN, not enough letters. Mmmmn, PREMONITION (?) No, that's too long-too many letters. To serve as a prediction-to serve as a prediction-to serve as a prediction-to serve-what about-no, it's got to have an S in it whatever it is that goes in here. Nearly lost a digit when he hustled me into the car and slammed the door on my fingers. Should have gotten someone to walk me to the parking lot. Who would have thought anybody would have the nerve to grab someone in an area as well-lighted as that? I should have put up more of a fight. Ugh! I can still taste his gloved hand cupped around my mouth, choking off the scream in my throat and heart before it ever got started. I should have put up more of a fight. I should have taken off one of my high heels and twisted around to gouge out his eyes. Right. That's easy to say now. Easy to know what to do after the fact. While it's actually really happening your wits scatter in all directions. Sure, I should have been prepared for something like – for something like that before I ever started out to my car. Yeah, that's what they all say. What I want to know is who ever prepares for the day they might be kidnapped and raped?

Where was I? To serve as a prediction-to serve as a prediction-to serve as a sign (?) A sign for what? A sign of things to come? A foretelling? No. A foreboding? No. A forewarning? No. A foretaste? Well, that has an S in it… no, that won't work-there are too many letters. I wish somehow I could get rid of the chill that runs down my legs and up through the root of me deep into the middle of the night when I wake up from another nightmare panting and sweating tears out of my pores remembering the ugly, snarling nicotine-stained teeth gritting behind the oval opening in the lint-filled red and black ski mask and demanding I take off my panties and throw them across the back seat. Let's try thirteen across-I don't know what seven down is all about.

Passageway or energy frequency. Just when I need it to get easier this puzzle gets harder. I should have seen it coming, but how was I to know? Passageway or frequency, I don't know that-let's try nine down. Maybe something will open up down there. Nine down. Nine down. The killer part about it was he parked that red Camaro of his right by my black Ford Focus as big as Life in broad daylight. How many times did I see him standing by that corroded ride of his, smiling at me, barely able to raise his hand in a nervous wave? A crew-cut, tinted glasses, a mustard colored mustache pasted across his upper lip, and all wrapped up in a navy-blue windbreaker that was obviously too big for him. Nine down. Nine down. I should have known, but what I want to know is where was Warren Melvander, our trusty old security officer, when the Sun went down and I stayed late to finish up my blueprints? What pains me is how I came off the elevator and told him how I would be right back because I needed to get the rest of my specs out of the car. I thought he would look out for me when I left the vestibule. I didn't think I would have to specifically tell him. After all, that was what he was–that was what he was–being paid to do. Hmn. Nine down. Nine down. The time that is to come. Um. That rules out the past and nix on the present. I know this one. The F in PROFESSOR has to be the–has to be the beginning of–yep! F-U-T-U-R-E. I know I should have parked closer to the front entrance instead of by the freight elevator. That still doesn't excuse Officer Melvander. I just want to know where was he when I was shivering by my car, with a furry hand cuffed around my mouth and the cutting edge of some kind of hunting knife poking at the underside between my breast and ribs. Sixteen across. Sites where battles are fought. How about Bunker Hill or Gettysburg? No, there are not enough letters in Gettysburg. I think maybe Pearl Harbor. No, I'm still a couple letters short. How about the parking lot adjacent to the Guarding Building?- There's a battleground for you. My own personal version of Hamburger Hill. Sometimes when I'm at home reading or watching television I can hear the voice of Rodger Ray Cook behind me as clear as a death knell.

"Remember me?"

Before I could give anything like an intelligent reply, I felt a gloved hand close about my windpipe and another around my lips. I thought he was going to break my jaw his grip was so tight. "Remember me? Just nod if you recognize the sound of my voice." I racked my brains all in a split-second as to who this could possibly be. "Don't try to scream. You cry out and I'll cut out your heart and store it in a jar with my own piss."

He pressed his head in my hair when he said this. Sometimes I think to myself that any passerby catching a glimpse of us from afar would have thought he was a lover whispering an endearment in my ear. Some sweet nothing from a maniac, wooing his prey. A shudder coursed through me and shook my entire body, but I uttered not one sound. The only thing that came out of me was the mist of my breath in the cold night.

"Open the door to your car." He whispered in my ear.

The keys trembled between my fingers. I pressed the button on the keypad and the doors to the Ford Focus burped open. The hand that was clasped about my throat reached down and snatched the keys from my hand.

"Get in the back and lock the door," he tells me, "you try and run from me and you will be one sorry mess of a sight."

Rodger Cook ushered me into the back and a thousand and one alternatives exploded in my mind like some kind of fragmentation grenade. I could have screamed, turned and fought, made a run for it somehow. The moment swelled around me and I attempted to steel my resolve, but whatever reserves of will I attempted to summon just seemed to wash out of me in a sick, queasy feeling of timorous weakness.

The moment passed and I was in the back like an obedient little waif. I heard the doors relock around me and all hope was shut out in a clacking finality.

"What is it you want from me?"

I heard myself saying it, but it sounded like I was listening to someone else take up my side.

"Just keep your hands in your lap, honey bunch."

"What do you want?" I asked the ski masked head in the rearview mirror. "Do you want money? I left my purse in the office, but there's some travelers' checks in the glove compartment. You can have them. You need my car? Take it. I don't care. Just let me out right here. I won't tell anyone."

I could have been mistaken, but it seemed to me he was chuckling to himself. I thought I saw him slowly shaking his head as though I just didn't get it.

"You really don't remember me, do you? Now keep your hands in your lap. You spring for that door and I'll break your arm. You scream for help and I'll slit your throat from ear to ear, but not straight away if you catch my drift. Are we on the same page now, sugar pie?"

"Who are you?" I asked in a resentful whisper.

"I think it will come to you in time." I hear him start the engine. "I don't want your money. I don't want your car. Now I want to make sure we have an understanding about this escaping business and this crying out for help stuff. Do you follow me, sweet thing? I need an answer right now, yes or no?"

"Yes,…" I heard my voice in spite of myself.

"That's better. Now that we're on the same page, we better get rolling. Let's go back to my place where we can talk."

"What do you want?" I mumbled grimly.

I felt the car lurch out of the parking lot. He was making his way down Michigan. Rodger Cook glanced at me with a curious, sneering smirk.

"Don't you know? I want you, honey bunch. I'll tell you what; take off your panties and give them to me."

"WHAT?"

"Calm down now, sugar pie, calm down. Don't make me come back there and put a bullet through your head. I want the panties. Give 'em to me right now."

This is it, I thought to myself, I'm going to die. This creep is planning to kill me. There. This is it. B-A-T-T-L-E-G-R-O-U-N-D-S. Sixteen across. Now eleven down. Things that conceal or disguise. Whatever it is, it'll start with an M and end with an S.

"Since you're going to murder me anyway, why don't you take off that ski mask so I can see who you are?" I challenged him bitterly.

"All in due time, darling, all in due time."

MASKS! That's what it is! Starts with an M, and now A-S-K- and ends with an S. That's it! M-A-S-K-S. Now seventeen down.

"I'll tell you what–" This idea flashes into my head from nowhere, "–let's make a swap. I'll hand over my panties and you hand over your ski mask so I can see who it is that's going to kill me."

"Where do you get the idea that you're in any position to bargain with me?"

"What–are you going to rape me wearing that ski mask? That's pretty kinky, isn't it?"

"What difference will it make to you?"

"Whatever happened to granting the condemned a last request?"

"What last request?"

"I want to see your face before I die. A girl should at least see the face of her attacker before she goes."

"Look, sweet thing, nobody's going anywhere and nobody's dying. You just be a good little girl and hand over those panties. Stop the pretense, little lady. We're not negotiating some bid on a condo here. Throw your drawers my way, sugar pie, and Daddy's going to take real good care of you. Forget all that Woman's Lib crap." I'll never forget how he turned and looked over to me while the Street lamps flashed ribbons of light across the side windows and upholstery of my car. "Unless, that is, you want me to make special reservations for you to have your own little private plot of land. That what you want, honey bunch? God's Little Acre for your little spring chicken be-hind?"

Seventeen across. Land measure or 43, 560 square feet. 'Let's Ask Architect Dorothy', brought to you by Procter & Gamble. Hmph. A-C-R-E. Twelve down. Unquestioning belief. Should be bias, but that's not enough letters. Should be prejudice, but that's too many. Same thing for obsession.

Some kind of term for fixed idea, but what could it be? Whatever it is, it has to have five letters. I don't know why it took me so long to place that voice.

"Don't you remember the letters you used to get when you were in college? Always signed the same way?"

Finally, it came to me, and I matched the voice to a face and the face to a name.

"R.C. Cola?"

"At your service, ma'am. There you go, in the flesh."

All my girlfriends used to give me the skinnies on how Roddie Ray Cook wallpapered his dorm room with photos of me. According to them, he would take his pictures while I was walking to and from classes. I was just an Architectural Design major at the time. He was studying to be a surveyor or something like that. The fellow seemed nice enough the few times I met him and talked to him in my classes. I never took much notice of him. A lanky, tall guy with a diffident manner, I would see him every now and then darting between the buildings like a ferret. Sometimes it looked like he was cradling a camera and sometimes no, but all the wild tales my girlfriends told me about him I just chalked up to idle gossip. There were plenty of guys on campus back then with the hots for me. Some I dated and others I did not, but with drafting classes driving me batty I had to concentrate on my studies. After graduation, the marriage proposals started coming in like fan mail.

I will have to admit it was all very flattering at the time.

All those letters! Some I opened and read, others I filed in the trash bin. Now I'm wondering, what could I have done with Ray Cook's letters? I don't know.

Fourteen down. Supreme male ruler. Four letters. Hmmn, it's not chief, it can't be boss, must be K-I-N-G. Yeah, that fits the N in BATTLEGROUNDS. One more. Fifteen down. What is this? Of the cosmos. Whatever it is, it's got to have an O and a C in it. Let me see, C-O-S-M-I-C. Yeah, that hits the spot. Now I'll go back and fill in the ones I missed.

"You never gave me a tumble," I heard something in his voice break that almost made me feel pity for him. "-never even as much as had a cup of coffee with me. Why? I'm just a good ole boy. Free, white and twentyone just like you are. What would one date have cost a pretty girl like you? Just one date with a nice guy like me. We could have gone out a few times and found out what we had in common-"

The car was slowing down, which told me we were nearing his place. He kept on rambling all that Lonely Hearts nonsense. How mortified he was and how rejected I made him feel. I kept inching my hand over to the lock button in the door console. I prayed to God that he didn't notice what I was doing in the rear-view mirror. While I was secretly groping to unlock the side passenger door, I nervously kicked a book or something on the floor with my toe.

That's it! The name of the book in my car! S-T-A-R-H-A-M-M-E-R!

"Do you always give potential girlfriends this kind of treatment?"

"Can't say that I have. But then, I guess there's a first time for everything, eh?"

"Look, you don't have to go through all this with me. Wha—what type of books do you like to read?"

"A few years too late for that, isn't it? What say we skip the preliminaries on this date, little darling." We were slowing to a crawl and I reached down for the book at my feet. Ray Cook turned to me and once again raised the hunting knife in his fist. "Now I asked you kindly for your panties, missus. Don't make me come over there. I'll slice them off if I have to an-"

I caught him with an awful whack under the chin, swinging the book upward with all my strength. Stunned, he reflexively slashed the hunting knife at my head and nicked me just above the brow near the crown of my head. My hands darted out in spite of the spasm of pain lancing through my temples. I mashed down on the lock button and levered the door open, spilling out in a desperate, tangle and jumble on the loose gravel and tufts of dry grass. He was pushing to open the door on his passenger side, and only pressed the lock button in a raging afterthought.

I was on my feet now with something wet curling around my right eyebrow and tracing itself through my hair and underneath my earlobe. I touched my fingertips to the edge of my ear and saw red on my fingers.

I could feel my heart pumping as Ray Cook bolted through the door on the driver's side to come around to where I was backing up in a terrified shiver. I took off one of my heels, having no other weapons to hand, and threw it at him. What else could I do? I saw the shoe bounce off his collarbone as he attempted to duck. I took off my other shoe to throw it as well, thought the better of it, and simply turned and ran for my life.

I was running without any idea where I was going. I looked back, because I knew he would be coming after me. I saw him trip and fall in a patch of wet grass, and that made me bear down and run all the harder. I managed to make it to the main road in about fifty yards. What I would have done otherwise I cannot tell you. I darted in my bare stocking feet between whizzing cars, their flashing headlights almost blinding me, and dodged at the blaring sound of oncoming horns until I made it to the other side of the road. The traffic everywhere was heavy and thick and it was providence that I didn't get run over in my crazy terror.

I could see Ray Cook on the other side between all the cars going both ways. I kept glancing at him out of the corner of my eye as I waved my arms wildly like a madwoman, hoping to flag a car down. Miserable seconds passed sluggishly during which I could see Ray Cook making his way through the traffic over to my side. Just as my heart sank that nobody would be having any of my troubles this night, a yellow checker cab rolled over onto the shoulder and flashing its red lights, cruised back in reverse towards me.

I ran, slipping and sliding with all my might.

I swung open the passenger door and hopped inside.

"Get me out of here!" I barely managed to gasp. "That guy—see that guy? Over there! Over there! That guy is trying to kill me!"

The cabbie was some young black fellow in a green windbreaker and a red beret. He clumsily slipped gears into forward drive. We lurched away off the shoulder and down the road. When we came to the first Police Station we could find, I filed a report. This took some hours, and the taxi driver who picked me up was also required to make a statement. After all, he was just about the only one who really witnessed anything. At least as far as I could tell.

Channel! C-H-A-N-N-E-L! Yes! That's it. A passageway or energy frequency. The E fits FUTURE and everything. Now it's time to clean up the ones that go down. Three down. A sailor; a seaman. Something like Ulysses perhaps? Now there's the R in Professor and the A in STARHAMMER. Mariner maybe? M-A-there's the A-R-I-N-E-and there's the R! Yep! Seven down. Seven down. Seven down … to serve as a prediction. Now I remember! Foretaste was too long—wait a minute! How about forecast! F-O-R-E-C-A- S-T! Just one more, twelve down. Unquestioning belief. It's got to have five letters. Maybe dogma, that has five letters. No, I need an A instead of an O. Ulp! What was I thinking? Faith! F-A-I-T-H! That's it!

Faith. Yep. F-A-I-T-H.

Uh-oh. I think the Mayor just introduced me. Yes, she's motioning me toward the podium. Better get going.

Tactile Understanding

N ever thought I would run into someone like Betty. I was without a clue as to what INFINITEX ENTERPRISES was all about. But thank heavens for Betty. She has really changed my life in so many ways…

We were a pair before we spoke a word to each other. I was just standing in the back of the elevator when it stopped at the third floor. Betty was the cheery cherry floating in a crowd of people that stepped forward. The car was packed within a few seconds as this well-built woman nodded at me. She flashed me a nervous smile as she attempted to turn around to face-front, but there was not enough time. The rush of people into the car against her back made her trip into my arms.

"Oh! Sorry," Betty exclaimed reaching for the papers spilling out of her file folder.

Before I knew it, she was standing on top of my feet, clutching the manila folder to her bosom. She looked up at me with blushing cheeks, glancing behind her with a gasp of distress as she was pressed even tighter to my chest. The feel of her big breasts thrust in a tight squeeze against me was as unexpected as the curl of her toes against the cuffs of my pinstriped pants. I really worked to keep from being aroused.

"Uh! Excuse me," Betty uttered again as she raised the manila folder over her head to keep her papers from falling out again.

"I'll hold that for you."

"Would you please?"

She placed both her hands against the sides of my neck. Our eyes were locked onto each other as I held her folder between my hands over her shoulders. The car seemed to swell with even more people until we were virtually glued thigh to crotch to each other. There was nothing to do but be adult about it and not embarrass each other.

A sense of incredulity grew in the expressions on our faces. We were pressed against the wall of the car. Nobody seemed to notice or be aware of how hedged in we were with all these bodies. We might have protested, but were having the feeling that it would hardly matter to the offending parties.

After all, where would they go while the elevator was hurtling to the upper floors with all of us in it?

Betty fingered the edges of my starched collar as the moments became an eternity of expectation. Our eyes remained fixed upon each other in mutual apology as we soared up through the shaft. We even seemed to share the same breath as I racked my brains for small talk to put her at ease. There was something about her wholesome beauty that melted my presence of mind. The way her body fitted into mine was also providing a real test to my professional decorum.

"Where do you get off?"

"Eighty-seven floor," she chuckled ruefully. "Oh, brother."

Before I knew it, Betty was pressed up against the snake growing in my pants.

"No offense," I whispered.

Betty licked her lips and gazed at me with twinkling eyes. "None taken."

"This could happen to anyone,"

"Don't concern yourself. I'll give you one of our cards."

"Thank you. I would like that."

"It's the least I can do. My papers would be all over this carpet without your help."

"Glad you see it that way."

"Just stop by the office. I'll give you a good estimate."

"Sure thing. First break I get."

"I'll be looking out for you."

The elevator mercifully stopped on the fifty-second floor. A trickle of businessmen stepped out. Betty came down from her toes and stepped off of my feet. She turned around slowly, straightening out the front of her Navy blue skirt.

I handed back the Manila file over her shoulder.

"My lord. I can breathe again!" Betty declared as her adorable caboose brushed around past me. "Thank you."

"Don't mention it."

The bell above the elevator rang again as it stopped on the sixtieth floor and the doors slid open. Nobody exited from the car, but a group of elderly women boarded with mincing steps as they chattered away. Betty stepped back again and gave me a pat of reassurance. She deftly slipped her business card into my pocket.

"Looks like we're not out of the woods yet, Tiger."

"Tell me about it."

Betty was fitted against me again. We shared our little secret until the bell above the elevator rang once more at the seventieth floor. The elevator was clogging up again and nobody could see me as I placed my hands around Betty's waist.

"Ever done any work with our firm before?" She asked me seriously.

"No. This would be a first for me. Although, I would have to admit I find your statistics for this year impressive."

"That's gratifying. I'm hoping you get an opportunity to see our year end projections."

"I'm looking forward to it."

We came to the seventy-seventh floor and the elevator stopped with the ding of the bell. Suddenly, there was a mass exodus and the car emptied out and we were the only ones left in the car. Betty leaned back and rested her head just under my chin. I could smell the fresh scent of mint shampoo in her dark brown hair. My hands went up the sides of her waist and cupped her breasts. The doors to the elevator were sliding closed again and she patted my hands gripped against the buttons of her blouse.

"This is my floor coming up. Please feel free to call for an appointment."

"Any slots available for today?"

"Bound to be a tight fit, but leave it to me. I'll squeeze you in somehow."

"Good, because I'm up for an accommodation."

"Just so you know—I don't normally do this kind of thing."

The bell rang for the eighty-seventh floor and Betty paced towards the opening elevator doors.

"I've just got this hunch you have a lot to offer," Betty said as she nodded at me.

"Should I bring my resume'?"

"No. Come as you are."

The doors slid closed again and I watched the numbers flash until the elevator came to my floor.

I found myself flipping her card between my fingers. I was at my desk shredding outdated memoranda and rechecking graphical information. All the monitors arrayed around me were blinking their usual coded columns of statistics. There were stacks upon stacks of paperwork to be seen to post haste. The last thing I needed was to have some busty brunette clogging up the pores of my attention.

I poked curiously at her business card again on my blotter.

The best thing to do I resolved was to get ahead in my work. At that point, I could take a break and give her a call on the auto-phone. I looked around through my glass lined cubicle at the thousands of others at work in their own cubicles. Nothing I was doing in my work routine could raise a hint of suspicion. The seconds and the hours pulsed and throbbed into documented record. Soon I was well enough along in my workload that I could sit back and take a moment.

I picked up her card again running my fingertips along its edges. The card gave off the scent of her perfumed hair and filled my nostrils. The feel of the embossed letters was smooth to the touch. I squinted at the lines of text.

INFINITEX ENTERPRISES

BANNEKER BUILDING

**NATIONAL ASSOCIATION
OF TEMPORAL ADJUSTMENT
AND SPECULATION**

**87th FLOOR–CALL OR POST
APPOINTMENT ONLY**

The lights went out in the cubicles around me. I saw my fellow workers here and there turn off their information pads and reach for their coats. A few meandered past the entrance to my own office and gave me a wave. Moment to moment, I felt more and more like a solitary cube of light in the expanding and swelling darkness.

I wearily rose to my feet. I was still holding her card in my palm. The door to my closet slid open as I thumbed back the stud on my desk console. I could see the blue light pulsing above the frame of the Intercom Monitor on the wall. The Monitor was automatically scrolling through all my unanswered calls when I saw her face.

I reversed scrolling until I came to the numbered code of her call. There was Betty, looking frankly at me with a wholesome, open smile on her face. She tossed a wave of hair over her shoulder before her voice reached out to me over the auto-phone. I slid my information pad back into my desk as I watched her speak.

"Coming down to see me some time, Tiger? Traffic volume is slow down here right now. Care to meet in the lobby and walk a girl to her transport?"

I glanced down at the time of the message flashing in green numbers. I was at a loss to determine how I missed her call. I reached for my coat and waved out the lights in my office. The message was only minutes ago. Perhaps I could just catch her, before she left for the day.

When I got down to the eighty-seventh floor I could see the vacuum drones hovering in the air with their lights clicking and flashing. All these machines were involved in a little light dusting up and down the hallways. Some were gliding along the molding underneath the ceiling suctioning out the grit and cobwebs. I could see others cleaning out the ashtrays near the windows and the elevators. Finally I came to the glass lined office for the National Association of Temporal Adjustment and Speculation. I could see the office-keeping drones gliding inches above the carpeting and cleaning under the desks.

I pressed my head against the glass and cupped my hands around my eyes. I scanned around the office but nobody seemed home. I sighed and shrugged and lifted up the coat that was draped over my forearm.

I walked with head bowed past the young and portly elevator operator who nodded at me as I passed.

"Good night, sir."

"Good night." I mumbled to the polished floor.

"Going down?" he asked.

The flicker of an idea startled me as his fingers hovered over the lighted console.

"Something you wanted to ask, sir?"

"Yes, now that you mention it. You wouldn't have happened to see a young woman pass by here a few minutes ago, would you?"

"A young woman, sir?"

"Yes," I handed him the card, "I believe she works for this company here…"

"Hmnn, 'INFINITEX ENTERPRISES'…" The elevator operator fingered the beginnings of his goatee. "Now that you mention it, I did pass a woman over there leaning against the window sill about half an hour ago. She kept looking over her shoulder like she was waiting for somebody."

The sensor sounded and the elevator doors gently closed. "You wouldn't recall her name by any chance?"

The elevator operator handed me back my card. We went whooshing down to the lobby floor.

"All I remember really was her leaning with her back towards me and her elbows on the window sill. She was…"

The elevator operator shaped the space in front of him and nodded at me with an approving glance.

"Well put together?'

"…uh, wearing her insignia and crest, I was going to say, sir. Did you have an appointment with her by any chance?"

"No. She just suggested I stop by and review her company's statistics."

"That's unfortunate, sir."

"Unfortunate?'

"Why, yes it is, sir. You saw the drones cleaning up the place, didn't you?'

"Yes."

"There. Now what does that tell you?'

I gazed at him with a flash of understanding.

"That's right, sir. INFINITEX ENTERPRISES is vacating the premises today."

There was silence for several moments between us as we clicked and pinged down past the floors.

"I'm a married man myself, sir," the operator spoke to his shoes, "but she was a masterpiece of design engineering as my drinking buddies would say. Several grades above – oh! Here we are, sir. The lobby…"

"Thank you," I mumbled, but could not say for sure he heard me.

I thought I sighted her a few times after that. Once while I was putting my Hover Car into autopilot and docking it to the ledge outside my floor. I looked through the windows and could have sworn I saw her pacing past one of our secretaries with a smile and a wave. But when I made my way down the ramp into the hallway she was gone. When I returned to the eighty-seventh floor after work one night on a lark, I could see the elevator operator was right. The walls and the floor were bare. Even the gold plate on the sidewall that read INFINITEX ENTERPRISES was removed. I also thought I saw her one night in a double-breasted coat walking and laughing with some friends. I was headed over to the parking lot for self-driving units when I was sure I caught her eye. But she seemed to look right through me and seemed different somehow. She glanced away as though she didn't recognize me and continued chattering with her friends as they disappeared through the sliding doors.

We were working on the specs for a new high-rise structure downtown. The office aide had brought in the data cube for the table projector and we were gathered around the holographic diagram on all sides in the conference room.

My business partner rattled off the numbers. Our secretaries took dictation on their lighted scroll pads. I punched in the calculated revisions to adjust the dimensions of the holographic projection, but a couple members of the team sensed my mind was somewhere else.

"Nothing to compare with the one that got away, huh?" My partner quipped.

There was amused titters from the secretaries. "What's that?" I muttered absentmindedly.

The blue and red lights began to flash on and off intermittently. The high-pitched burp of sirens pierced the air at close intervals. Everyone looked around with a sense of foreboding that blanketed the mood of the room.

My business partner waved away everyone's concern.

"Air Raid drill. Let's just keep working on this."

"Alright then," I began as I pointed forward.

The holographic projection spilling upwards into the air shimmered in response to the concussion from the first explosion. The next blast threw all of us simultaneously to the floor. Secretaries and business aides alike crawled frantically beneath the tables and the desks. The ceiling to the conference room buckled as one of the walls caved in and chunks of loose debris shot past our heads amidst ejaculated screams and scary moans of whispered prayers.

The ashen-faced office aide came stumbling back through. The door to the conference room was ajar and off its tracks. He looked around at us trembling with disbelief.

"What are you still doing here? The building is under attack! Everyone is to report to the Hover Car Dock for the floor or take the elevators to the parking lots. NOW!"

He reached out first for the secretaries who formed a living chain holding hands. They left the room whimpering and shrieking at the rain of dust and smoke pouring into the room.

"Turn that off and grab that data cube!" My business partner rasped in the choking air. "I'll download and retrieve all the pertinent documents and send them to our parent site."

"Hurry!" I demanded as I snatched up the cube. "Come on! We can take my Hover Car to a Shelter if we leave now!"

We reached for our coats. The building seemed to lurch and sway hurling us over tables and chairs.

"Are you all right?" I asked as I helped my business partner back up to his feet.

"I – I think so…" He coughed, slipping the company record discs into his coat. "Where is your car?"

"This way. Follow me."

We made our way around the corners and turned along and down all the aisles until we stumbled and limped into the main hallway. Office workers literally by the thousands were herding into the dozens of elevators on our floor. The ones left behind when these were packed banged and clawed on the closed elevator doors with sobs of despair.

"How much farther?" My business partner asked in desperation.

"We're almost there. Just ahead where you see the Dock windows."

I pulled out my key fob and pressed it to undock my Hover Car. I saw the Dock windows begin to shiver and creak. The giant windows began to crack and we only stopped just short of being buried with many others under an avalanche of shattering glass. Huge chips of masonry seemed to flutter in the air like confetti from some great height.

They came crashing down to crater the floor or bury some unfortunate worker in a tomb of rubble. The debris piled up so high it blocked our route to my Hover Car.

"We can't go that way," I wheezed to my business partner.

"Nothing for it now." He spat and coughed. "We'll have to take one of the elevators out of here.

I replaced my key fob back inside my coat. There was no way now for me to know whether or not my Hover Car had successfully undocked. The Dock windows were blasted down and that could have left my car still in hover mode.

I just did not know whether or not my car had gone down in the blast. We headed back the way we came amidst cries for help. Many were the bodies we helped to uncover from the rubble before I saw someone I recognized. A head and a hand in all that smoke and dust waved us over. "Ho! Sir! Is that you?"

"Who's there?" I cried out.

The elevator operator with the goatee emerged into a flash of light.

"I'm here, sir. This way. Bring your friend. There are still some down at the farthest end where the last elevator is located. Here, let me help…"

He threw my business partner's arm over his shoulder and began to shepherd us over.

We stumbled and shuffled forever down a hallway that seemed unending. Between the constant blaring and burping of the Air Raid sirens and the constant streaking of the blue and red lights against the walls and the ceilings, it felt like such a futile business. I did my best not to slip in anybody's blood or trip over all the charred rock that was scattered over the floors. I was longing to lean against something and catch my breath, but the efforts of our friend on the other side of me never seemed to flag.

Finally we came to a knot of people being herded into the last elevator at the end.

"Here we are, sir." The elevator operator ushered us through. "I'll have us down into the lobby in no time…"

We crowded ourselves into a space that could easily accommodate a hundred and fifty people, but which now seemed clogged to absolute claustrophobia. The air inside the elevator was rank with sweat and vomit and the stench of burnt metal and plastic. There was weeping and wailing that punctuated the constant background rumble of shock, dismay and consternation. I keep backing up with mounting exasperation as more and more people were herded inside.

"Going down!" The elevator operator announced to grateful relief of everyone.

I felt soft hands that smelled of lotion and perfume close about my eyes. "Looking for me, Tiger?"

"I can hardly tell blindfolded like this," I admitted uncertainly.

"Here, let me help you with that." I heard her voice.

I could feel her breath against my neck. She took my coat off the crook of my arm. Gently she slipped my arms through the sleeves of my coat and folded back its collar before giving me a little pat on the back.

I turned around and Betty was looking up with a mischievous chuckling glee. I saw there was oily grime across her forehead, nose and cheek. She was that very same beauty I remembered her to be, but I sensed something different about her that I just could not quite put my finger on.

"Where are your boots, my little man?"

"The Weather Man said nothing about dressing for an Air Raid."

"Betty? Who is that?" A woman behind Betty groaned.

"Just a friend who can help us out of here, Donna."

"That's right, isn't it, Tiger? You will help us out, won't you?"

My business partner nudged me with a hiccupping smirk.

"That the one that got away, fellow?"

Before long the doors to the massive elevator were sliding open. Hordes of people staggered out into an already cluttered lobby where medical teams were scrambling around vast numbers of cots. Levitated stretchers were being marked with color sensors for triage and sailed throughout the lobby in fleets towards the Hover Ambulances awaiting them. The air became filled with the plaintive cries of emergency sirens on their way to clinics and hospitals.

We helped my business partner limp over to one of the levitated stretchers.

"Better get checked out. I wouldn't want to wake up tomorrow paralyzed from the waist down for something that could be handled easily right now. How about you?'

Before I could speak, Betty wrapped her arms around my waist. "I'll see that Tiger gets checked out properly," she insisted.

"No doubt you will," my business partner quipped. "You have the data cube with you, right?"

"It's in my coat."

"When we arrive wherever they're taking me, I'll contact you from there, alright?'

"Alright."

"Thank god! Here come the sawbones heading off the reporters at the pass! Nice meeting you, miss..."

A doctor calibrated my business partner's stretcher to be neatly installed in one of the Emergency Vans.

We waved as the levitated stretcher bore my partner sailing away in the air.

"How are you getting home?" I asked Betty.

"That's a good question. Things are such a mess around here about now. Think there might be SDVs around here someplace?"

"We can take a look."

We took a walk out of the lobby onto the crowded main corner. Corner Marshals were vying with doctors and reporters for rights of way. Self Driven Vehicles were in short supply and people were fighting frantically for them.

That was when I remembered the key fob in my pocket. I took Betty hastily by the hand.

"Tiger! Where are you taking me?"

"Come with me to the North side of the building, Betty. I've got a hunch..."

There it was! My Hover Car was undocked from where I had originally parked it at the Docking Station. The vehicle was still hovering in midair next to the flaming and smoking devastated side of the Banneker building. I took out my key fob and fingered it gingerly.

"Barring any serious malfunction," I muttered to myself as I manipulated the key fob and keyed-in the vehicle identification number, "our ride home may be awaiting us for departure..."

There was still that incessant sound of voices behind me. Out of the corner of my eye I could just catch the looming silhouettes of people pattering their way towards us.

Betty and I looked up with anxious expectation.

Sure enough the ring-shaped doughnut chamber drifted silently from on high to a position just a few inches above the ground before us. I pressed the key fob again and the circular doors on either side opened up like gull wings. I turned to Betty and now gestured for her to take the passenger seat. I watched her eyes open wide as she stabbed a finger into the air over my shoulder.

"Oh! My Lord! What about them?"

"Wha–!" I barely caught my breath enough to exclaim.

The rush of silhouetted bodies piling up into my Hover Car nearly knocked the key fob out of my hand. There were shrieks and screams and fervent exhalations of thanks from the stammering female voices wedged in at all angles tight against my body. I scrambled for a foothold in the driver's seat crushed against Betty. There was no time to register a protest, and it was all I could do to maneuver into a position where I could lower the gull wings on either side of me.

"By your leave, sir." Betty nodded nervously as she took my hand. "You may take me home now. I would like to thank you in private for an ever so thrilling evening."

I sat down with Betty straddled across my lap and closed the see-through doors. There was love light in her eyes as we attempted to catch our breaths and regarded each other face to face. The din of voices wailing their trauma in this closed space made it difficult for us to say much else to each other. The darkness cast its strong shadows upon us from the shattered street lamps. This made it hard for me to grasp the faces and the identities of our additional passengers. But no one disputed we should leave the site of this invasion as soon as possible. I shifted the Hover Car into gear manually and with voice command lifted up.

Betty and I took off for her home, but I could not shake the feeling still that there was indeed something different about her this time.

Now everything is plain to me.

We showered together and washed all the sweat and grime of our experience down the drain. Everything was cleaned away but the trauma of that event. Except for the odd bruise here and there I was basically all of one piece. Scrubbing Betty down from head to toe I was amazed at the symmetry of her physique and form. There was something newly minted about her. She bore no birthmarks, scars or blemishes of any kind. You could not have put together a more attractive woman from a blueprint.

We made love and she left nothing to the imagination or held anything back.

She seemed to read my thoughts as to what I needed and wanted in a lover. So when she asked me what a 'data cube' was nestled in bed with her head against my chest, I told her what she wanted to know. I held nothing back and denied her nothing.

"May I see it? That is, before you hand it over to your business partner?"

There she is now, admiring the information receptacle as she holds it in the palm of her hand. She is to me still the most admirable form of woman, lying naked across the couch and kicking back with an easy, natural grace. She hears a voice at the door and turns to me.

"Better see who it is, Tiger. You can tell the mailman I'm not at home…"

I go to the door. But of course it was her voice all along. She gives me a kiss as she brings in the groceries.

"Hello, Tiger. Did you miss me?'

"I thought you would never get here."

We turn as we hear someone vigorously brushing her teeth in the bathroom.

"She just got up," I explain to Betty, "better see what she wants for lunch."

Betty comes out of the bathroom in her nightgown with her mouth filled with toothpaste holding the handle of her toothbrush between her puckered lips. She gestures to me to hold on for a moment. She rushes back to spit the toothpaste out in the washbasin.

She emerges radiant, standing barefoot inside the bathroom door. "I'm not going to be choosy at this point. I'll eat whatever you feed me, Tiger."

There is a voice again at the door.

"Go see who it is, Betty." I tell Betty as she takes the groceries into the kitchen.

"Right, Tiger. Just give me a moment to set these things down."

Betty goes to the door and it's Betty. She is dragging a long fiberglass box into the apartment. I run over and give her a hand.

"Hey, Tiger! Is this the kind of table projector your company uses at the Banneker Building?"

"Let's take a look. Yeah," I tell her, "the serial numbers seem to match. Somebody get a knife, a couple of screwdrivers and a pair of pliers."

Betty comes out of the bedroom. She yawns and stretches with the Sun fingering her beautiful bare body through the open window. She is carrying a Yoga mat.

"All that stuff is on the top shelf in the closet, Tiger. I put your toolbox up there just in case of emergencies."

"Did you get a good night's sleep, Betty?" I ask as she wanders over and I kiss her on the neck.

"Easy, Tiger." She wags a finger at me. "I know what's on your mind. I've got to be at INFINITEX in about an hour. No time for the hanky-panky."

Betty rolls out her yoga mat and begins practicing her poses in the nude.

We set up the table projector in no time. It is a collapsible affair that can easily be stored under bed. But now that it's all set up, I have Betty insert the data cube and make sure it is properly connected.

"Here, press this here," I take Betty by the hand and place her finger over the sensor stud. "That's it. Now try it…"

The holographic projection shot a tower of light straight to the ceiling. "Yah! It works!" Betty applauded with glee. "I love it when you bring your work home, Tiger! This calls for a celebration…"

Betty peeled off her nightgown and sat back on the couch.

I go to the window in our living room because I can hear somebody calling me from a Hover Car.

"Who's calling for you, Tiger?"

"Looks like Betty," I say tentatively squinting my eyes, "yeah, it's her…"

"Why don't you tell her to come on up?"

A couple of my Betties ran for the door while Betty elbowed me on either side of the window looking down…

Techtown Book Club

Professor Powell found it quite awkward. Rolling down the aisle way between the raked seats on either side, shielding his most attractive student from flying bullets. But what could he do when that fool lifted up that gun from the lectern and it went off? He did not expect her to reach out for him like that while he was brandishing that weapon at her. He also regretted tripping over his own big feet. But he knew it was best to cup his hand over her mouth before her scream made matters worse…

"The problem I find when I cover this subject with the high school students I teach, Professor Powell…" said Robin with a sigh of exasperation, "—is how to get past all the giggling and shocked expressions of surprise in order to discuss Human Sexuality in an intelligent and mature way."

"I can see how that would be quite a challenge, Miss Lancaster…"

She would sit there in his classroom after all the other students were gone. Robin normally paid him no mind as she continued going over her notes and marking paragraphs in her hardcover books with a highlighter. He found her the beautiful soul of propriety sitting in her white Reeboks and sweatshirt shuffling her papers.

"Be sure to turn off the lights when you're finished, Miss Lancaster."

"I will, Professor Powell, thank you very much…"

Powell closed the laptop and placed it back within the leather frame. He stacked the test papers together. Robin glanced his way as he placed them carefully within one of the accordion-like pockets of his briefcase. He could tell she was going out on the town tonight. She was scribbling as usual across the papers she was grading with blue and red felt tip pens. Powell did what he could to keep his eyes from straying the length of her shapely legs as she crossed and uncrossed them. But it was hard not to note the idle way she tapped her toe from time to time in her red high-heeled sandals.

A woman with beautiful legs and feet easily becomes the center of attention in an empty room. Even more so when she lets the long yellow tresses of her hair drape down a shoulder of her sleeveless blue party dress.

"My students are always asking me about pre-martial sex, Professor Powell…" said Robin with a hint of concern, "When I tell them they would be better off to save themselves for marriage, they snicker at me as if to say, '-what planet is she from?' Just the expressions on their faces make me feel like I'm out of touch. Almost like I can't relate to what's really going on in their everyday lives."

"Are you their Physical Hygiene teacher?" Powell asked with a weary sigh.

"No, I mostly teach them Social Studies and Physical Science. I've filled in for Mrs. Anderson's African American Literature class from time to time…"

"I see."

"What do you think, Professor Powell?"

"About what?"

"About pre-marital sex, Professor Powell. How would you address the subject should it come up in your classroom?"

"I don't think I would address it at all."

Robin cast an eye his way with a troubled frown.

"That is, unless I knew I was qualified to speak upon the subject to the benefit of my students."

"How does one know that?"

The silence in the Lecture Room grew heavier with each moment that passed. Powell hissed another sigh in exasperation. He got up and soberly took his coat off the back of his chair at his desk.

"You strike me as an intelligent young lady, Miss Lancaster. I have confidence that you will come up with a satisfactory solution to your situation."

"Thank you, Professor Powell."

"Afterwards, write up your solution and be sure to include three references. I want it on my desk by the end of the month. Do you understand?"

"I understand, Professor Powell."

"Have a good evening, Miss Lancaster. Be sure to turn out the lights when you're finished."

Powell carefully made his way out through the Lecture Room door. He started to gently close it, but the sight of Robin's perplexed expression verging upon despair made him decide against it.

He shook hands with a couple of grateful students after his lecture. Robin came down from her desk holding a brown binder. She was professionally dressed in a green tweed jacket and skirt and wearing grey wingtip Rockport shoes. He watched her come down from her perch regarding him with an imperious gaze. There was no doubt she cut a splendid figure of professional bearing. Powell noted she was even more beautiful without makeup and was somewhat startled as to how this could be so.

She placed the brown binder upon his desk and slid it forward with a sullen grace. There was a slight puffiness beneath her eyes and she seemed tired and haggard despite her well-scrubbed appearance.

"My paper. I included the three references that you required."

"Thank you, Miss Lancaster. I'll take a look at it tonight."

"Thank you."

Powell marveled at how the students hustled and bustled around them. Now in the blink of an eye it was just the two of them alone in the Lecture Room. Robin nodded at him and then turned for the door. She started to turn the knob with a bowed head before her hand trailed away. Robin turned again, her back against the door and her arms crossed tight over her Samsonite Flapover Briefcase. She cast a defiant look his way through squinted eyes.

"I have a question for you, Professor Powell."

"Alright, Miss Lancaster."

"I unfortunately had to help pull a couple of students apart that were fighting in the hallway…"

"Your question, Miss Lancaster?"

"I was getting to that. One of the students used a term I'm not familiar with and I thought perhaps you would know it."

"I'll do what I can, Miss Lancaster."

"Have you ever heard of the term 'spur tongue', Professor Powell?"

"Yes, I have, Miss Lancaster. Did you Google it?"

"No, I thought it might be best to consult with you first."

"Why don't you Google it and see what you come up with?"

"Okay. I have my laptop with me…"

"There's no hurry, Miss Lancaster. Google it and hand in a short paper no longer than two pages the next time we meet for class."

"Alright, Professor Powell."

"Make sure you have the paper with you and we'll discuss it fully after class."

Powell sat down at his desk again to arrange his papers. He let out a sigh and when he looked up again Robin was still leaning with her back against the door. There was something in the dour expression on her face that was noticeably brighter.

"Oh, don't bother about the lights." Powell said as he picked up her brown binder. "I'll douse them once I'm finished here."

"What did you find out?" Powell asked as Robin plopped down in the chair next to his desk. "Did you get any answers for your questions?"

"Oh, I think so, Professor Powell. I'm not sure how I can use any of this kind of information to improve my teacher performance, but here it is…"

Robin slid her two-page paper onto Powell's blotter.

"I found two definitions for that term I mentioned to you last time," Robin told him as she swept her hair out of her face. "I'm certain the young boys in my class weren't talking about a dental appliance."

"I'm afraid I'll have to agree with you there."

"So the definition related to 'urban slang' seemed to be the most applicable."

"I agree," Powell nodded as he briefly looked through her paper, "does that give you any insight into the situation you found yourself encountering?"

"I think so, Professor Powell…"

"Good enough."

Powell rummaged inside his briefcase and brought out her brown binder.

"I was pleased to see you included the work of Steinburg in your references. I also respect what The Diagram Group has done on the subject as well. So, you have my congratulations there, Miss Lancaster. I am familiar with the work Gunther Hunold and Rudiger Boschmann and their participation with the EURASE Institute for

Marriage Counseling. However, the presentation of some of their information I feel might be too graphic and sensational for young people. Remember, we are trying to graduate our children through their teens so that they can experience what it would mean to be responsible marriage partners and beyond that even parents."

"I understand, Professor Powell. Thank you."

"Make me a copy of your paper and I'll add it to your grade as extra credit."

Robin looked through her paper in the binder. She saw where points were taken off for a few typos and errors in grammar. She undid the flap on her own briefcase and replaced the brown binder inside.

"I'll have it for you the next time we meet for class, Professor Powell."

"Now this term 'spur tongue'. How did you come to hear it being used, Miss Lancaster?"

"I thought I covered it fairly clearly in the paper you instructed me to write, Professor Powell."

Powell heaved another sigh and flipped the stapled paper back to its beginning. He read it through more closely this time and the expression on his face grew more grave. Briefly, Powell looked up at Robin just as she was beginning to feel like she was not there in his mind at all, and then resumed reading again.

"I see..."

"Professor Powell?"

"So this term was sort of an indirect insult aimed at you."

"Goodness, Professor Powell, I don't know as I would go so far as to say that."

"Here you write, '– Deshante yelled at Marion once I separated them, 'Now you can run back to Miss Lancaster, nigger. Have her let you stay after school so you can lick her spur tongue.' "

Robin gazed at Powell stonily while blushing furiously.

"Naturally, his parents were called in for a conference."

"Yes, sir."

"Did that settle the matter to your satisfaction?"

"I think for the most part, Professor Powell. I did notice how some of the students were snickering behind my back after the incident."

"I see. How has this affected your classroom management, Miss Lancaster."

"I still get my 'props' as the kids might say. I run a pretty tight ship, Professor Powell."

"That's good to hear, Miss Lancaster." Powell placed her paper inside his briefcase and closed it. I noticed you used the word 'props', Miss Lancaster. I hope you're not trying to deal with those students on their level."

"Why not, Professor Powell?"

"Because that's not your job, Miss Lancaster. Your job is to raise them nearer to your level through dint of application to study and by increasing their knowledge."

"I understand that, Professor Powell. But I'm sure you would agree a little love and understanding goes a long way."

"All I remember is what Yul Brynner once said, 'Never deal with people on their level. They'll beat you every time.' "

"Yul Brynner, Yul Brynner…" Robin furrowed her brow. "That was before my time, but wasn't he a movie star or something like that?"

"That's right, Miss Lancaster. He was also quoting someone else at the time as I remember on the Dick Cavett show."

Powell watched with relish as Robin's beautiful face contorted into a frown.

"Let me see if I read you right, Professor Powell. You're asking me to accept as truth a quote from an actor who in turn was quoting someone else, is that so?"

"That's exactly what I'm asking you to do, Miss Lancaster. Now how does that strike you?"

"Forgive me, Professor, but that strikes me as specious reasoning. Why should I make an untested assertion part of my working methodology as a teacher and educator just on your say so? I mean – forgive me, Professor Powell, I would have thought…"

Powell's face was shining with impish glee.

"But I thought you understood, Miss Powell. Don't you like me, even just a little?"

"But Professor Powell! That doesn't mean I-I—"

"Should what, Miss Powell? Should What? Turn off all the lights and let me do your thinking for you? Why not?"

There was a long silence between Powell and Robin as they stared at each other long and hard for several moments. Emotions of wonder, offense, humiliation, anger, rejection, admiration, acceptance and mystification flickered across the many faceted comeliness of Robin's face. She felt as though Professor Powell was playing some kind of delicious trick on her. He was both laughing at her and laughing with her. He was shutting her out and yet at the same time inviting her inside in the most intimate and congenial way he knew how. She was all churned up inside and closed the flap over her briefcase as she prepared to take her leave.

"I think I should go now…"

"Exactly. May I offer you a Kleenex?"

"Thank you, Professor Powell."

"Wonderful, isn't it?"

"What's that, Professor Powell? I'm not quite sure I follow you…"

"But you will think the matter over, won't you?'

"Why, yes, of course, I will, Professor Powell."

"Wonderful, Miss Lancaster, wonderful…"

Robin sat outside in the hallway. She frowned as she checked the time on her cellphone. She noted she was still a quarter of an hour early even though it was well into the late afternoon. Robin opened the box that was placed next to her on the long wooden bench where she was seated. She was holding one of the printed flyers up to the light and squinting at it. She hastily replaced it back into the pasteboard box as she heard Powell's lumbering footsteps and saw him coming through the glass doors.

"Miss Lancaster," Powell nodded at her as he fumbled his keys out of his pocket. "I take it you're here for your appointment."

"Yes sir."

"You have your corrected version of your paper with you, I take it."

"Yes sir."

"Very well then," Powell opened the door to his office, "let's see what you have to relate today."

Robin followed behind Powell to a chair set next to his desk. She sat down quickly as she placed her briefcase on the floor and set her box of flyers in her lap. She reached down into her briefcase and took out her brown binder again. She placed the paper next to his blotter.

"Why don't you put that in the 'Pending' basket right there, Miss Powell." He told her without looking up from the form he was filling out.

"Alright, sir."

Powell was signing his signature to the bottom of the form with a flourish. He slammed his hand down on top of it with relief.

"Now! What can I do for you today, Miss Powell?"

"The whole class signed up for appointments with you, Professor Powell. I signed up for this date."

"I understand. How is class going for you? Is the information proving to be useful to you in your professional activities?"

Robin bowed her head and moved the lid on her pasteboard box up and down in her lap. She looked up at Powell with an ironic smile.

"I suppose you could say that in certain respects."

"What respects would you be unable to say that, Miss Lancaster?"

"Sometimes I feel my students and I are in two different worlds. Truth be told, they bring a lot of the street into the classroom and I'm just not used to that."

"One of those," Powell muttered aside to himself as he locked his hands behind his head and regarded Robin thoughtfully.

"What are you not used to exactly, Miss Lancaster?"

"Their conversations at times, I suppose. They're very frank and direct with each other and their indulgence in vulgarisms goes off the charts and can be off-putting."

"I understand. Now this is affecting your classroom management?"

"No, I can't really say that. It just seems like they are one way with me and another way when they're interacting with each other."

"Excuse me, Miss Lancaster. Isn't that to be expected? After all, they are teenagers and you're an adult. No?"

"That's not what I'm talking about."

"What are you talking about, Miss Lancaster?"

Robin took a deep breath and folded her arms across her ballooning bosom.

"Sometimes I feel like I'm just not making a connection with them, sir."

"What kind of connection?"

"I don't know exactly. The kind of connection that changes lives for the better, I suppose."

"How are their test scores, Miss Lancaster?"

"Fair to good, sometimes better than that."

"When their test scores improve would you attribute that to your influence?"

"I don't know…"

Powell took his hands from behind his head and began fingering his key ring with both hands upon his desk.

"Do you think you would feel better if you could quantify and qualify that influence?"

"Excuse me?"

"Your teaching experience, Miss Lancaster, your teaching experience. Would you feel better about your teaching experience were you better able to evaluate your influence upon your classes?"

"Isn't that why I'm here taking classes at this University?" Robin answered with a frosty air. "I'm here to hone my teaching skills if I can."

Powell was finding it hard to quell the feeling he was playing a bit part in some kind of Hollywood movie sitting across from Robin. He cleared his throat and she bowed her head again. He dropped his keys on the desk blotter with a clatter.

"What did you mean?" Robin whispered under her breath into a corner of the room.

"About what, Miss Lancaster?"

"When you said, I was 'one of those'? What did you mean by that?" Robin looked up and gave him an accusatory glare.

"I heard you," she stated simply. "What makes me 'one of those'?" Powell regarded her with a frank, dry expression.

"Everyone is different," Powell began with an expansive gesture, "you're one of those 'heart' people, in my opinion, Miss Powell. You judge everything by the way your heart is touched and by the way you touch the hearts of others."

"Is that bad, Professor Powell?"

"Hard to say, Miss Lancaster. It could be a good thing if you're Helen Keller or Mother Theresa. Heart with a little feistiness can go a long way."

"What are you implying, Professor Powell? That I'm not tough enough to make it over the long haul?"

Powell sat back and locked his fingers behind his head again. He rocked in his chair, peering at her through slitted eyes.

"Tell me, Miss Powell, what attracted you to the teaching profession in the first place?"

"I've been told I'm good at helping people learn new things. I suppose."

"Who told you that?"

Powell felt Robin's confidence sink as she crossed her legs and pouted at him. She started to scratch at the elbows of her blouse as she looked away. Powell looked up at the ceiling rocking to find a delicate way to continue with her.

"We'll let that go for the time being. How do you think your students regard you, Miss Lancaster? What do you think you represent to them? What do you think they see when you walk into the classroom?"

"Their teacher for the day I would imagine."

"Let's say I was a student in one of your classes. What do you think I would see, Miss Lancaster?"

Robin gazed at Powell with a hint of asperity.

"Enlighten me, why don't you, Professor Powell…" Robin replied near hissing.

"The first thing I would wonder, Miss Lancaster, is whether or not you had ever been a contestant in beauty pageant. The next thing I would wonder is whether or not you were planning to pursue a career as a model or movie actress. Finally, I would be wondering what you were doing in a classroom with a face and a body like that. Why you chose teaching when your physical gifts seem so overwhelmingly to point you in the direction of doing something in the entertainment industry."

"That sounds awfully sexist to me, Professor Powell."

"I'm just talking about the image you present at this time, Miss Lancaster. You look like a movie star or a model moonlighting as a teacher because she's on the run from the mob."

Robin's mouth dropped open as her eyes widened in protest and her expression froze on her face.

"I – I do my best to dress in attire suitable to my profession and to observe classroom decorum at all times. I don't see why my looks should get in the way of what I have to give as a teacher."

"But it is; isn't it, Miss Lancaster?"

There was a long silence and you could hear Robin's breathing almost crumble into a sob.

"What do you think I'm doing wrong, Professor Powell? I work so very hard to be the best teacher I can be and I really care about my kids."

"A lot of what you have to teach is what you are, Miss Lancaster. Sometimes it can take awhile to make sure that works for you instead of against you. There will be plenty of time for us to craft a persona for you as an effective teacher."

"I want to succeed as an educator in the worst way, Professor Powell."

"I'm sure you shall, Miss Lancaster, I'm sure you shall."

Robin looked down to nervously study her shoes and the floor. "What's that in your lap, Miss Lancaster?"

"This here?"

"Yes."

"Oh. We're starting a Book Club in Techtown. We've printed up flyers and everything. I wanted to put some up around the University, but I found out I have to get them stamped by the Department Head before I can post them."

"Are you going to put up all those here at the University?"

"As many as I can, Professor Powell."

"Alright. Leave as many here as you intend to post around the campus and I'll have my secretary stamp them in a couple days. You can stop by my office Friday after class and get them."

"Thank you, Professor Powell. That would be a big help. We're doing a Science Fiction Reading program this first year. You're welcome to come whenever you have some free time."

"Thank you, Miss Lancaster. I'll keep that in mind. I would suggest you write a three-page paper about how your activities with the Techtown Book Club might improve your experience in the classroom as teacher. There's no rush. I'll help you with this assignment."

"Thank you, Professor Powell. I really appreciate your input. I'll be back Friday to pick up the flyers."

"That will be fine. Is there anything else I can help you with, Miss Lancaster?"

"No, I'll see you in class Friday, Professor. Take care."

Robin got up and put out her hand. Powell shook it and watched her gently set the box of flyers on his desk and wave herself out of his office.

Now as she paced amongst the buildings to the Research Library, Robin could not help but break out intermittently in smiles with her head bowed. There were her flyers for the Techtown Book Club plastered everywhere she looked on the bulletin boards and in the lobbies of the Admissions and Student Union buildings. They fluttered on the glass pillars and walls adjacent to the walkways on campus. Professor Powell was as good as his word and she took the steps up to his classroom hugging her briefcase to her bosom.

The first thing she saw as she stepped up towards her seat in the back was another of her flyers on the bulletin board next to the door marked with Powell's stamp. She timidly waved at Powell as he grunted, his head bowed over a stack of papers he was in the process of grading.

"Thank you," she mouthed diffidently to him in the silence as she took her usual place in this room packed with classmates.

Powell lifted up his eyes and gave her an almost imperceptible nod. He finished the last of the class papers and rose to begin his lecture.

The students began filing out and Robin carefully took her stapled paper out of her briefcase. She made her way down the raked levels and stopped at Powell's desk.

"Anything I can help you with, Miss Lancaster?"

"I have my paper here, Professor Powell."

Powell recapped his red sharpie and look up at her with mild surprise.

"Is that right, Miss Lancaster?"

"Yes sir, and I want to thank you for having my flyers posted. I was going to do that myself after you stamped them."

"You're an educator, Miss Powell. There are plenty of student assistants here at my beck and call happy to render that kind of service."

"I'm just glad it's done. Our first meeting is tonight at 7:30. We would be honored to have you drop by."

"Techtown. Is that right?"

"Yes, sir."

"I can't promise you, but I'll see what I can do."

"Yes, sir."

Powell leafed idly through Robin's paper on his desk.

"Hopefully this 'book club' will have some remedial value for students who need to improve their reading."

"Oh yes, sir! We have a computer lab and access to the Internet among other available services. My paper—"

Powell opened up a drawer and tossed Robin's paper inside. "Anything else, Miss Lancaster?"

"No, I—"

Powell noted how the ceiling lights glinted magneta in Robin's blue eyes.

"Hope to see you there, sir."

Powell nodded and returned to grading his papers.

"I'll have your paper back to you by next class session, Miss Lancaster," he muttered to the desktop.

Robin returned his nod as she turned on her heel and moved out into the hallway traffic.

Powell watched her go out with amusement.

Robin sat in the back of the vast lecture hall as Professor Powell shuffled through his notes. He coughed and cleared his throat as he continued to address the class now keening in on him with increasingly rapt attention.

"The real question you should be concerned with as you continue your reading of Dostoyevsky's novel is the motivation of the protagonist Raskolnikov. What primarily moved him from being a student to being a murderer? As Malcolm Muggeridge once observed, CRIME AND PUNISHMENT is not as much a 'who-dun-it' as it is a 'why-dun-it'? Why did Raskolnikov, a bright young man capable of forging for himself a bright future, choose to smash that future with the commission of such heinous acts? How much did being impoverished influence his decision to kill? Did he really plan these acts essentially as an intellectual exercise of will? Can you point to any of his experiences as a student that led him to conclude he could exercise the ability to take a life as his right and privilege?"

The click of the 9mm semiautomatic palpably heightened the interest in the room.

"What have we here, Donald?" asked Powell looking up from his notes curiously.

The young man with a three-day growth of beard rose imperiously to his feet. There were gasps and suppressed screams as he held his weapon aloft.

"What does it look like, Professor Powell?"

"Looks to me like you have something you would like to say to the class, Donald…"

Robin grasped at her necklace over her thumping heart. She watched with alarm while Donald glared down at Powell from the middle row. A young, slight girl removed her glasses and put them back in her case. Quietly, she attempted to make it from the side aisle where she was sitting to the door.

"That's right. I do, Professor Powell." Donald trained his gun on the young girl just as she was rising from her seat. "Where do you think you're going?"

The young girl looked uncertainly between Powell and Donald.

"Return to your seat, Alicia. It's alright. I'll let you know when class is dismissed."

Powell wearily removed his own reading glasses and set them on the lectern. The young girl resumed her seat with a moan.

"Alright, Donald. Now that you have our attention, what's on your mind?"

Robin watched the back of Donald's head as he shook it from side to side.

"No, no, don't," he declared as he took a step towards Powell. "– I've had it up to here with all this crap. I'm sick and tired of your bullshit, Professor Powell –"

"I take it we're beyond the point of discussion. Is that it, Donald?" The roar of the semiautomatic shattered the slate blackboard behind Powell.

"SHUTUP! You think I don't know what you are doing? SHUTUP! I know what you are doing!"

Students ducked for cover under the seats and in the aisles.

"PROFESSOR POWELL!" Robin exclaimed as she sprung out of her seat from the back of the room.

The briefest flicker of surprise registered on Powell's face. He looked up at Robin and swore softly. He regarded the rebellious student again with consternation.

"Alright. I'm listening."

Donald bounded to the front of the room and locked the door in triumph.

"Now! WHAT!!"

"I'm listening, Donald. Do you want me to take a seat?"

Donald considered this for a moment.

"Yeah! You go have a seat…"

He then motioned Powell away from the lectern. Powell made his way half up the side aisle towards Robin now standing and gestured to her to find a seat and sat next to her.

"What in the world are you doing here, lady?" Powell whispered to Robin as he kept his eyes fixed on Donald.

"I'm–I'm sorry. I just wanted to thank you –"

"Email me next time. The last thing I needed was for you to add some Hollywood to this drama –" Powell told her sternly under his breath.

Silence once again seemed to circle and outline the encounter between Powell and this disorderly student. Donald diffidently moved behind the lectern as he continued glaring at Powell.

"Looks like you need a friend, Donald." Powell observed dryly.

"WHAT?"

"I just said it looks like you need a friend. Perhaps to help you collect your thoughts?"

Donald tapped the semiautomatic pistol against the lectern with a sardonic snicker.

"Oh, so NOW you want to be my friend. Am I hearing right, Professor Powell?"

"Apparently I have failed as your instructor, Donald. Right now I would say you could use a good friend."

"So NOW you want to be my friend!"

"That's right, Donald. Your career as a Wayne State University student is over. Once you brought that gun to class and shot the blackboard you made sure of that. But that doesn't mean you can't still have friends who will want listen to you and help you out."

"So NOW you want to be my friend? It's too late for that, Professor Powell."

"Why?"

Donald paused to reflect and unable to find the words raised the pistol at Powell again in frustration.

"WHAT?"

"Why?"

"WHY WHAT?"

"Why are you doing this to us!"

A voice exclaimed in desperation. Heads turned towards the soft, tremulous voice at the side of the aisle.

It was Alicia wiping away her tears and sobbing.

"Alicia –" Powell said with a gesture of admonishment.

"I'm sorry, Professor Powell, I'm sorry. I haven't done anything to you, Donald. I barely know you. None of us here have done anything to you. Why are you doing this?"

All faces in the class turned to Donald once again.

"I hate this place." Donald confessed with a hiss. "I hate Wayne State. You're all out for yourselves and none of you care about nobody. I'm sick to death with trying to fit in here. You're all just here so you can get a better job or because your parents told you to. This is all such bullshit. There's no real learning going on here. Just a bunch of fake people walkin' around in a daze and earning fake credits so that they can graduate into more fake positions, that's all."

"Oh Donald," Robin said to him in sympathy, "I'm so sorry you feel that way –"

"Robin, please –" Powell gestured her to silence.

"Look Donald, somebody is sure to have heard you when you gave the blackboard the business," Powell continued, "so the odds are good that somebody has called the police and they're on their way even as we speak. We don't have a lot of time. What I would do about now if I were you is make sure that I wasn't holding that gun when they arrived."

Donald glared at Professor Powell with growing resentment.

"But you're not me, Professor Powell. You don't know anything about me. You don't care what I think or feel —"

"Donald, we are both grown men here, so I'm not going to sugarcoat this for you. You have brought violence onto this campus. Right now, you're liable for a damaged blackboard and that's about all. You decide to go out in a blaze of glory, taking half a dozen or more of us with you, it would be a profound disappointment to everybody here."

"Right. I bet it would."

"All I want to know is what purpose would it serve to end up with your face on the Nightly News or have shrinks engage in psychobabble about you for Newsweek or Time magazine? Sure, you will be important and famous and everybody will know your name and that you mattered and all that for a minute. But after that rot, you'll just be another corpse who earned his claim to fame for all the wrong reasons."

There was a pounding on the door to the lecture hall. Powell could hear the muffled sound of someone calling out his name. He regarded Donald grimly with a knowing nod.

"Are you finished, Professor Powell?" Donald took a deep breath and reluctantly set the gun down on top of the lectern. "Because now I'm going to tell you what I think —"

The lecture hall door finally burst open to the thunder of repeated battering.

"LOOK OUT! I think he's got a gun!"

Powell grabbed Robin as she started for the troubled student. He closed his hand over her mouth and found himself falling and tripping over his feet. He covered her body between the lecture seats as the bullets flew past them.

Robin passed out the syllabuses in their black folders before the bank of computers that lined the back wall in the conference room.

The bruises on her hip and thigh were rapidly healing and she walked with less of a limp now. She anxiously checked the time on her cell phone, worried that no one would show up at the Techtown Book Club this first evening.

"Umph! Umph! Umph! Disgraceful!" Grace Alma exclaimed to herself as she walked around setting the books on the long conference table along with their plot summaries and synopses. "Don't make no types of sense."

Robin sat gingerly in the last seat before the lighted monitors of the computers.

"Give it a rest, Alma! I'm so over that at this point. I would have thought by now you would be too. After all, it happened to me, not you."

"I'm through with it then, honey. We got this First Year Program up and running, and that's all I care about. Powell said he was sending some of his students over, right?"

"Uh huh. He said he would see what he could do."

"Alright, then. Let's see what he can do. You know, we really ought to have something special for Black History Month. Grab me some of those plot sheets over there."

"Here you go, Grace…"

"Umph! Put that fool under the jail, I say!"

"Right. Let's hear it for increasing the prison population."

"That brother earned his prison suit. I say give him what he has coming to him."

"Oh yeah, and you call yourself a Christian!"

"Sho' you right. But fair is fair and justice should be about more that ' just us'."

"Now we're playing the race card, are we?"

"When the shoe fits, honey. Fix us some more of that tea."

Robin and Grace Alma sat on either side of the front desk in the conference room. They looked nervously up at the wall clock as they chatted and sipped tea. Every once and a while the two women would trade turns calling students committed for the night. Robin circled with a red Sharpie the ones yet to be reached on a sheet. She was tapping out numbers on her cell phone when a thin, dark boy in a green windbreaker peered timidly through the door.

"Uhh," he drummed lightly on the doorjamb, "– is this where the Techtown Book Club is meeting?"

"Yeah, honey. You here for that?" Grace Alma asked him as she riffed and stacked her papers. "Here you go –"

The young man held up a forefinger and looked down the hallway.

"C'mon, y'all! This is it here!" He called and gestured inside the door. He looked back at Grace Alma and Robin nodded at him warmly. "I'll be back. I've got to go get my friends –"

"How did you find out about our Book Club? Are you coming over from Wayne State?"

"Yeah, yeah. Professor Powell sent the whole class over. He told us he would mark us down a full letter grade unless we showed up. Here they come!"

Robin peeked through Professor Powell's office door.

"Excuse me? Is Professor Powell here this afternoon?"

The secretary glanced from the cell phone at her ear.

"No, he won't be in today. Did you have an appointment with him?"

She started to rise from her seat behind the desk as she smoothed out the wrinkles on her blouse.

"Well,–I –" Robin began and faltered off into silence.

The secretary hitched her glasses onto the bridge of her nose and swept her bangs off her forehead.

"Yes?"

"Oh, never mind. I'll just Email him, I suppose. Thank you."

Robin stepped back out and closed the door to Professor Powell's office still peering through the glass window. She looked down the hallway to the lecture room where workmen were still piecing together all the hell that had broken loose. Robin gingerly made her way down the hallway and momentarily stopped at the open room. There was yellow tape barring her way inside.

She caught her breath now as her fingertips came to her lips. She could see the chipped and shattered frame of the chair where she sat when Powell threw her to the ground and covered her with his own body. Robin craned her neck and barely caught sight of what looked like a gun shot hole in the bulletin board on the back wall. The memory of the sound of the shots came back vividly as a burly worker came over and blocked her view.

"Hello there. Sorry Miss, you can't come in here right now."

"Oh. Okay. You wouldn't happen to know where Professor Powell will be holding his classes now, would you?"

"Couldn't tell you."

"Alright."

Robin left closing her jacket over her blouse in the chilly hallway. The memory of Professor Powell scrambling to shield her on the floor returned. The vivid sensation of his arms wrapped frantically about her body and head filled her with a pang of terror. She made her way carefully down the steps to the exit. Nothing could keep her nipples from rising erect against her bra with that lingering sense of dread. Only the mental image of twisting around and looking up into Professor Powell's grim and determined face gave her any solace.

She resolved to somehow catch up with him to thank him in person for sending all those students over for the opening of their Techtown Book Club.

"I just wanted you to know how much we appreciate the help we've received from you, Doctor Powell," Robin began as she crossed her legs in his office. "Thanks to the input of the classes you sent over, we were able to meet our initial quota for program certification. I can't say we've been approved for additional funding yet, but we have filed our survey sheets and completed our applications. I feel our chances are good that we will be licensed for a five year contract, but we'll have to see what happens."

Powell peered at Robin over the steeple of his fingertips.

"You'll keep me apprized of all future developments, Miss Lancaster."

"Yes, of course. I was hoping I could consult with you from time to time about the selection of the books we intend to include in our reading programs. I hope you'll feel free to comment on our review process. That is, whenever you feel it is warranted…"

"Email me all the pre-test results in PDF files, please. Keep me briefed particularly about the students I have sent you. I intend to monitor their progress."

"Yes, sir."

"That should just about cover it for now, Miss Lancaster. Any questions you have for me should be typed double-spaced and sent to me through my secretary. Once I have given them due consideration and have formulated an appropriate response for solutions, I'll contact you. Is that understood?"

"Yes, sir."

"Is there anything else, Miss Lancaster?"

"No sir. I suppose not. I just want to thank you again for all your help and everything…"

Robin rose as though on cue to Powell's perfunctory nod and tentatively extended her hand.

"Oh, that's right." Powell dipped his head and reached into his briefcase. "Your paper. Miss Lancaster…"

Powell placed the three-page paper complete with its folder in her outstretched hand.

"Now. Is there anything else I can help you with, Miss Lancaster?"

Robin opened the folder and briefly looked over the copious notes written across her pages.

"No sir."

Robin closed her folder on all the red marks she saw written in the margins.

"We hope you'll come visit us, Professor Powell..." Robin said evenly.

Powell resumed scribbling on top of the stack of papers he was grading. He nodded again at Robin and grunted without looking up.

Robin helped Grace Alma decorate the rooms for the Grand Opening of the Techtown Book Club. Books were scattered everywhere on the tables, on the desks beside the computers, even perched inside the open windows next to the fluttering green drapes. Robin carried over piles of books spilling out of the sofa chairs in the corners of the Study Room and handed them to the portly Grace Alma, who was standing on a folding chair in front of a wall framed with wooden shelves. The matronly woman took each volume from Robin and slid them into their designated places on each shelf by subject and author. Robin looked around for the box of bookmarks and found them still resting on the glass counter by the front entrance. She picked a rubber-banded stack out of the open cardboard box and began placing them on the desks beside the computers like playing cards.

"You send that invitation to Professor Powell?" Grace Alma asked over the hard covers she was shelving.

"Why on Earth would I do that? Professor Powell is not going to show up at our little affair."

"Says you, honey. Where did you put those posters?"

"Over there by the broom closet. What makes you think Powell would show up at our little Shindig anyway?"

"Get them posters. He'll come all right, if you take the trouble to hand deliver his invitation personally. Bring over that bunch I matted. They're in there with the ones of John Coltrane and Carter G. Woodson."

"Oh, so now I should deliver his invitation personally, is that right?"

"He your Professor, Robin. He did loan you all those students of his."

Robin handed up the framed and matted posters for Grace Alma to place between the bookshelves on the walls.

"Go get some more masking tape, will you?"

Robin headed to the rack up in the broom closet where they kept most of their cleaning supplies. She pulled out the little stool inside and stepped up on it. She leaned onto her tiptoes and searched around the upper shelf for the tape.

"The last time I saw it, it was up around here someplace. You haven't been using it since the last time, have you?"

"Just to matte these posters here. That's all. But I put it back where I got it from."

"Funny, then it should be here."

Robin kept rummaging around until she felt her fingers close upon it.

"I got it," Robin declared at last as she descended from the stool, "I'll help you put up some of those posters."

"Yeah honey, take a couple over there and put them between those book cases, will you?"

Robin headed over to the opposite wall with her posters.

"Did you want me to fix us some tea?" Robin asked Grace Alma.

"I beat you to it. Let's take a break after we're done putin' up all these posters, okay?"

Soon the life size posters were strategically placed between all the bookcases lining the walls. Robin and Grace Alma sat across from each other at the entrance desk blowing through pursed lips over their raised cups. They sipped their Chamomile and Chai Spice tea with care.

Halfway done with their tasks, the two women surveyed the vast empty room with its decorated rows of long tables and banks of monitors and keyboards. There were four low boxes filled with mauve colored envelopes still sitting flat between them inside their cardboard lids.

"How many of these invites we still got to send off, Robin?" Grace Alma asked Robin as she swirled drops of honey into her tea.

"Less than four hundred and fifty by last count," Robin remarked, cooling her tea. "We've already sent out a thousand by post and Email."

"Now wouldn't that be sumpthin?" Grace Alma exclaimed cackling with glee. "You really think we could pack a thousand people into this joint?"

"I have no idea."

"What you gon' be wearing, sweetie?"

"Now Alma," Robin said after a sip and wagging her finger, "I refuse to answer on the grounds that it might incriminate me."

"Aw, now how that sound, Robin? How you know anybody is going to show up anyhow to 'in-crim-i-nate' yo' behind?"

"That's what I mean, Alma. For all we know, we'll be sitting right here, dressed to nines and sipping tea all by ourselves."

"Says you, honey. I got family to represent me. My boys know what time it is they don't make it through that door."

Robin and Grace Alma went back to thoughtfully sipping their tea.

"Hmnn, what have we here…" Grace Alma thoughtfully reached into the box marked, 'P-Q-R' and pulled out an envelope. "It says, 'PROFESSOR POWELL'…"

Grace Alma slid the envelope across the desk at Robin and it fell off the edge into her lap. Robin placed her cup onto the coaster at her side. She gingerly picked up the envelope by its corners. Grace Alma watched her make a face, handling the object as though it were dirty linen and chuckled.

"Don't be like that, Robin. After dodging bullets with the man, you know you two got history now."

Robin cast a look of protest, and then patted her mouth with the envelope.

"That cold fish. He'll never come…" Robin grumbled with a frown. She tossed the envelope back on the box it came from.

"He posted them flyers for you, didn't he? He sent them students to us that first day, right? The man wasted no time being a human shield for you when guns were involved and the chips were down." Alma observed Robin coolly. "Seems to me if you can get a man to risk his life for you without having to ask, you should be able to get him to do anything you want."

Robin sat back and crossed her arms under her bosom. She regarded Grace Alma solemnly and felt her objection die in her throat even before she uttered a sound. Finally, she fixed her gaze on the floor with a sigh.

Robin reached for the envelope again, found her purse and deposited it inside.

Robin went through her wardrobe searching for just the right outfit. She rummaged through the heap of skirts, gowns and blouses massed upon her bed. She wanted to wear something appropriate for the Grand Opening of the Techtown Book Club. She looked for something cheerful and inviting, but not too revealing. She struggled to put together attire that would be flattering to her generous curves and yet resolve her appearance in a dignified manner.

The thought occurred to her that the best person to test it out upon would undoubtedly be Professor Powell. She clicked on her cell phone and started to take pictures of herself in several of the outfits she had selected. There was the red dress and the green gown and the blue skirt with the peach blouse. She also set several pairs of shoes at the side of her bed to try on with each of her outfits.

After modeling the various fashions that were racked inside her closet before a mirror and making a photo opportunity out of them, she transferred each to a spare thumb-drive at hand. She posed with a book in most of them; holding up the cover to 'Great Expectations', 'The Great Gatsby', 'Things Fall Apart', 'The Sun Also Rises' and 'Moby Dick' among others. Soon there were over twenty pictures on the thumb-drive and she slipped it into the envelope that bore Powell's invitation.

"Professor Powell?" Robin called him at his office several times. "Oh!" She would exclaim whenever his secretary answered in his stead. "I understand. When he comes in would you have him call me, please? Yes, that's correct. I'm one of his students."

At other times she simply left a message, heeding the request of the mechanical voice at the other end. Finally all these abortive efforts to reach Powell made her resolve to catch him somehow at his office or in one of the lecture rooms where he would be holding a class.

She kept the invitation always in her purse now while mentally rehearsing what she would say to him when she presented him with the thumb-drive as an added incentive. Robin was haunting his office and just missing his lectures owing to the press of her teaching duties at the high school. There were other classes she needed to study to complete her graduate degree, and when she was not putting the finishing touches to her lesson plans in the evening she was at the library flipping through pages of books for them.

Robin was walking the halls between the reading rooms one afternoon when she thought she heard the distinct sound of Professor Powell's voice around a corner. She rushed towards the voice only to find that Powell was sitting at a table with Donald. He was pointing out something to him in the dictionary and the two were sharing eager confidences.

"Professor Powell? Donald!"

Robin stopped in her tracks bumping up against the table. She was facing one of many wooden tables in the room where students were gathered together in clusters around open books and dictionaries. Some of them looked at her quizzically before returning to hushed conversations in their study groups.

"Donald has been granted permission to work in our Literacy Program." Powell said with deliberation. "We were going over some of the tasks he'll be required to assist the students in performing."

"Miss Lancaster," Donald began with reticence, "I – I hope I can make it up to you and the other students I threatened. Professor Powell talked to the judge and this is part of what they required of me."

"Required of you?" Robin remarked with a hint of asperity.

"Yes. I have to fix up the lecture room too and help pay for damages."

"Damages?" Robin repeated pointedly. "Have you any idea what you put us all through, Donald?"

"I'm trying to understand. Professor Powell said I – I might understand better if I looked at things standing in his shoes and – and yours, Miss Lancaster. I should see what it's like to try to help people, he said, instead of acting to hurt them. I'm ready to try, Miss Lancaster."

"Is there anything we can help you with, Miss Lancaster?" Professor Powell asked quietly.

Robin glanced between Donald's hopeful young face and Powell's stern, severe countenance.

"There was a matter I wished to speak with you about."

"Good. I'll be in my office around four o'clock tomorrow. Why don't you stop by then and we'll discuss it?"

"That would be fine, Professor Powell. I'll see you then."

Professor Powell went back to pointing something out to Donald in the dictionary. Robin could hear the two of them laughing together and sharing conspiratorial asides and whispers as she walked out of the reading room. There were the usual brazen stares and murmurs of leering approval that her exceptional beauty elicited and she winced with annoyance as she walked towards the exit of the library.

"Now, Miss Lancaster, what can I do for you?"

Professor Powell asked as he sat down behind his desk.

Robin was standing at the door, holding her purse as though it were a shield.

Powell gestured with stiff formality at the seat next to his desk.

"I won't keep you long," Robin began as she undid the clasp on her purse, "Grace Alma and I were talking about inviting you…"

"Please, won't you have a seat, Miss Lancaster?" Powell insisted with a question in his smile.

"I won't be staying long, I don't want to keep you from your duties."

"That's very kind of you, Miss Lancaster."

"I just wanted to take this time to personally invite," Robin began again.

"Please be so considerate as to,"

"We were hoping you would do us the honor," Robin took out the envelope as she spoke to a spot above Professor Powell's head.

"Miss Lancaster?"

"Yes, Professor Powell?" Robin's eyes engaged Powell's eagerly.

"Please do me the honor to be seated as we discuss this."

"I – I can't stay long, sir…" Robin shifted from one foot to the other.

"I understand that."

"I just wanted to thank you for all,"

"You're most welcome, of course, Miss Lancaster."

"I just – I just – why are you helping Donald like that?" Robin blurted out.

Professor Powell regarded her as he cocked his head upon his hand.

"What would you have me do, Robin?"

Robin. He finally called her by her first name, she mentally noted.

"I'm sure that's not for me to say, sir. I just don't think you can blithely discount the fact that he threatened all our lives. He has to answer for that somehow."

"What would be the best way to handle the situation as you see it, Robin?"

She waved the envelope in her hand as she shook her head all in a fluster.

"I'm sure I have no idea, sir. I just object to how close the two of you seem after everything that has happened. My Lord, dear, he fired a gun at you for goodness sake!"

Something halted in Robin's mind. What was that she just said; was it 'My Dear Lord,' or 'My Lord, dear…'?

"I'll tell you what, Robin," Powell said with his hand cupped under his chin, " just between us imagine that it WAS for you to say. Imagine that you did have an idea on the best way to handle this situation. Go ahead. You have my permission to use your imagination and have an idea that is the best solution from your point of view."

Robin perceived an insult and glared at Powell.

"Now you're playing with me, Professor Powell. I don't appreciate being talked down to, I'll have you know."

Powell sat back rocking with an air of amusement on his face. He feasted on how gorgeous Robin looked in her black silk jump suit and open-toed black high heels. The broad brown belt banded around her narrow waist was a perfect compliment to her entire outfit. He enjoyed watching how the ceiling lights sparked flashing highlights in her silken blond hair spilling like sunshine over her shoulders.

"What's the matter?" asked Robin as she went back to shifting her weight on her feet.

"Nothing. Just waiting."

"Waiting? For what, may I ask?"

"Why for you to use your imagination and have an idea, of course, my dear."

Robin caught her breath with heart thumping at Powell uttering the words 'my dear'.

"I have no objection to you retiring to the little girls room should you need to do so." Powell observed drolly.

"The little girls room? I'm not a child, Professor Powell, what makes you think,"

"I suppose it's just the way you keep dancing with all those ants on the floor. Please feel free to call me Claude."

Robin cast a look of mortification upon Powell. Here she was all dressed up and appearing as though she had to go pee. She assumed an air of wounded aloofness.

"Claude?'

"Yes, Claude."

"What kind of name is 'Claude'?"

"I was named after Claude MacKay, the African American poet. MacKay is my middle name."

"Claude MacKay, huh?"

"That's right."

"Never heard of him."

Powell looked at her bristling and Robin could barely conceal her chuckle before they both broke out laughing.

"Be seated, Miss Lancaster. You said you have something to give me?"

Robin clicked with rueful gaiety over to the vacant seat next to Powell's desk.

"Yes I do," Robin sat down in the padded chair and crossed her feet at the ankles, "I came here to personally invite you to the Grand Opening of the Techtown Book Club."

She handed him the envelope. Powell took it and put it next to his ear shaking it.

"What's in the Crackerjack's Box?" Powell wisecracked.

"A prize and a preview of coming attractions. That is, should you choose to accept this mission…"

"I'll have to consider it. Give me time to put my team together."

Robin tossed her hair off her shoulders and shook her head.

"Afraid there isn't time, sir. The clock is ticking. You can show up with your buddy Donald, since you and he appear to be getting along like gangbusters these days; or you can take me back for a glass of punch."

"I'm afraid you have me outclassed at the moment with regard to attire, Miss Lancaster. I'll have to go home and dress up for this."

"I'll be happy to help you pick something out…" Robin touched Powell's hand before she could catch herself, "–that is, that's appropriate for the event."

Robin drew back her hand and looked down at her feet. The silence grew between them as the sound of footsteps down the hallway signaled classes letting out for the evening. Soon even these echoes died away and left them alone in Powell's office.

Each could hear the other's breathing.

"No time to waste, then," said Powell finally as he reached for his briefcase. "I think this time your assistance might prove indispensable, Robin. Why don't we take my car and after I've suited up we drop off to Techtown?"

"Sounds like a plan," said Robin beaming, "you wouldn't happen to have a tux in your closet by any chance, would you?"

"There's a distinct possibility I just might have one racked for occasions such as this one."

"That would be fortunate. I can see you sporting that Master of Ceremonies look. Much better for the Grand Opening of the Techtown Book Club."

"I'll get your coat and you turn off the lights, okay?"

Robin felt Powell's hands lightly about her shoulders as she slipped her arms through the sleeves of her coat. He put his own coat over the crook of his arm and stepped outside the door of his office into the hallway fingering his keys. Robin doused the lights and came out as Powell quietly locked the door.

There was the sound of a bucket wheeling towards them from far down the hallway. Robin turned to see the janitor pushing it forward with the handle of the mop in his hands. She flinched as he waved their way.

"Goodnight, Professor."

"Goodnight, Jeremiah," Powell returned his wave as he linked arms casually with Robin. "Are you coming down to the Techtown Book Club tonight?"

"Soon as I clean up here. Got any free books for my kids?"

"Bring 'em and find out."

"We'll be there."

Robin turned her attention from the janitor to Powell.

"How does it feel to hold me when there aren't any bullets flying around?" she asked.

Powell regarded her with a broad smile.

"Let's find out. Afterwards, I want a complete report with at least three references and be sure to Google Claude MacKay."

"Yes Professor." Robin said, clutching Powell's arm.

Their footsteps echoed softly before they descended the stairs and exited through the glass doors onto the campus grounds.

Land Of A Thousand Cries

There is this thing. Before it nothing comes. From it everything proceeds. This has been said before and in many places better than I am telling you now. Nevertheless, it all comes back to this. There is this thing. Nowhere a man looks can it be found. No place where a man can put his hands can it be touched. There is no force to move it, and the flow of time does not alter its condition. You will not see it ebb and flow or rise and fall.

"What Mon cannot imagine does not exist." The cocky young African tapped his finger on one of the x's he had crossed on the crude map of the world he had drawn. He made the last mark on the brown toilet paper and handed the pen back to Niagra. He took off his cap, scratching his close cropped woolly head and then continued, "Aaaa-see these 'X's?"

All things depart from this source only to return once again. All things that rise and fall with the flow of time depend upon it. Wherever a man touches there it can be found. Whatever moves whatever it moves, would not move without it. Because it all comes down from the same thing. All goes back to the same thing. Coming from and going to, this is the way of our universe.

"All these places I have been." The gravel voice of the African sounded like he was scraping coals against the basement of his throat. "I have seen and experienced many things. There was a Mon in Iceland, who, when he saw me, my dock skin, his mouth fell open in shock. He could not imagine and he told me so himself- how the same God who hod made him could make a mon as dock as I. And when I told him that across de ocean a whole race of men and women such as I existed, he called me a liar! He could not conceive of such a thing in his mind!"

Now all things that ebb and flow and contain feature for the mind to know come from it.

Imagine blackness as the all encompassing all. Space a black room without walls. No ceiling for us to know what is up and no foundation for us to know what is down. Look straight into this and see a speck of light amid the blackness. No bigger than a grain of sand upon the beach of eternity or a pinhole upon the canvas of the mind's eye, peeking light. Now watch it grow as it comes toward us. See the speck spin, grow, expanding now its pinhole contours in the black room of our consciousness. See the light. Now see the light spin, grow, whirling to expand.

"It just could not be to him! Why he might have even thought that I was an hallucination talking to him from somewhere–inside a nightmare!" The African leaned his stocky frame forward once more. He tapped once again the line he had written across the top of his makeshift map of the world. "Remember this." The African's fiery eyes became branding irons. "This is the only thing of which from all my travels and education I am absolutely certain. What Mon cannot imagine does not exist."

Around and round the great wheels spin in our universe, oceans of light and sound and life now bounded only by continents of Space. These oceans churn with the action of exploding suns and the spinning of planets. See the light and hear the light spin, grow, spiral and expand. These great wheels are the long-playing discs of eternity. Their churning rotation contains the music of the Spheres.

We do not hear this music because we hear it all the time...

"You mean as far as he is concerned."

The African took a cigarette from his shirt pocket and stabbed it into the corner of his mouth.

"But naturally, since any Mon is really only concerned this far." The African smiled shyly.

"You got a match?"

"I dun' smoke."

"That's right you don't."

The African leaned down and caught the attention of a fellow worker at the far end of the table. He gestured at his cigarette with both his hands and a book of matches came down the table and slid to a stop in front of him.

"So how did a globe-trotter like you end up here at Mack's Stamping Plant?" Niagra said as he leaned on his elbow.

The African wrung out his match and his mustache fogged as he sucked in the smoke. As he finished exhaling, a halo of smoke issued from his open mouth perfectly wobbly round.

Spinning, growing, spiraling and expanding, see this speck of light become the spinning disc that is whirling across the arena of the mind's eye. All manner of jazz can be heard upon this disc. Ranging upon this great wheel, this spinning disc, can be heard the note we emanate. We are no more than the cymbalist who gives his clash at the proper time in the symphonic work. Let the symphony of the disc play to the very end and you will not hear that note again. But the cymbalist has his note to play; and with each new playing of the disc his note returns again. Clear and true, in the right relationship with all that came before and with all that will come after. We have our note to play. Earth has its note to play within the Cosmic Jam Session. Our note constitutes its own symphony within the equinoctial dance of summer Sun and winter Seasons.

Our Jam Session and Symphony contains the notes of a certain kind of music.

We hear it all the time, the sound of living things surviving and perishing. This is the history of our race within the wheel of eternity. Man plays all manner of jazz upon this earth, but it all comes to but a note of a note within the Cosmic Jam Session.

We hear it all the time, because this is the land of a thousand cries. Men make groups to play pain and pleasure against each other and the womb of the planet. We hear it all the time—the clash and thunder of bombs bursting upon the continents of this green earth counterpoised with the sound of eggs in nests cracking, birds chirping, children laughing and the new born babe crying out life.

We hear it all the time, important seeming men making a great noise in the world about nothing to their snoring constituents while a housewife wipes blood off the steps in the morning light from the fight the night after she sighed and cried in her lover's arms, "Oh! Papa! Love me! God love me! Oh, God love me! God love me! God! God! God!"

BANG! Exploded the rifle as it spat its red flame, its ejaculation of terror and pain into the frosty night air. What could have brought death here this time?

"Financial difficulties have brought me to this state of affairs." He smirked at Niagra and shrugged his shoulders. "But whaw de fuck, in my country there are places whar a Mon is paid thirty cents for a whole week's work in de mines. This situation would be heaven to him!"

"Well, it's hell to me!"

"But quite naturally. Because you connot conceive of a situation that would be considerably worse." The African's eyes narrowed as he leisurely held his cigarette between index finger and thumb. The smoke trailed from his nostrils. "There are many things worse than work in the factory."

The '65 Cutlass sped down Woodward and the barrel slid back from the window and under the seat. He never saw the bullet his body took in that parked car, this dude, as the ambulance lights winked red and the cigarette he had bitten into at point of impact still dangled twixt his lips, his cigarette lighter slapped flat down in the street, the wind long ago snuffed out the flame from the wick. The flower of blood that sprouted from his temple dripped red dew on his shoulder.

Mae sighed and sobbed for the husband who drank himself on rumor to puking vomit down the alley the evening after and caught her hair and wound it in his hands. She ran. They struggled. Mae struggled and ran. He caught her in the kitchen and the butcher knife went wild in her hands. Mae lopped at her husband's body as though it were a slab of meat. Wally cried and sighed in her arms, this man she really loved, about their good thing gone wrong. She wondered truly too, but live steer meat went down the conveyor to be slaughtered just the same. Who heard their cries or were they just in vain when the blade cut sharp and well?

Sonny screamed and cried, pulled back, he needed to be held by his mother and father both before the Doctor could pierce his skin with the syringe. Velma screamed too with stockings torn and blouse ripped, trapped in a garage and cowering for a way out. The scent of whiskey more like incense from a savage rite held upon an altar of lust.

She struggled under his drunken thrusts as the fire sirens turned the night into a roar and glass shattered as he thrust for more.

The young pregnant mother came running, carrying, leading, and clutching as many of her sleep dazed children as she could from the fiery blaze. The whole of her family could hear the cries of her little daughter still trapped in the topmost room. The little girl's screams burned in her brain. She turned in a despairing wail, but even she could see that the flames were too far gone.

Niagra skeptically raised his eyebrows. "Hey–but where were you last Friday when we were humping overtime on the line?"

These words struck sparks in the African's eyes. He leaned forward with a piercing glare.

"Listen to me, I work in the White Mon's Foctory because I choose to, but don't nobody tell Uh-tog-bay what he got to do!"

Niagra laughed nervously. "Okay, Ethagbhe–okay man! You ain't got tuh get 'JAWS' about it!"

The African was still glowering. "Do you know what my name means?"

"Hey look —"

"I said–DO YOU KNOW WHAT MY NAME MEANS!"

Niagra hissed with exasperation. "Naw man, whut's it mean?"

The African leaned back proudly. "Ethagbhe means: 'I'll join my Father's side.' But my full name is Ethagbhe Opamelu Aghba. Opamelu means: 'I can do it.'"

"Do what?"

Their eyes locked for a moment. The African swallowed craning his neck at the Ebony girl in the blue jeans who had just entered the lunch room. "Uhn?"

"What can you do?"

The African turned back to Niagra. "Why any God-Damn thing I want to do! I can get up on top of this foctory and howl like a dog- 'I am Ethagbhe Opamelu Aghba! Nobody tells Uh-tog-bay what he got to do!'"

This is the land of a thousand cries. Come through the tunnel of tears and the cries in the night. All manner of jazz is played here. Come through the blood-drenched screen of clashing knives.

Hear shattered shards of pain and agony flash and fly like sparks in the night while the full moon watches from its numinous halo. Come through, come through to the continent that wears the glove on its little toe. All manner of jazz is played here. We hear it all the time.

The whine of the whore as her pimp beats fifty dollars from her face, creates a space within her clenched fist wherein he cops, takes the money and runs his race against time blind. The moon in its illuminated buttery glow watches. These cries churn in the night, trouble-trouble, bubble–rubble of busted things and broken screams. Piteous dreams evaporate like bubbles against the neon glare of the asphalt nightmare. Come through, come through to America! All manner of jazz is played here and upon this glove of earth and forest, concrete, brick and glass, factory horns howl and factories belch gas and smoke and the raw waste of writhing souls. The full moon watches in mute testimony while Eugene, apprentice O.D., also howls running through the wild streets amongst swarms of milling people with an old woman's purse in his trembly fist. She also cried for a meager reward that was flying away from her retired grasp on fleet feet. Come through, come through Michigan to the corner of the thumb of the glove. Here voices cry within a rectangle of space as streams of people flow among towering monoliths of glass, steel and stone. Squares of light from homes and apartments serve as searchlights in the night.

This is the night Eugene came running down the alley at length collapsing against the backyard fence of a two-family flat. No one heard him as the fire sirens came whining down the street to the house next door, glass smashing as the woman spirited away as many of her children as she could from the fiery blaze. The cries of her little daughter still left her dazed and burned in her brain while the '65 Cutlass sped down Woodward.

Who other than the moon knew that next door within the upper-flat above, within a cube of green walls, making the grand escape through all doubts, and insecurities and fears to a place of ecstatic certainty, rushing like a torrent of lava through all the trap doors, like a river swelling and surging and pulverizing a storm beset dam on a dark cloudy day, starkly lit by flashes of lightning in high winds, Niagra came screaming out of his fearsome and angry need and into the clear still pond that was Odessa, rising and surging to meet him and accept his gift.

The moon made searchlights of her eyes as Niagra cried and cried and cried and cried and cried and cried and sighed and cried and sighed and cried and sighed and cried and sighed and cried and sighed and sighed and sighed and sighed and sighed and sighed and sighed and the last of his cries merged with Odessa's cries and the last of his sighs merged with the last of her sighs and the heat of Niagra's passion breathed like summer through the cinnamon woolliness of her African hair.

Now Odessa's full brown breasts rose and fell before the fluttering blue curtains in the evening wind. Surprise flickered in the moonlight over the fine features of her face. The cracking echo of a shot pierced a jagged edge through her lambent reverie. She rose, her naked body a black silhouette against the window framed moon. The shapely form of her became a question mark as she turned to Niagra.

"Baby, you hear that? Come here-hear them sirens?"

"Yeah sugar-I know-there's a fire next door. Come on back to bed. Let the firemen take care of that."

"Naw Niagra—that's the poe-lice! C'mere an look!"

Odessa turned when she heard Niagra slap the mattress. "God Dog- Odessa! Why you got to talk about that now?

Niagra rose. He moved over to the window scratching his head. "Why now——" He started as Odessa pointed out the window.

"See? I tole you it was the poe-lice!"

The firemen were falling back, scurrying like grouse once the shot was fired. Niagra could see a big, muscular, light-skinned man holding a little boy off his feet at pistol point. He just now emerged from the front entrance of the house in flames and the police, dark blue foreshortened figures crossing the street in front of flashing red lights were already attempting some kind of verbal negotiation. The full moon watched while the little boy cried.

Odessa and Niagra could hear his cries echoed by his little sister Keesha, still trapped in the house before them. The little girl; was standing in front of the window just across from them. The window billowed smoke, and she screamed as the curtain in front of the window swept by the wind crackled ablaze.

"Niagra! We got tuh do something!"

"WE got tuh do something?!" Niagra's expression was incredulous. "WE ain't got tuh do shit!"

"Please—Niagra! All them books you got up in this crib and you cain't think uh nothin'? What kind uh man is you?"

Niagra's eyes angrily locked on Odessa's round moon face, her expression truculent and yet somehow imploring. He opened his mouth in protest and closed it with a sigh of resignation.

"C'mon, baby, we got tuh think uh somethin' now!"

Niagra sighed again and looked out the window, past Odessa wringing her hands to the full moon outside.

He could barely make out the little girl clutching her doll in terror through the folds of the curtain and the billowing smoke. The light from the flames flickered on her tear stained face and that was what got to him. He sighed again and cursed under his breath, looking over at Odessa as though it were all her fault.

"Put your clothes on and tie some bedspreads together. Don't blame me if this shit don't work–"

"Yeah baby, c'mon nowww-"

"All right now, tie one end around that bicycle pump on the floor. Listen now, you got to do like I tell you to do this thing right, you understand?"

"C'mon, Niagra, cain't you see-"

"Look-tie one end around that bicycle pump on the floor. Listen-listen now! You got to throw it from here over to her window—"

"Okay-okay—"

"Naw, it's not okay! Listen now! You gotta somehow talk her into tying her end around a bedpost or something that won't move. That's the hard part. Do you think you can do that?"

"Yeah, I-I-I guess I can—"

"Only one way to find out—get to it then! I'll see to the little boy."

Niagra slipped on his clothes and went over to the window. He could see the huge, light-skinned man holding the little boy, his legs dangling off the ground. He was coming down the steps of the front porch as the house behind him roared in flames. The police were continuing furiously in their efforts to reason with him.

Niagra's eyes went to the cabinet in the corner of the room.

The shadow of the light-skinned man loomed large across the street. He was glistening with sweat, still holding the pistol to the little boy's temple. Niagra slid the storm window up a little.

"Niagra!" Odessa turned to him in distracted anxiety. "Come help me tie these here sheets together-"

"I'm comin'-"

After stripping the sheets from the mattress, Niagra helped Odessa fix together a makeshift rope and bound up the bicycle pump with one end. They worked quickly, as Niagra's eyes kept flickering to a cabinet in the corner of the room. Odessa started muttering something to herself, but Niagra didn't pay her any mind.

"I know what!" Odessa said, an idea flashing across her face.

"What?"

"I'll sneak around the backside and throw these sheets up from underneath her window! She'll be sure to get it that way! What you think, Niagra?"

"Sounds good to me. Better get going."

"What you gon' do?"

"Huh?"

"What you gon' do, Niagra?"

"I already told you, Odessa. I'll see to the little boy-"

"You goin' down to help talk Mister Lamont out of hurtin' that child?"

"Look, Odessa, I got this. You just go do what you got to do. Hurry 'fore it's too late!"

Odessa started to say more, then stifled the question that was on her face.

"All right baby," Odessa headed for the door with the knotted up sheets over one shoulder, "- be lookin' out for me, hear?"

"Go, Odessa, go!"

Niagra pressed his back against the wall next to the window once Odessa was gone. He could feel every bit of will and determination and resolve ooze out of him, and leak from between his toes as he heard her footsteps pound down the stairway from their apartment. Niagra felt his knees buckle as he slid slowly down the wall with a sickening sensation pooling in his stomach. He wound up sitting on the floor and facing the locked cabinet.

He found himself laughing a soundless little mocking laugh. Since when had he ever talked anybody out of anything? He knew about hunting from going with his Uncles to chase away hawks and buzzards and wolves. But what did he know about talking it over with a next door neighbor he barely knew who was bound and determined to blow his little boy's brains out? He would bet sooner on what success he remembered having downed opossum and deer, than pin a young boy's hopes on the precious little practice he had with the arts of persuasion. The shouting outside in the night air startled Niagra and he got to his feet again. He sighed again and wearily went over to the cabinet to fumble on top for the key. He unlocked it, and then carefully pulled out the sporting rifle his Uncle Richie once gave him as a birthday present. He got down on one knee and sighted along the barrel. Uncle Richie always told him he had a good eye.

Niagra tested the bolt on his rifle and then adjusted the scope. The thing might not even work right, it being so long since he last used it. Niagra went back inside the cabinet and fumbled some more. He could hear the volume going up on the shouting out his window, and he nearly dropped the small box in the dark.

"Don't kill him, Lamont! He yo' son!" The young mother wailed at her husband in a chant. "Don't kill him, Lamont! Sonny yo' son!"

"SHUT UP! Ah keel him rite now ya'll don' lemme thru-you hear? YOU HEAR!"

Odessa came down the back steps of their house, barely making a sound. She carried the rope of knotted bed sheets over her shoulders. She stood back from the house until she could see the little girl in the window. She stepped back some more, waving and calling until she could get the little girl's attention. When she finally did, that was when she decided to throw the bed sheet rope through the window.

Odessa cursed her way through several tries before the bicycle pump sailed through the smoking window. The bed sheet rope trailed from the window and Odessa pulled and pulled on it until she felt something catch. She stepped back with the sheets in her hands and waved wildly at the little girl clutching feverishly to her little doll and racing about the room.

"HEY! Climb down! Climb down, honey, Climb down! HEY!"

After an eternity of wheedling and coaxing, Odessa finally got the little girl to throw her the doll. Some time later, Odessa got the little girl to put one leg out over the window sill and hold onto to the bed sheet rope. Odessa cursed herself, because she had forgotten to tell the little girl to wrap the end with the bicycle pump around something so that the rope would hold fast. She kept tugging on the rope until it became taut in her hands.

The little girl climbed gingerly down the rope. The sound of people arguing full blast out in front of the house grew louder and louder in Odessa ears. She listened for Niagra's voice in the din of the rumble and the ruckus, and hoped he wasn't making too big a fool out of himself. The window above the little girl burst into flames, and the part of the bed sheet rope held fast in the window caught fire. The young girl screamed and jumped, just as Odessa heard a shot come from somewhere and reached out for the little girl to break her fall!

The flames ran through and took a final death grip on the house, plunging it down into an inferno. The young mother took one last look at her ravaged home as Odessa, making her way through the press and rush of firefighters and policemen, gently placed her daughter Keesha in her arms. The astonished woman screamed with tearful joy for her daughter's deliverance. She took two quick steps forward, as though to show her husband Lamont that Keesha was still alive. But Lamont lay stretched out across the lawn, his son pounding on his chest for him to wake up. The fingers of one hand were still protruding through the trigger guard of the pistol he had brandished against his son. There was a hole drilled clean through both sides of his skull.

Odessa heard someone in the alley, but paid it no mind. Eugene, the apprentice O.D., lifted himself up from against the fence at the sound of the shot and continued running. The strap of the stolen purse was still dangling from his fingers.

Elsewhere, the '65 Cutlass rolled to a gravelled stop on an open lot to the west of Paul's Cutrate Drugs, and the driver sat in the dark sepulcher of his car, his forehead pressed against the steering wheel.

The police were charging up the back steps to Niagra's flat now as the firemen fought to contain the blaze.

Niagra heard their voices coming up through his bedroom door. Odessa looked up towards the window of their apartment, and with a grim sinking feeling realized all of a sudden that Niagra had never intended to come down to talk Mister Lamont out of anything.

The clouds congealed through the rest of that long night, until the watchful eye of the full moon was entirely blotted out. But the thunder rain was washing the heavens clean too late.

The flames were now too far gone…

Sex Education

He finished the questionnaire with relish. Stoner MacKay glanced around at the computers blinking statistical colored results. He sat back and stretched his legs before the secretary approached with the findings of the Institute. She was tall and bespectacled and wore a severe expression in a wrinkled, green, short-sleeved dress. She handed MacKay his papers and a CD in a paper jacket.

"Sign here," she pointed out to him as she handed him a pen, "-and here…"

"Do you have the date?" Mackay asked as he finished writing out his signature.

"I'll fill that in," the secretary assured him as she looked over his papers to make sure that nothing was amiss, " just make sure you file a weekly report with us every Friday before twelve."

"When do my classes start?" MacKay asked sheepishly.

"You'll be contacted by your instructor once all your paperwork has been assessed and is on file. Check the computer on your wall at home for posted dates."

The secretary scanned his paperwork before casting a wary eye his way.

"You have completed and submitted your companion profile mock-ups, I take it. Is that correct?"

"That's right, Miss Kroner."

The secretary shuffled his papers together. She regarded MacKay with an air of presumption. The question that was forming upon his lips faded in the glare of her professional gaze. Miss Kroner made him feel like a fact sheet in three-dimensional relief.

"I believe we have everything we need for now. The Institute will keep you abreast as to any changes in your program. That's all for now, Mister MacKay."

When the house tone sounded he rushed eagerly to the door screen. He could see her image as it flickered onto the monitor. He looked up at her just above the front entrance to his apartment. The intelligence in the grey-eyed brunette's face struck him forcefully. She lifted her dimpled chin and looked into the hallway camera with a frank expression. There was a hint of amusement playing at the corners of her mouth. He fumbled for the stud on the wall console so as to open the door. The 'ping' of computer identification went off as she entered his apartment. The matching pictures of her winked away from the wall as he took her coat.

"Hello there! Did you get a chance to review my information?"

"Yes, it was quite comprehensive."

"I should think so. The Interview Department really gave me a going over. How about you?"

MacKay regarded her in silence as she took a brush from the flat purse under her arm. She idly ran it through the dark brown strands that fell straight past her square shoulders. Now that MacKay could compare his study partner with all her pictures on file, he was embarrassed to admit to himself there was no comparison. He watched as the beauty replaced her brush with the dutiful poise of a student assistant.

"Uh – I'll have to admit there were a lot of questions and forms to fill out. Uh – is there anything I can get you?"

"We better check our identification cards against each other and run them through our computers. Have you got your Lesson Tag to hand by any chance?"

"Sure. Right here."

MacKay raised the inside of his wrist to her view so that she could see the glowing numbers. He watched as she raised her own wrist to display the glowing numbers that qualified her for tonight's research session. They pressed their wrists together for the recorded digits to flash off once again becoming invisible under the skin.

"That should do for the Home Office. Can I see your wall computer? I need to run my card through it."

"Sure. Over there."

MacKay nervously gestured down the Hallway.

"Alright now," she looked back at him as her card came out of the slot under his monitor again, "I saw the study room you prepared on the video clip you submitted. We better check it out now to make sure all the points in the manual are covered."

"Yeah. Course. Right this way –"

"Stoner?"

MacKay turned towards her again as she slipped out of her shoes.

"I'm going to take my clothes off now. I think you should do the same and escort me to the study room."

"Oh."

MacKay could feel her amused smile on his skin like warm sunlight as he slowly undressed. He slipped carefully out of his clothes and watched her disrobe with a gray shudder of modesty. He knew you could not make an android do that.

"Could you come here for a second?"

"Okay."

MacKay leaned against her shoulders as he unlaced his shoes and removed his socks. She giggled at the feel of his fingertips against her back.

"Ready to begin the lesson?" She looked at him with a serious demeanor. "I am whenever you are."

"Yes," coughed MacKay into his hand, "I think that would be best at this point."

MacKay took her gently by the hand and walked her into the bedroom where they would begin their studies. He passed his hand over the shining blue sensor in the wall to connect the circuit and the lights grew brighter. "Mmmm, this is nice," she observed as she made her mental notes, "I like where you've placed the cameras..."

MacKay watched as she moved over and caressed each of the walls with practiced precision. When she came to the large room monitor above one of the mirrors she nodded at him with beaming approval.

"This is really quite excellent. Everything seems to pass Institute Standards in my view."

"Thank you."

"We better take our roll call pictures for this class session before we get started. Don't you think?"

"Sure. Right over here –"

MacKay directed her over to stand on a yellow circle before one of the full-length mirrors. He nervously set the timer on the wall console looking over to her.

"Five seconds alright?'

"Fine by me," she said as she tossed her hair off her shoulders.

The computerized voice seemed to come with a cheerful murmur from everywhere inside the room. A bell sounded each time the camera clicked a still photograph.

"Front View... Right Profile... Back Profile... Left Profile...

"Identification Complete. Thank you and welcome to class!"

She stepped off the yellow circle smirking at him with a sigh, glad to be done with this silly ritual.

"Your turn..."

MacKay walked over and placed his feet carefully upon the yellow circle.

The secretary blinked onto the wall monitor shuffling papers and looked up. The expression on her face as she parted her lips seemed to indicate she was taken by surprise. Now she cleared her throat as she adjusted the resolution of her image pressing studs on her desk console.

"May I help you, Miss Strumbold?"

The woman sat in the Institute chair and appeared somewhat shaken. She held her arms folded beneath her full breasts conservatively attired in a three-piece grey woolen suit dress. There was a grim expression on her face.

"I recently submitted my first lesson for evaluation."

"Yes, you should have your results soon. Everything going all right thus far?"

"That's what I came to the Institute to discuss. I was wondering might I be assigned to another study partner?"

The secretary arched an eyebrow with a quizzical air.

"Something the matter, Miss Strumbold?"

The woman shifted uncomfortably in her chair, rubbing the soles of her shoes against the carpet.

"I have the feeling I might not be entirely compatible with my partner."

"Oh? Has he registered a complaint?"

"No, nothing like that. He finds me satisfactory as far as I can observe."

"That's excellent! I take it then these are entirely your issues we are about to discuss."

"That's correct, Miss Kroner."

"Very well. Where do you believe things have gone amiss?"

"Something happened between us – I mean to me – while we were performing the 'Blanketing Exercise'…"

"I see. Tell me more."

The woman swung her knees from side to side in her chair.

"Perhaps I'm the one to blame," she reluctantly went on, "but I didn't entirely care for the emotional discharge that we accomplished…"

"I see… go on, Miss Strumbold…"

"I – I – I don't really know how to put it. There is all this hate and anger; and fear I believe inside him. At first I thought we were discharging it, and I experienced some relief. But then it would just build up again more intensely than before, regardless of whether I was lying on top of him or he upon me."

"I understand, Miss Strumbold…"

"This angst he attempts to discharge through me amounts to some kind of murderous rage. I can feel it already, despite the fact that we've only done the 'Blanketing Exercise'. Truth be told, he scares me. I don't feel safe or comfortable in the study room with him."

There was a silence in the Interview Hall. The woman timidly looked up at the bespectacled face on the monitor.

"That's very informative, Miss Strumbold."

"At this point, I'm not certain it would be appropriate for us to continue as study partners, feeling as I do. I suspect he already senses what I have told you."

"A pity. The fact of the matter is he has no criminal record of any kind for all that."

The woman bowed her head with a frown while shaking it in reluctant disapproval.

"All I can say is that I have a bad feeling about this. I know how important the concept of pair bonding is, but at this stage, I doubt our ability to mutually attain the best learning experience."

"Yes, I see. We know that first impressions do count for something. Naturally, it will take some time to reference your revelations with the data we have on the both of you. Do you have your PTFM assignment to hand by any chance?"

"Yes, I do, Miss Kroner."

The woman reached for her purse and pulled out a small flat blue oblong tube barely as long as half her index finger. She walked over and guided the tube into its slot under the monitor before returning to her seat.

"Fine. At least this part is going according to schedule. I'll transfer your data onto the required channels and get back to you. At this point, we'll have to do a fresh interview with your study partner to get his impression of the situation. Hopefully, a solution will be found that will put your mind at ease and your fears to rest."

"Thank you, Miss Kroner."

The woman picked up her purse and turned to depart.

"Just a moment, Miss Strumbold."

The woman watched as the flat blue tube extruded itself out of the slot under the monitor again.

"I've just added your PTFM assignment to your study partner's database and transferred his PTFM to your files as well. Best you review it and take notes until we get all the troublesome details of this situation ironed out."

The woman sighed and returned to the monitor with her purse. She retrieved the small blue tube from the monitor and sullenly deposited it in her purse.

"Take no action just yet. The Institute will contact you and let you know what your next step in the program will be."

"Thank you, Miss Kroner."

"Your quite welcome, of course. Good Day!"

The monitor flashed to black as the woman strode for the door, barely able to muffle her audible groan.

"There are matters that have come to our attention. It would appear that your study partner finds your participation a less than satisfactory learning experience."

Stoner McKay registered a puzzled expression on the Institute monitor.

"I don't understand."

"Evidently Miss Strumbold feels her studies might be more successful with a new partner."

MacKay showed genuine surprise.

"I don't understand. What did I do?"

"The Institute cannot offer you an objective analysis without gathering more data. For the time being we feel it would best for the both of you to explore the problem under guidance and supervision here at the Institute. We have study rooms available here for just such a purpose. We will set up a new schedule for you to refer to with Miss Strumbold. Check the postings on your screen at home. Until then, we have determined it would be best that you keep your meetings with Miss Strombold strictly within the premises of the Institute at all times until further notice."

MacKay lifted his face up to the Institute monitor. He stiffly attempted to mask his wounded feelings and dashed hopes. He slouched down in his chair despite assuming an air of indifference.

"I don't wish to cause any trouble. I'll…" MacKay looked away with a sigh of resignation. "…be happy to be assigned to a new partner if that's possible. If that's not possible, I won't ask for any refund. I'll just thank the Institute for giving me this opportunity…" MacKay sighed again with a deepening sense of dejection. "…and be on my way…"

"There is no need to foster a negative attitude, Mister MacKay. Have no fear, the Institute will get to the bottom of this and resolve matters to the satisfaction of all parties concerned. Until then, check the postings on your screen at home."

The face on the Institute Monitor flickered out before the next question fully formed in MacKay's mind or he could remember to say 'Thank You'.

The walls were lined and checker boarded with holographic monitors. After removing the last of her articles of clothing and folding them neatly onto the pallet that slid out of the wall slot, she stepped gingerly across the foam padded floor. The monitors twinkled on full like the multiple lens you find in the eyes of a fly to reveal her presence in the room. The modulated tone of a mechanical voice broke the silence.

"Olivia Theresa Strombold! Please submit your Identification Number…"

She raised her right wrist to display the glowing numbers. A thin band of red light ran horizontally down the wall from the ceiling to the floor. It caught the glowing numbers on her wrist with a pinging sound akin to a bird call before flaring out at the edge of the floor.

Olivia frowned when she saw MacKay timidly make his way through the door gliding open across the room. The pallet automatically protruded out of a slot in the wall in answer to his presence. MacKay began to remove his clothing glancing at her with wary diffidence.

"What are you doing here?" She uttered with a hiss of cold reserve.

"I–I checked the postings. This was my next assignment."

"We're not compatible."

"Why do you say that?"

"Call it 'women's intuition'."

"We were matched by computer."

She looked down as she folded her arms beneath her breasts, making a mark with her big toe on the foam-padded floor.

"I guess somehow human error reared its ugly head."

"You really think that's possible?"

"Face the facts, Mister MacKay. You're a pervert in sheep's clothing."

"What did you call me?"

Olivia glared at him with stony defiance.

"You're a pervert."

"That what you think about me?"

"Uh huh. We're not suited to each other. I can't discharge all the hate and anger that's inside you. At any rate, I would be afraid to try."

Moments passed as they confronted each other. Finally, MacKay bowed his head in defeat.

"What do we do now for new partners?" MacKay whispered to the floor.

"We? I don't see that there is any 'we' to this. I told you there's nothing between us."

"Alright. I heard you. I just don't understand why they sent me your PTFM assignment knowing how you feel about this whole thing."

"I imagine they were counting on me changing my mind."

She leaned against the wall behind her and coolly regarded MacKay's dejected figure mirrored in the holographic monitors all around them. He made half-hearted gestures towards her that seemed to die in midair. Finally, he turned to the slot in the wall, his body shuddering with suppressed sobs.

"I–I better get my clothes then," he mumbled to the wall before him.

"Pardon me?"

"I said let me get my clothes and I'll be on my way."

MacKay was too busy keeping his tears from running down his face to notice how Olivia's expression almost imperceptibly softened on all the holographic monitors. He waited while the pallet was sliding out of the wall again before fumbling amongst his things. He barely heard her voice as he reached for his undershirt.

"I have got to be out of my mind." She muttered to herself again. "You know, you masturbate like a serial killer. Did you know that?"

"What did you say?" MacKay sniffed as he flicked his fingertips away from his eyes.

"I said you masturbate like a serial killer."

"What difference does that make now?"

"There is plenty of data on it. I took notes."

"Sorry the Institute made you waste your valuable time."

"All I'm saying is you should take your time and relax. Slow down and act less like you're handling a sub machine gun or something."

"I'll take that under advisement. I noticed you seemed to be enjoying yourself."

"Oh? So you took notes, too?"

"I did my assignment."

"At least we were on the same page in that regard."

"Sure. Thanks for the opportunity."

"I suppose I came across a little like one of those old time porn stars."

"I did my assignment. I evaluated you according to the set of criteria I was given by the Institute. I don't feel I'm qualified to judge you in any other way than that."

MacKay began to squirm his way back into his underwear.

"Hold on."

MacKay looked askance at the hand on his shoulder.

"Mind if I scan your evaluations first? I've been told I look heavenly when I'm pleasuring myself."

"No doubt about that. Help yourself. I put everything on file."

"Hold on. I want to see what you said about me."

She tapped a row of buttons that lined the edges of one of the monitors. Written text instantly presented itself. MacKay felt uncomfortable as he stood next to her naked well-proportioned body. Now that she desired to end their partnership he no longer saw any point in talking. This must be her way of letting him down easy, he thought to himself.

He watched with resentment as her lips moved from time to time before the lighted monitor; the written text was interrupted by scenes of her dutifully demonstrating her Personal Technique For Masturbation. She turned and regarded him with discerning amusement. MacKay reached for his pants in despair.

"You take good notes." She told him softly.

"Thank you."

"Hold on."

"You don't have anything to fear from me. I won't be coming back to the Institute and I'm not plotting to take any revenge on you. You say we're not compatible, so I see no use in arguing or belaboring the point. I'll be out of here in a minute."

"Hold on. Let me help you with that."

She started to unbutton MacKay's shirt again and slowly pulled up his undershirt.

"What are you doing?" MacKay asked as she pulled away his shorts.

She thoughtfully took his underwear in her hands. He was caught in the gaze of her grey-blue eyes as she carefully and neatly folded his clothes and placed them back on the pallet. She leaned her tailbone and hips against the hanging shelf and spoke to herself reflected in all the holographic monitors arrayed on all the walls.

"I would feel more comfortable doing our assignments at the Institute for awhile. Do you approve?"

"But you just said –"

"I've changed my mind."

"Why?"

"I liked reading your evaluation about me."

"What's that got to do with anything?'

"That's what I've decided to find out."

"What if I agree with you now? I might just see your point now. Perhaps you're right and we're not compatible with each other. I–I don't need your pity."

Olivia looked down at MacKay's erection betraying his feelings with swelling urgency. She looked up into his face with the frankest expression.

"That's a relief. Because I don't have any to give."

She moved around the pallet and pressed the button that retracted it back into the wall.

"I just want you to know I have my pride, too." MacKay informed her. "Your behavior thus far has hardly been a confidence builder."

"Stoner. Stoner. What am I to do with you? Relax. I see now that there is a faint possibility we might be able to learn something from each other. At least for the time being. What do you say we find out one way or the other?"

"What–what made you change your mind?"

"I have no idea. I have to be out of my mind, right? Should I get the blankets and the sheets now?"

Stoner nervously chewed his lip as his indignation faded.

"Yes. I think it's best we follow the directions for the assignment."

"Alright. I'll get the sheets."

MacKay went over to the wall and tapped on a set of buttons that raised a padded rectangular platform up from the center of the floor.

"Do you remember what the first part of our assignment was to be?"

"One hundred kisses." Olivia reported as she fitted the sheets and the blankets to the platform. "I'll set the counter, okay?"

"Okay."

"Best we begin standing, Stoner. Do you feel comfortable with that?"

"I think so."

"Good. I'll stand right here, okay?"

"Okay." Stoner came over and put his hands on her shoulders as he carefully remembered where to place his feet. "Is this alright?"

Olivia took MacKay's hands and replaced them about her waist.

"There. That makes me feel a bit more comfortable."

"Alright."

"Ready to begin?"

"Any time you are."

"Why don't you go first?"

"Alright."

MacKay planted a kiss on Olivia's closed lips. One of the monitors behind them flashed a red number one that then changed into a number two as they followed the directions of their assignment.

The female voice over the intercom blared its soothing caress into the research room with mechanical efficiency.

"PREPARE FOR END OF SESSION IN FIVE MINUTES, PLEASE –"

She continued to fold the sheets with MacKay now that the two of them were fully clothed again.

"We better getter ready to get out of here," MacKay suggested as he stacked a folded pillow case on top of the protruding pallet, "no need losing study points over a technicality."

"At least we finished our hundred kisses assignment on time." Olivia remarked with relief. "Here let me help you with that fitted sheet."

"Alright."

"Watch me, Stoner. See? Take corner number one and fold it over corner number two. Now slide down and take corner number three and tuck it in. Slide down again and take corner number four and tuck that in."

"Like this?"

"Uh huh. Now straighten those two edges and we'll walk it over to the pallet. Here we go! I'll fold and fluff this end for you. There. Now we fold it in fourths. That's right. Fold it into fourths again and there we are!"

"That was easy. I can remember that. That looks like everything to me. I'll close our pallet back into the wall now."

"Okay."

MacKay pressed the buttons between the holographic monitors. The pallet was retracted once again into the wall.

The two of them looked around the room with a bit of wistfulness. The green palm fronds, ferns and grassy carpet that were holographic projections began to dim down and evaporate all about them. This event was a final signal that the session was indeed coming to an end.

"What made you change your mind?" MacKay asked again.

"I can't really tell you at this time. I suppose I'm attracted to the challenge you represent to me."

"I don't understand."

"Usually a normal is paired with another normal. Perverts are paired with perverts for rehabilitation."

"There you go with that again!"

She started at MacKay's pained expression.

"Pardon me?"

"There you go with that again. Putting labels on everything. For all you know, I could be the normal and you could be the pervert. We could even both be perverts for all the data we have about each other."

She looked at him with a mixture of stifled anger and sympathy.

"I'll have to admit there is something about you, Stoner. Perhaps we'll both be a higher order of normal after all this."

"Whatever that means."

"CLASS PERIOD HAS NOW COME TO AN END. PLEASE PREPARE TO DEPART THE RESEARCH ROOM."

She flushed a dark pink as the pinging sound alerted their attention.

The doors on either side of the padded room were now sliding back.

"I suppose that's it for now, Stoner."

She glanced up at him shyly as though waiting for something.

"What do you think our grade will be?" MacKay asked with a stiff glare.

"I think we did alright."

"How do you know?"

"All I know is I enjoyed the French Kissing. Once you stopped chewing and drooling all over me."

"I–I'll do better next time."

"I'm sure you will."

She surprised herself by reaching for his cheek. He winced away from the touch of her hand. She shrugged to herself as she collected her things and headed for her exit. When she came to the open doorway she turned to him one last time.

"Do you want to walk me to the shuttle train?"

MacKay stood glowering at her. The light framed him inside the doorway of his own exit at the opposite side of the room.

"I don't like being called a pervert." He uttered with a low hiss.

He was speaking so softly she was unable to make out exactly what he had said. She stood there waiting for him to approach her. Moments passed and the doors slid closed, finally separating them from each other's view.

Olivia reluctantly made her way down the hallway past the rest of the students. She held her books to her bosom with questions forming in her mind. She wondered to herself what kind of relationship could turn fear into courage, anger into something more constructive and productive, and perhaps even hatred into something at least bordering upon love. There was no telling at this point, but the whole thing was an interesting challenge to say the least.

She resolved to make an appointment with a student counselor as she left one of the Institute's main buildings. She ignored the gangs milling about the service pods and sidewalk kiosks, hooting admiration for her physical charms and slinging sexual slurs her way. After alighting onto one of the moving walkways that led to her shuttle train, she stepped off again. Olivia came with the milling crowd to the slope that led to the tunnel.

She walked along to the sound of her own echoing footsteps until she found a bench. She looked up at the lighted schedule posted before her in the tunnel and sat alone waiting for the I-505 to arrive according to schedule.

When it finally came, she decided to go to an all-night library rather that drop off straight home.

She entered one of the larger rooms with its banks of lounge chairs. Olivia carried the large book nestled in the crook of her arm to one of them. She plopped the book down on the padded seat and snatched up the audio-phones from the headrest. Olivia carefully placed herself within the foamed contours of the lighted and numbered lounge chair.

Olivia irritably ignored the furtive glances of various male patrons of the library. The striking beauty stretched out her shapely legs and opened up her book to read.

A rectangular screen telescoped itself out of the foot of the chair so that she could review text and do quizzes.

The book she was reading was entitled 'CASES AND CATEGORIES OF SEXUAL PERVERSION'. Olivia sighed as she quickly scanned the index until she finally came to the chapter, 'Obsessions and Compulsions in Sexual Perversion'. She squinted down the paragraphs until she found what she was looking for and swiveled around the keyboard in front of her. She typed out what she needed to be recorded on the screen before her and printed on her way out.

She was deep in study when a fellow classmate and girlfriend strolling past startled her.

"Olivia! Is that you? What are you doing here?" The pudgy, sandy haired young lady inquired in a flash of recognition.

"Doris? Doing a little research. How did you come to be here this late at night?"

"Cramming for a test, what else? How are your studies coming?"

That pained expression returned to Olivia's face as she frowned.

"Rather not talk about it."

"That bad, huh?"

Doris quickly came over and sat her portly frame on the edge of the lounge chair.

Olivia realized that once she told Doris she would rather not talk about it, her friend would be determined to make sure she did.

"Come on, Olivia. You can tell me." Doris nudged her confidentially.

Olivia drew up her legs and wrapped her arms around her knees. She knew there was no getting rid of Doris now.

"Come on." Doris turned and brought her legs together, now giving Olivia her full attention.

"What can I say? I was assigned to a pervert. We've been doing our assignments at the Institute to prevent me from being found dead in me bed."

"Really? How did you confirm he was a pervert?" Doris asked as she pulled her black silk dress around her hips and thighs.

"I've got a six sense about these things."

"Uh oh. There you go again."

"What? I know what I'm talking about!"

"Sounds like another 'snap analysis' to me, Olivia. You've got to stop judging people so quickly and jumping to conclusions. What data do you have to support the claim that your study partner is a pervert?"

"He's always looking at me. His eyes seem to follow me everywhere I go."

"That's a bad thing?"

"There's something too obsessive about it; too intense. He wants me too much and I don't feel comfortable with that."

Doris drummed her fingers on her knee.

"You're going to run out of study partners at this rate, Olivia."

"I know. I requested a new study partner, but evidently the instructors want me to work out my issues on my own with this one."

"Can't say I blame them. You're going to exhaust the supply the way you're going about it, Olivia."

Olivia set her chin on her knees as she stared ahead blankly.

"Right now, we're only supposed to meet within the premises of the Institute."

"You brought that upon yourself, Olivia. Now the instructors will be making a special study out of the both of you."

Olivia idly covered her knees with the edges of her skirt.

"At the end of our last assignment…I tried to get him to violate policy." Olivia admitted as she glanced into Doris' expression of shock.

"What? Why, Olivia?"

"I thought if I got him to violate policy, I would be assigned a new study partner."

Olivia regarded Doris coolly with an air of indifference.

"What did you do this time, Olivia?" Doris asked, narrowing her hazel eyes in an accusatory manner.

"I just asked him if he would walk me to the Shuttle Terminal. We're only supposed to meet within the premises of the Institute at this stage in our study because of the issues I raised. But I knew if I could get him to walk me to the Shuttle Terminal that would violate our agreement and we would be separated. That way, I could get a new study partner."

"You didn't, Olivia!"

Olivia looked at Doris soberly and nodded.

"What did he do?"

Olivia placed her chin on her knees and shrugged.

"He just stood there."

"Probably saw right through your little plot."

"I don't know. Either that or he was having too hard a time making his way over past that erection he was trying to hide from me."

Doris' eyes popped open in an instant and she hid her giggle in her hand.

"Olivia! They're going to burn you at the stake!" Doris exclaimed, slapping her on the shoulder. "You're absolutely wicked."

Olivia shrugged again and with a confidential glare at Doris, stifled a giggle of her own.

"How many assignments have you completed so far?" asked Doris.

"Only two. We did the blanketing exercise until I was radioactive. When we did the kissing assignment he was all over me. I could barely catch my breath long enough to kiss him back."

"Yep. Sounds like you've really got problems, Olivia," Doris muttered. "What's next?"

"Oh my Lord, Stoner, relax, will you please?" Olivia exclaimed.

She was straddled over MacKay and recalling her notes. The holographic monitors were projecting their surroundings as a warm summer beach. She stroked his pulsing and throbbing manhood with slow, gentle caresses.

"Now breathe deeply in rhythm with what I'm doing. That's it! There we go now. There we go. Therrrre we go ... see? See? Isn't that nice? Isn't that better? Now look up. There we are, dear, look at me. That's it. Look up at me. See me? See how I'm smiling, Stoner? That's it. Breathe deeply and look at me. You're doing good now. That's better..."

MacKay was looking up at her, his face flushed with a glorious enchantment.

"You're so beautiful, Olivia..."

While not very original, at least it was heartfelt, Olivia thought to herself.

"Why, thank you, dear. Just relax, now."

"I'm learning a great deal, Olivia!"

"Are you, lover? I am too, I must admit. I think learning how to pleasure yourself gives you insight into how to successfully pleasure others. What do you think?"

"What's that?" MacKay exclaimed with a shudder as he gripped Olivia by the hips. "I didn't quite get that."

"Oh, never mind. Now relax and do try to stop frowning, dear. You're not at the doctor's office getting a vaccination shot. That's it. Now get a grip on yourself, honey, and let's see if we can make this last on both of our behalves…"

MacKay took another deep breath and managed a weak smile.

"I'll try… I'll do my best…"

"That's what I wanted to hear, my dear. Now you just relax and try not to come in my face. At least not right now."

"Okay…"

"We don't want to have to be dealing with premature ejaculation this early in our studies, now do we, lover?"

"No…"

"Now. Mind if I lie beside you for awhile?"

"Be my guest…"

"Thank you, my dear Stoner. Here, put your hand on me right here. That's it. I'm going to lie down now. Hold onto me, lover…"

"I am…"

Olivia lay back against the fluffy pillows on the inflated blue blanket with MacKay.

"There. That's it. Right there, lover. That's it, on either side of my clitoris. Just like that. Feel free to stick your fingers inside me at any time. Just be gentle. Just be nice. Take your time. I'm not going anywhere. There we are. Much better than all that machine gun stuff, don't you think, lover?"

"Yes … yes…"

Olivia held onto him between his legs as she lay on her side and pressed her toes against his own. She brushed his cheeks and mouth with light kisses. Out of the haze of passion she and MacKay were generating, she could see from the corner of her eye the flickering red letters on the monitors. A familiar female voice also spoke out of the intercom in soothing tones.

"SESSION TIME FOR 'INTRODUCTION TO MUTUAL MASTURBATION' IS NOW COMING TO AN END. PREPARE FOR END OF SESSION IN FIVE MINUTES, PLEASE –"

Stoner MacKay heard the buzzer sound and turned off the drill and the laser welder. He reached for his lunch underneath in the storage compartment and pressed the stud on his elevated seat to descend to the factory floor. He quickly headed down the line past the frames for the electric hover cars and took a shuttle to the cafeteria.

"How's your study going at the Foundation, Stoner?"

Stoner spotted his friend Grindor stumbling into the shuttle with his helmet and insulated gloves. He took the vacant seat next to the huge chunk of a redheaded man and shrugged as he twiddled with the latch on his lunch cylinder.

"What's the matter, Stoner? Are you learning anything down there?"

"I'm getting along, I suppose."

"You are, huh?" Grindor scratched the bread crumbs out of his neatly trimmed beard. "Surprised they haven't tossed you out on your ear by now."

"Why would they want to do that?" Stoner tossed back defensively. "I'm doing my assignments."

"Is that right? So this is the new and improved Stoner, is that what you're telling me?"

"No."

"So you haven't violated any policies yet. That the update, Stoner?'

"No. I'm making progress. At least I'm working to better myself. Not like you."

There was raucous laughter among the other workers holding onto their lunches as the shuttle lurched its way through the plant to the cafeteria.

"He's got you there, Grindor." Rantel chuckled as he pointed a lanky finger at him.

"Oh, he does? What are you supposed to be now, Stoner?" Grindor screwed his heavy bulk around to squint for the cafeteria. "The 'Model Student' or something?"

"Who are you, Grindor? I don't have to tell you nothing."

The grimy shuttle lunged to a stop. The assembly line workers hopped out through the sliding doors and treaded through the plastic shavings for the cafeteria.

Stoner calibrated the timer on his lunch cylinder to reheat his soup. He looked up with a hiss of resignation as Grindor loudly planted his bulky frame across the table from him. Rantel hobbled over with his revolving tray and sat next to Stoner slapping his cap against his knee.

"Man! To get off these feet!" Rantel exclaimed as he rubbed his legs.

"What I can't understand is how you even qualified, Stoner." Grindor mused as he pulled out half a chicken from his open canister. "A notorious pervert like you."

"I'm not supposed to share the details of my Rehabilitation Program with outsiders." Stoner muttered.

He glared at Grindor as he slurped his soup.

"Hey Stoner!" Grindor mumbled through a mouthful of chicken.

"What?"

"Let's see the flicker disc on that piece of meat they paired you up with."

"Dream on, Grindor."

"Don't tell me they teamed you with a machine." Grindor gave Stoner a probing look. "A plastic doll maybe?"

"Yeah. You wish."

"Just being realistic, my friend. Who's going trust you alone with a real live female?"

"It's none of your affair, Grindor."

"Aw, come on, Stoner. Let's see the dog they leashed you to, my fellow."

"Get your girlie pictures somewhere else, Grindor. I'm not here to feed your lust."

"CLASS PERIOD WILL BEGIN IN TWENTY MINUTES. PLEASE PREPARE TO ENTER THE RESEARCH ROOM."

Stoner and Olivia regarded each other carefully after shuffling out of their clothes and folding them into neat little stacks on the pallets extruding out of the walls.

"Ready to study the topic for today?" asked Olivia as she set her books and papers with related materials on a bureau beneath the monitors.

They stood naked before each other and cast gazes at the glowing numbers on their wrists.

"I finished all the quizzes." Stoner said defensively with a stiff expression. "I am as ready as you are."

"I hope for your sake you are. The Institute will be putting our Research Session in the next edition of the ENCYCLOPEDIA OF HUMAN SEXUALITY for reference in the future. Are you sure you are ready?"

Olivia pressed a stud and her pallet retracted back into the slit in the wall.

"I already said I was ready."

Olivia gave him a last searching glance.

"Alright. I'll do everything I can to put you at ease. I know Oral Sex is not an easy technique for everyone."

Stoner pressed the stud that sent his pallet to lock back into the wall.

"I'm here to learn."

"Fine, Stoner, Fine. Let's take our showers now. Make sure you brush your teeth thoroughly and gargle with the mint mouthwash I requested you use. I will do the same, of course."

They pressed the inside of their wrists together and the glowing digits vanished beneath their skin.

"Just remember to take your time and let me know when anything feels awkward or uncomfortable or even unpleasant. I'll keep an eye on the monitors so don't worry about that."

"I understand. We should take our showers now." Stoner stated with resolve.

"Alright. Let's meet back here in twenty minutes."

Stoner and Olivia turned on their heels and headed in opposite directions. Steam poured out as the panels in the walls slid back. Between the winking monitors they padded barefoot into their separate showers.

The couple scrubbed themselves with washcloths and sponges inside billowing clouds of smoke until they were glowing red in the heat of their own sweat. They could see each other preparing in the monitors arrayed around the full-length mirrors lining the walls. Stoner enjoyed viewing Olivia's admirable form as she bathed; even watching her brush her teeth was a visual treat to him. Olivia could see everything Stoner did to aspire to Institute Standards of Cleanliness and was impressed with his exhaustive efforts. Each of them went through the sliding doors and down the narrow hallways drenching wet as jets of warmth air-dried their bodies.

The two of them came out into the padded Study Room. Olivia stopped halfway and holding her hands in front of her waited for Stoner to activate the platform. The holographic projection of a sandy beach loomed up and surrounded them.

Stoner went over to the wall and tapped out the code that would serve to raise the rectangular platform out of the center of the floor. The padded platform elevated to the height of their waists. There was a pinging sound in the room and both Stoner and Olivia stepped forward until they were face to face and their noses nearly touched.

"PRESENT RESEARCH SESSION WILL COMMENCE. BE MINDFUL TO CAREFULLY PERFORM ALL POSITIONS AS LISTED IN THE TEXT."

Olivia took Stoner gently by the shoulders.

"Hold onto me, Stoner."

Stoner put his hands at Olivia's sides.

"This how you want it?"

"Yes. Let me do you first, alright?" Olivia lightly brushed his cheeks with kisses.

"I'll give you the signal when we should alternate."

"Yes, of course, Stoner…"

Now Olivia lightly kissed her way down his body. She softly teased her tongue and lips down his chest and abdomen and gently pulled at his pubic hairs with her teeth. Soon she was down on one knee and looking up at him as she ran her fingers up and down his throbbing penis. Stoner was aware of the ceiling lights glinting in her grey-blue eyes between the giant monitors over head as she silently took the head of his organ into her mouth and worked her tongue around it.

He felt as though he were floating as he held her other hand and feverishly grabbed the hair behind her head with the other. Olivia massaged Stoner's penis in this way for several moments before looking up again into his own eyes for confirmation that he approved of what she was doing. The rapt expression on his face told her all she needed to know.

Now she was kneeling upon both knees and Stoner placed his fingertips on either side of the crown of her head. She continued a little more before looking up at him again.

"How is this working for you, Stoner?"

"This is quite acceptable. I'm finding it most enjoyable."

"Good. I'll note that. Let me know at any time when you would like to alternate positions."

Images of Stoner with a gang of youths chasing naked women through flaming riot torn streets sent a shiver and a chill through her.

She did all she could to focus her concentration on all the points to be covered in her assignment. The more she ran her warm tongue along the length of his penis and sucked him out the more the mental images of Stoner's past seemed to flood into her consciousness. Images of hate and rape where there should be love and some mental reference to dates and close female companions in days gone by; images of fear of discovery as Stoner looked over his shoulder and fled with his cohorts from the scene of some crime. Now there were images of anger erupting from Stoner as he responded to unexpected rejection or emotional slights with ringing slaps and fists. Here she was bonding with a partner whose texture of mind was more that of a criminal than a lover. Olivia wondered as she held onto his rigid member where might she possibly end up in all this quagmire of negative and violent emotion?

The room seemed to resound with a pinging sound that brought her out of her reverie.

"ALTERNATE POSITIONS AS SOON AS POSSIBLE ONCE SATISFACTORY AROUSAL IS ACHIEVED AS PER TEXTBOOK."

Olivia felt Stoner tap her twice on the shoulder and squeeze her hand. This was the signal that they now could alternate positions. She released him and sat back upon her haunches, looking up at him through narrowed eyes with a guarded expression of expectation.

"How was that? Satisfactory?" Olivia asked as she ran her hands over her bent knees.

"More than textbook, I would think," Stoner responded as he caught his breath.

Olivia kissed and licked her way back up Stoner's abdomen until she circled the nipples on his chest with her tongue and found her way back into his mouth.

"Do me a kindness, Stoner?" Olivia said between kisses.

"What's that?"

"Lift me up and set me on the platform"

"Yes, I will…"

Stoner grasped her just underneath her hips and lifted her off the floor until his face was pressed just against the bushy hairs of her pelvis. Olivia was surprised at this unexpected display of strength. He carried her over to the platform as she wrapped her legs around him and he set her somewhat gently on the edge. Olivia lay on her back, her breasts heaving like pink hills of flesh with every breath.

Now Stoner knelt before her and opening her legs a little wider, began to explore the folds of her labia with his fingers and his own tongue. Before long, Olivia found herself lost in the swirling haze of her own pleasure and surrendered moaning to the sensations. Stoner eagerly did what he could to increase her pleasure. Soon there was a pinging sound as the sensors in the platform registered her panting in full release.

"NOW RECORDING FEMALE PARTNER HAS ACHIEVED ORGASMIC RESPONSE IN ALL PARAMETERS AS PER TEXTBOOK"

"Stoner…slow down a little, Stoner, control yourself…that's better, that's better…you did it…"

Soon they were on top of the platform together and mutually pleasuring each other. They lay on their sides with their heads between each other's legs, kissing the scent of the soapy shower from their bodies. Stoner would roll on top, thrusting himself into Olivia's mouth with urgent force. Olivia would respond rolling onto of him as he licked her pubic hairs slick. She pressed her breasts against his stomach and crossed her feet in the air.

"Careful, Stoner…careful…take care not to hurt me…"

"I will…I will…" he gasped under his breath.

All while they performed their assignment, Olivia deliberated as to whether or not she would ingest his seed. This was purely optional, but it seemed to her that mostly for aesthetic reasons this might be best when their research session was logged into the Encyclopedia. Now that the issue was resolved in her mind, she wiggled and tumbled back on top of Stoner in order to bring their session to a more successful conclusion. She glanced up at the monitors as Stoner began to kiss her feet. Yes, their session would compare favorably with any of the other sessions involving couples doing research for the Institute. Better to end this on a high note somehow.

"Stoner?"

"Yes! Olivia?"

"Any time you care to ejaculate would be fine with me…" "Yes!"

"Just relax and I'll do it for you, okay?"

"What – what are you going to do?"

"Let me explain later. You can put this in your notes for later reference. Is that okay?"

"Okay!"

"There won't be any mess to the business because I'm going to swallow all your ejaculate. Is that all right with you?"

"Yes! That would be fine…"

Olivia tossed her shoulders and swung her hair behind her. She raised Stoner's member up to her mouth and searched for that spot along the underside between the swelling head and the trunk. Lightly she dabbed this area with the tip of her tongue.

A grateful smile traced her lips for the briefest of moments as she heard the ping of the computers go off in the room and she closed her mouth over Stoner.

"NOW RECORDING MALE PARTNER HAS ACHIEVED ORGASMIC RESPONSE IN ALL PARAMETERS AS PER TEXTBOOK."

Stoner lay on his back, convulsively rocking his hips and pelvis into Olivia's bright, reddening face. He clutched her skull in his hands and clenched his fingers in her hair. Olivia's Adam's apple bobbed up and down as she swallowed, her silent attention on completing the assignment was punctuated only with Stoner's groans.

"Olivia!" Stoner gasped.

Olivia silently kissed her way back up Stoner's body when she was done and closed his lips with her fingertips. She wrapped herself in his arms as though she were pulling up covers around the both of them.

"There, there, Stoner, just hold me." she murmured softly, "We did good. We did good. You just hold me."

"SESSION TIME FOR 'TECHNIQUES OF ORAL SEX' IS NOW COMING TO AN END. PREPARE FOR END OF SESSION IN FIVE MINUTES, PLEASE –"

The couple came out of their end of session showers. They pressed the studs under the monitors on the walls to retrieve their clothing. Stoner thought there was more rose in Olivia's color as they picked out their underwear from the protruding pallets.

He wondered how she felt about him now and whether or not she would still call him pervert. Olivia glanced up at Stoner as she strapped herself into her bra and he pulled his undershirt over his head.

"We did good, Stoner." Olivia said simply as she shimmied into her slip.

"We did?"

"Yes, we did."

"Alright if we review and exchange notes before we file our reports with the Institute?"

"Sure, Stoner. I'll download mine once I get home, okay?"

Olivia collected her things and put them in her duffel bag. The door in the wall came up and she headed for the exit.

"I can walk you to the shuttle train if you want, Olivia."

Olivia smiled at Stoner with a look that bordered almost on affection.

"No, you can't, Stoner."

"How come?"

"Our activities are confined to the rooms of this Institute, Stoner. You walk me to the shuttle train and you will disqualify yourself for this program. I know Student Policy is so detailed you really need a lawyer to go through it all, but it's all there in print."

"But I thought you wanted me to –"

There was dawning understanding on Stoner's face as Olivia regarded him with a look of chagrin.

"You wanted to be rid of me." Stoner murmured with a hint of resentment.

"Yes I did, Stoner."

Stoner turned brusquely away and began thrusting his things into his duffel bag. Olivia looked at his back in silence and shrugged intending to exit, but then turned back.

"Face facts, Stoner," she began again, "you used to run the Plazas with the Swoop Gangs. You've preyed on women and raped them; sometimes in concert with others and sometimes cornering your victims all by your lonesome. You've actually raped and sodomized many men and women. Occasionally you've even recorded the acts to be viewed with your gang of friends later. The thing that astonishes me is how you've never been caught and have no criminal record at all to show for it."

Olivia waited for Stoner to turn around and deny all this, but he kept her looking at his back.

"How do you think you know all this?" Stoner said quietly.

"Oh, your secret's safe with me, Stoner. No need to murder me to keep me quiet about it all. Besides, what's said within these walls stays within these walls."

Stoner kept stuffing his things in his duffel bag as the silence grew around them.

"What do you want me to say?" Stoner whispered to the floor. "I would never hurt you. I'm a good person ... at least – especially now..."

Olivia stood there weighing this last statement in her mind.

"There's no need to say anything, Stoner. Let's just keep 'knowing' each other like they do in the Bible and maybe I'll wind up telling you lots of interesting things about yourself."

Olivia walked over and put her hand on Stoner's shoulder.

"Look, we did good. Let's just leave it at that for now…"

She could feel him sobbing under her hand and looked around to the sight of tears streaming down his face.

"I'm a good person," Stoner protested with a sniff, "and I've been very careful. Very careful."

Olivia stepped around and leaned against the edge of Stoner's pallet.

She looked up into Stoner's face with stalwart sympathy.

"At least these relationships are consensual, Stoner. You don't have to chain me to a wall or tie my hands to a railing to have your way with me. Right?"

Olivia unzipped her duffle bag, reached in for her purse and extracted a cleanse wipe.

"Right?" She patted Stoner on the back. "Here…" Olivia began to wipe his cheeks.

Stoner took the cleanse wipe from her and blew his nose.

"There. Isn't that better? Now you don't have to go home and jack off about me; fantasizing all the while about how pleasurable it would be to take me by force."

"How do you think you know these things about me? I would never hurt you, Olivia."

Olivia remembered the line on her application that required her to list all her special gifts and talents. When she listed 'Psychic Empathic' she was hoping then she would be paired with someone of a similar bent. She had hoped for somebody young and handsome with impressive accomplishments to know all about while together they underwent the various exercises to add to the general database of the Institute. Instead she was paired with this Stoner, a man reeking with the promiscuous thoughts of a pervert and repressing all manner of criminal tendencies. What brought the two of them together admittedly was a puzzle to her.

Unless there was some kind of design to their pairing engineered by the Institute notwithstanding her protests and initial disappointment. Whatever could that be?

Olivia bowed her head in thought next to Stoner.

Perhaps the Institute was working from the principle that opposites attract. After all, loving for Olivia was as natural as breathing and talking. How Stoner could ever know what love was barricaded behind the force field of all that hate, anger and fear was beyond her.

That must be it! The matter was simplicity itself. Olivia slapped her thighs. Maybe it was computer logic, after all, ultimately binary in nature, but dimly a sort of rationale began to suggest itself to her. She was capable of love, both the giving and the receiving of it. But Stoner was shuttered up in a dark room where his own hatred, anger and fear permitted little if any light. She could give love and he needed to be loved. This essentially was the basis of their relationship. The Institute was somehow calculating that it would be a transformative one for the both of them.

"At least you will allow that all I have said about you and the nature of your past is true," said Olivia reaching out and stroking Stoner's arm.

Stoner glanced at her with a pang of terror.

"I – I admit nothing."

"That's alright, Stoner." Olivia said, continuing to rub his arm. "I enjoy knowing you." She got up and gave him a wet, opened mouth kiss. "I just hope one day you will enjoy knowing me."

Olivia got up and grasping her duffel bag headed back towards her exit.

"I – I'll see you next Research Session?" Stoner said sniffing at Olivia.

"You can count on it, lover. Now that I've swallowed your cum, how can I refuse you anything?"

Stoner returned Olivia's chuckle with bitter resignation.

"We better get going, Stoner. Somebody else may need to use this room. Be sure to send me your notes, tonight. Right?"

Stoner nodded and taking his duffel bag, made his departure through the exit in the opposite wall.

Stoner sat in the cafeteria at work glumly sipping his soup. How did she manage to come to know so much about him in such a short time? He reached for his shiny lunch cylinder and poured himself a cup of mineral tea. What should he do now? He was of half a mind to quit this rehabilitation program altogether and looked guiltily around. Grindor casually tossed jibes his way to the tittering mirth of the reedy Rantel. The soup was hot and it was all he could do to keep from hurling the contents of his bowl into Grindor's face.

When they did the recommended exercises together, she made him feel as though he might somehow emerge from the shadowy degradation of his past and forge a new life for himself. But afterwards, when they would make their attempts at casual talk, he could still sense himself standing on the other side of the gulf between them. He the card carrying pervert and sex criminal; and she the full-fledged normal doing her charity work for the good of mankind and using him as a suitable test case. At least he was fit for that, Stoner thought to himself bitterly. He found it strange that she never considered to at least credit him for that.

"What's the matter, Stoner?" Grindor said, scratching between his rolls of beefy fat. "Did your lady fair revoke your study pass?"

"Yeah. You wish."

Grindor drew on the straw until the ice rattled in his plastic cup and he burped. He wiped his mouth with the back of his hand. Rantel looked askance at him with a trace of irritated annoyance as an inaudible curse parted his thin lips.

"Great to get your hands on the real stuff again, isn't it, Stoner?" Rantel nudged Stoner playfully with his bony elbow. "Looks a little to me like she's got you spooked at this point, my boy. Don't be cowed by the pussy, friend."

The workers all looked up as the welded frames for the hover cars floated above them. They were locked into the mechanical pincers to be slowly lowered onto the moving lines and blocks of chassis.

"What makes you such an authority, Rantel?" Stoned said to his soup.

"On the job training, friend," Rantel leered around at Grindor, "on the job training plus a fifteen year sentence in the married state."

"Yup. That'll do it. That should qualify you." Grindor swirled his straw around in his cup.

Stoner wondered how she saw through him so quickly. He punched in his badge number and put in a hard day's work just like anybody else now. He drilled his quota of frames and welded his engine assemblies to company standards. He was certainly a working man now and that ought to suit all concerned. So how was it she found him so transparent as to see clearly all the crimes of which he was never even accused?

The thought occurred to him again that he ought to terminate this rehabilitation program. Who would really miss him should he disappear from this Metropolis altogether? He could then return to those prior activities which registered such disgust upon his study partner's face. She could be re-paired with someone whose thought atmosphere was more compatible with her own. He was not really sure he wanted to be involved in all this 'knowing' she was doing with him anymore; what with her assumption of such a superior air and all.

He was nearly finished with his soup and about to take his leave of Grindor and Rantel. Stoner reached for his helmet and insulated gloves and half rose before he halted. He could see the shuttles coming and going from high on the rails overhead to descend gracefully to the trough of tracks gouged throughout the length and breath of the factory floor. Minutes remained for him to return to his work post, and he would have departed but for the menacing mass of muscle seated at the other end of the long table he shared with his work mates. The grinning block of granite in the grey and black creased uniform beckoned Stoner to come his way. Grindor and Rantel nodded and timorously headed for the next shuttle. They mumbled something to Stoner as they carefully avoided the gaze of the figure planted at the far end of the table from them. Stoner seized up with fear as he raised himself to his full height with a shiver.

There was nowhere to escape to as far as he could see. So Stoner stepped forward with downcast eyes to see what errand Quadurk required of him now.

"Afternoon to you, Quadurk," Stoner's words trailed of into nothing.

Quadurk wolfed down his breaded veal before cracking open a hard roll and thrusting butter inside with a table knife. Stoner could see muscles clenching in his face as he chewed. Quadurk gestured to the empty seat next to him.

"Sit down, Stoner." Quadurk stated simply without looking at him.

"I – I have only a minute to give you," Stoner began weakly, "I'll be written up if I'm late for my work post."

"I have spoken to your superiors, Stoner," Quadurk mumbled through cheeks puffed full of food, "have no fear. You won't lose any of your 'goodie points' due to our having this discussion. Sit down, sit down."

Stoner looked around again as though he were deliberating the best route of escape.

"Sit down, Stoner." Quadurk repeated with a gaze of stone. "Now."

Stoner let out a sigh mingled with exasperation and resignation. He sank into the seat next to Quadurk with pained reluctance.

"I understand that you have been spending your off work time engaged in some kind of rehabilitation program with a study partner?"

"According to the requirements of my release papers, sir."

"Yes, there is that. You have chosen to become involved in some kind of research project for the Institute of Encyclopedic Studies. Is that not correct?"

"That's correct."

"Something to do with the subject of Human Sexual Congress, I believe..."

"Yes, I applied for enrollment and was accepted."

"The study partner assigned to you is quite beautiful to my understanding, Stoner."

At this point Quadurk reached into his pocket and set the holo-disk before him on the table. He clicked the stud in the rim of the disk and a three-dimensional projection of Olivia sprang up from the base of the disc. Quadurk looked up curiously at Stoner.

"Where did you get that?" Stoner whispered indignantly.

"Oh, I have my ways, Stoner, I have my ways..."

"I – I hardly see what my educational activities have to do with my work performance here."

"Oh, don't be so defensive, Stoner." Quadurk waved him off. "You remember what we used to say when we were running with the gangs, eh? 'Share and share alike...' we always said..."

"I – I have nothing to share with the likes of you."

"Oh, but don't you though?"

Quadurk fingered the disc and looked fondly at the projection of Olivia.

"All we need are the entrance codes to the Institute and we could have ourselves quite a party indeed."

"Who's 'we'?"

"Don't be obtuse, my dear Stoner. All our old pals would love to meet your new 'study partner'."

Stoner locked gazes with Quadurk and divined his meaning with disgust.

"I'm afraid I can't help you there. Besides, I'm thinking of dropping out of this project soon anyway."

Quadurk nodded to Stoner with a knowing sneer.

"Off and running again, are we? Sounds just like you, old boy." Quadurk tapped his finger on the holo-disc and the image of Olivia flickered before them. "Oh well, I guess that will leave us to our own devices then…"

"Look, Quadurk, if you touch her…"

Quadurk looked up with mild amused interest. He clicked the stud in the rim of the disc and the projection of Olivia shrank away into nothingness.

"You'll 'what'?" Quadurk inquired as he replaced the disc back into the red sash that hung around his tunic. "What will you do, pray tell, Stoner? Pass the wine and the narco-bliss tablets like all the other times before?"

Stoner shrank under Quadurk's gaze. He could hear the man chuckling as he lowered his eyes. Quadurk rose to his feet and left Stoner the echo of his footsteps.

"What's the matter, Stoner?" Olivia asked with a curious expression. "Here, let me help you with that…"

Olivia carefully adjusted the glowing circular sensor pads on all the pressure points of his naked body.

"There. Here," She swept her hair away from the nape of her neck. "I always have a hard time putting that one there.

Stoner placed the sensor gingerly at that place just under her scalp. The red dot in the center of the sensor pad flared and expanded covering its whole circumference. Olivia glanced over her shoulder at him with concern.

"Stoner? Is there something troubling you? You can tell me…"

Stoner kept looking down at his feet. Every time he glanced up at Olivia she appeared to him more beautiful than ever. The sight of her made it all the more difficult to speak.

"I don't think I can do this." Stoner confessed to the floor.

Olivia placed her hands on her hips and regarded him quizzically. "Well, now is a wonderful time to get cold feet, Stoner."

Olivia whirled gesturing at the holographic projections all about them. They were surrounded with images of couples successfully copulating in the various attitudes of the missionary position. She stepped through one of the projections and knelt down, eyeing Stoner's growing and swelling erection with a studied gaze.

"Look, Stoner, all you have to do is follow the holographic simulations. I'll help you out with a little guidance here and there. Besides, the sensors on our bodies will go off should we really get something out of sequence. Remember? Plus we have these practice dummies to refer to when all else–"

Stoner began to open his mouth to reply when the lights in the Session Room began to flicker erratically. He shrank back against the wall as the projections began to shimmer and flash on and off with pulsing irregularity.

Olivia cast about, gazing at the ceiling until her questioning eyes came to rest upon Stoner again.

"What is this? What's happening here?" Olivia asked Stoner as she whirled around and watched the various simulations start and short in static about them. "What's going on, Stoner?"

Stoner sank to the floor and his voice came out in a barely audible hoarse whisper.

"They're coming for you." He stated simply.

Shadows began to curl about and cloak their naked forms.

"Coming for me? What on earth are you talking about, Stoner? Who's coming for me?"

Stoner glared at her with trembling lips. He watched Olivia look at him and then suddenly touch her heart. He saw her face turn red with a swift and sudden pang of comprehension. She turned round with narrowing darting eyes as thin red bands of light enclosed the spacious room and sliced running down the walls. Olivia returned her gaze to Stoner, her breasts nervously jiggling as the glowing sensor pads pulsed with her attempting to catch her breath.

"Stoner! What have you done? Tell me!"

Stoner wrapped his arms over his head in anticipation of Olivia's blows.

"I'm sorry – I'm sorry–" he wailed, "they would have killed me if I had refused to give them the codes…"

"Codes?" Olivia started with an incredulous expression. "What codes? Stoner you can't mean – oh, Stoner!"

Olivia rushed over to Stoner and knelt around him as though to shield his body with her own, cradling him in a hug with her arms and legs. She sobbed for several moments against his neck with her hands wrapped about his knees.

"Stoner! Stoner! What have you done to us? Just when I was beginning to have feelings for you…"

Stoner, somewhat taken aback at this sudden display of affection, attempted to reply. He barely opened his mouth when Olivia thrust him away from her with all her might. He was sent sliding and sprawling across the slick floor and marveling as he cowered in a corner of the room at her passionate strength. He looked up and saw her pacing the floor and wringing her hands.

"No! No! This can't be happening! I did nothing wrong. I'm just a student! I was just trying to help you, Stoner!"

Stoner raised his hand to her from the floor when she whirled again to face him.

Now she regarded him with nothing but distaste and disgust in her expression, and she exuded a wave of revulsion that stunned him.

"I was right about you all along," she hissed nodding vindictively.

"I'm sorry – I'm so sorry…" he moaned to the floor.

He looked up at her and even now watching her take heaving breaths, treasured the sight of her as he wallowed in his own overwhelming regret.

"Get up." Olivia spat at him.

Stoner snapped to attention suddenly as though given a command.

"Get up! You pervert!"

"Don't call me that!" Stoner cried out cringing.

"You heard me!" Olivia rushed over cuffing and slapping Stoner about the head and shoulders. "You get up, you perfectly hideous pervert you!"

"Stop calling me that!" Stoner roared as he rose to his feet grasping Olivia by the wrists.

He wrestled with her squirming form through all the static, short-circuiting holographic projections that were supposed to act as visual aids for their study until he had slammed her against the wall. She spat in his face and eyed him with distain.

He pinned her hands on either side of her head and squeezed and squeezed until she flinched in pain.

"You're hurting me, Stoner." Olivia uttered with an attempt at cool reserve and just a hint of menace.

Stoner felt his grip slacken in spite of himself. Olivia pushed him aside and moved quickly over to the slits in the wall where their clothes were stored.

"We've got to get out of here, Stoner." Olivia said, as she pushed the studs on the wall.

The pallets extruded that contained their clothes.

"There isn't time." Stoner lamely uttered.

"What?" Olivia recoiled, covering her breasts.

"I'm sorry. The exits are covered. Either way we try to leave we'll be intercepted by … them."

Olivia started forward and then stepped back indecisively. She was like wary prey sensing she was trapped.

"I'm sorry…" Stoner whined again as he reached out a consoling hand to her.

"Don't touch me."

Stoner let out a cry that was half a sob and half a groan.

The couple stood there trembling before each other, their bodies polka dotted and dappled with glowing test sensors.

"What are we to do now, Stoner?" Olivia asked with wounded indignation. "Since you've brought this down upon us. I can see the plan now that you hatched up with your Swoop Gang pals. First disable all the alert mechanisms…"

Olivia looked about as the holographic projections shorted and fizzled out one by one.

"– then they'll be coming through the Session Exits … won't they, Stoner?"

Stoner nodded silently.

"Once you've introduced them to your Dream Girl what becomes your role in all this, Stoner?"

He could see the green vein in her neck pulsing as she regarded him with level contempt.

"Let me guess…" Olivia continued spitefully as her eyes began to well with tears.

"I suppose that's when the party begins. Is that right, Stoner? A little vapor wine and a few narco-bliss tablets to loosen me up … and then I get passed around so that each of your friends can have a turn testing my orgasmic response and seeing who can get the highest readings on those gauges over there … that's about the size of it, isn't it, Stoner? I'm the main act for tonight's entertainment, aren't I?"

Olivia could see Stoner mouthing yet another apology and shook her head in disgust.

"Stop it. Just stop it." She insisted, pre-empting his reply. "No use me removing my sensors now, I suppose."

Olivia moved over to where the practice dummies were lying all awry on one of the session tables. She sat one up testing the padding on various places in its anatomy.

Now poking and probing here and there she grew pale as she heard the footsteps coming her way.

Olivia regarded Stoner quizzically as she held the head of one of the female dummies next to her own.

"What do you think, Stoner? Does it look like me?" asked Olivia bitterly.

Stoner sank down on the pallet where his clothes were stored and groped for words. Olivia continued on past his forlorn silence.

"What do you think, Stoner? Do you get the first serving of me or do you get the leftovers after all your pals have finished? Huh? I'm asking you what do you think? Do I get tossed aside like one of these practice dummies when you've used me all up, or do you steal me away from this Institution of Higher Learning to prowl the streets with you once I've been broken in and know the routine? Come on, Stoner, don't be shy." Olivia held the female practice dummy beside her as though it were her favorite doll. "Don't you think she looks like me?"

Stoner made a few futile gestures with his hands, looking down at his feet. It was only when he looked up at Olivia sitting next to the practice dummy that an idea flashed haphazardly into his head.

They were still wearing their sensors!

Olivia started in terror when Stoner hopped off the clothes pallet and came her way. She scoured the whole area for something hard to throw at him or to arm herself with. A shoe maybe or a nail file or belt buckle…

"Don't come near me, Stoner. You keep your distance or I'll –"

The Judge sounded the witness chimes for order to resume in the court. He then nodded for the witness to continue. The learned counsel continued his interrogation as the hover mikes and court cameras relentlessly relayed today's proceedings to all available media outlets Worldwide. The courtroom was filled to capacity with law students and high officials from the Institute of Encyclopedic Studies. There were also an inordinate percentage of gawkers here and there listening intently in the hallways and spilling out onto the streets where various groups held up their flashing signs in support for or against the defendant.

"At this point the defendant approached you, is that correct, Miss Strombold?"

Olivia cleared her throat and lifted her chin up against the oglers with steely defiance.

"Yes, that's correct."

"What did you assume his intention to be at that time?"

"How could I say? I didn't know what to think. I simply knew that things were not going according to the standards and protocols of Institute Study Procedure. I felt betrayed and no longer considered myself working with a student who shared my same desire to learn."

There were murmurs in the courtroom, a few titters and a guffaw that made the Judge sound the witness chimes once more to restore order.

"So would you say you were apprehensive as he approached you?"

"Very."

Olivia glanced Stoner's way and blinked nervously.

"Apprehensive of what, Miss Strombold?"

Olivia felt unsettled under the learned counsel's grizzled, beetle browed gaze.

"Well," Olivia crossed her legs defensively, "as I was already aware of his past history, I feared that I might be subject to the same kinds of victimization he was known by me to be a party to in other prior events."

"That so?"

"Yes."

"I take it therefore at this point you prepared to defend yourself."

"Yes, I did. To the best of my ability."

"Did your fears indeed prove to be justified?"

Olivia shifted uncomfortably in the witness seat. She looked over at Stoner with a warm albeit guarded smile. She crossed her legs again and pulled her skirt over her knees to keep from encouraging the murmurs of the oglers.

"I am relieved and gratified to report that they were not."

This comment evoked a renewed buzz in the courtroom and the Judge was compelled to sound the witness chimes again.

"Do you remember what the defendant said to you at this particular time?"

"Yes, I do"

"Look, let's take our sensors off, Olivia. Hurry, you hear them coming! We'll slip back into our clothes and put the sensors on the practice dummies."

"What?"

"We can couple them together and crank the motors up to have them simulate the missionary position. I'll dim the lights so they appear in partial silhouette. Hurry! We don't have much time!"

Olivia and Stoner hastily replaced their sensors on the dummies and shuffled back into their clothes.

"Now you came in through that way," Stoner pointed to Olivia's Session Exit, "I'll stand beside you. When they come through, I'll help you escape back through your exit and seal it off. At that point, with some luck, I'll be right behind you or I'll make my way through the other exit. What do you think?"

Olivia gave Stoner a puzzled frown.

"Sounds sort of half cocked and awfully dicey, Stoner." Olivia commented to Stoner ruefully as she pulled her blouse over her head.

"What do you want from me? I'm doing the best I can here, Olivia!"

The learned counsel at this point casually leaned against the Witness Pod. He surveyed the men and women of the Tribunal. He directed his next question as much to them as to Olivia.

"Now was it at this point that you would say the Security Measures of the Institute were indisputably violated?"

"Yes, I most certainly would. Soon after we redressed in our attire we observed two men making their way through the Session Exits without prior authorization."

"Do you see those men present here in the court today?"

Olivia narrowed her eyes at the two hulking men glaring at her with grim, deadly expressions.

"Yes, I do," she said with a tremor of diffidence.

"Would you be so kind as to point them out to the court now?"

Olivia and Stoner made themselves small behind the pulsing frame of her Session Exit. The door finally slid open and Quadurk came through with his favorite variety of vapor wine and magnetic shackles. Stoner nodded to Olivia as Quadurk lumbered into their Session Room. Quadurk beheld the silhouette of the practice dummies simulating the missionary sexual act and chuckled.

"Just couldn't wait for us to join the party, eh, my good man?" Quadurk exclaimed as he raised aloft his jug of wine. "Ho! Grindor! Look at our boy go!"

Grindor made his way through the sliding door at the opposite end of the room.

"The lad is certainly showing our new recruit some tricks, isn't he?"

"She seems to be a looker from here, Quadurk! Fresh meat for the Open Market, wouldn't you say?"

"Product testing is already underway, methinks." Quadurk smacked his lips. "Did you bring the branding iron and the stamps?"

"Right here in the tool box." Grindor assented cheerfully.

"Good, man. Let's help young Master MacKay inspect the merchandise before shipping and handling."

Olivia was hard put to keep her stomach from turning.

"Now, Olivia, now!" Stoner whispered harshly.

He shoved her through the Session Exit before the sliding door closed again.

"Yes, I do." Olivia rose to her full height and pointed a steady finger. "That man there. The one beside him also."

There was a sustained rumble throughout the courtroom and the witness chimes were sounded again and again. Reporters dashed off down the aisles to their computer feeds outside the courtroom. Here the rumble reverberated even more so and the Judge directed the court attendants to quell the brewing commotion out in the adjacent hallway.

"Good Ladies and Gentlemen," The Judge admonished them all sternly, "you are being permitted to enjoy a privilege, not a right. I advise you one and all to consider again how best to conduct yourself with the proper decorum as befits these chambers or you will find me compelled to clear this court of all likely offenders. The learned counsel will now continue his examination without distraction."

The witness chimes sounded again.

Olivia tripped her way through the Session Exit. She staggered forward as she heard a thump and a pounding. The sliding door to the Session Room closed shut. She thought Stoner would be close at her heels behind her, and several times she glanced back expecting him to be racing to catch up at any moment. She heard the echoes of shouting and thought she felt footfalls behind her, but these things were hard to make out being muffled by her ragged breath and the sound of her pounding heart.

Running as hard as she could, Olivia feverishly pressed the alarm bands. She broke the wave circuits of the warning beacons down and through every hallway she passed.

Where were the proctors and the regents and the instructors? Olivia knew she would never feel completely safe until she was once again in contact with the authorities.

She stopped and cupped her hands to her mouth, fearing for what might have become of Stoner MacKay.

"Stoner? Stoner!" She called down the way she came hearing only an echo for an answer. "Stoner! Are you there? Where are you?"

The learned counsel pointed as well to Grindor and Quadurk.

"Let the court note that the witness has identified these two men as the ones who violated security procedures at the Institute of Encyclopedic Studies and put her in fear of her life."

"The court notes this and would suggest the learned counsel continue his examination of this matters," the Judge advised dryly.

"Indeed I will, Honorable Mediator, Indeed I will." He turned his attention again to Olivia. "We would be correct in assuming you effected your escape owing in some part to the assistance of the defendant seated before you? Mister Stoner MacKay?"

Olivia looked with sympathy Stoner's way.

"Yes, that would be correct."

"Did you encounter him again once you found yourself safely out of harm's way?"

Stoner sat there in the courtroom remembering how Quadurk hurled him over the tables and Grindor gleefully kicked him with relish rolling across the floor. He threw things at them and evaded their blows as best he could, but once he had gotten Olivia safely through her Session Exit and closed the sliding door behind her, he became fair game for all the punishment they generously meted out. He thought his last moments were upon him when Grindor put a choke hold on him, and he was fast losing all consciousness when he somehow managed to convulsively grasp the handle of Grindor's toolbox and club him with a satisfying thud. While Grindor recoiled and howled, Quadurk grasped him by the lapels and banged him against one wall after another. He was close to passing out a few times, until while sailing over the pallet where his clothes were stored, he caught up his duffle bag and pulled out his welding torch. He twisted the flare switch in the handle and the flash blinded Quadurk just before he finally found the stud that reopened the sliding door to Olivia's Session Exit. He dragged himself kicking and rolling through the opening, and limped and hobbled his way down the passage to the shouts and curses of his pursuers ringing in his ears.

Olivia took this time to catch her breath and was of a mind to proceed on toward some kind of safety for herself when she heard the faint thumping of footsteps gradually growing louder and coming her way. She kept calling out Stoner's name, all the time dreading that she was alerting Grindor and Quadurk as to her whereabouts. But finally her calls where answered and she could recognize that it was Stoner's voice.

When she saw him come around a bend in the passageway, she was shocked and horrified at his bruised, bloody and battered appearance.

"Stoner? Is that you?"

"Yes," he wheezed, "this is me."

"My god! You look awful! What have they done to you?"

"Never mind that now. Those thugs may still be behind us. Give me a hand, would you?"

Quickly Olivia reached out to steady him. They stumbled down the hallway in a panic to anyplace that would put them out of the reach of danger.

"Do you have any more questions for this witness?" The Judge inquired of the learned counsel.

"I would say not at this time, my Honorable Mediator."

"Good." The Judge sounded the adjournment chimes. "Considering the lateness of the hour, I think it would be best for us to resume these proceedings tomorrow morning at the appointed time. Please note this on your schedules. However, before I leave you ladies and gentlemen to take care of the responsibilities and matters that at present require your attention, I would like to express a word to Mister Stoner MacKay. Young man, would you please rise?"

Stoner MacKay reluctantly rose with his head bowed, expecting a rebuff and perhaps even a word of censure.

"Mister MacKay, whatever judgment this court finally renders, I hope you will see fit not to forsake your studies. Study is, after all, an excellent way to improve one's character and standing in Life, regardless of one's prior circumstances or background. The Institute of Encyclopedic Studies is proving to be a useful institution for helping dispel and remedy the ignorance and hypocrisies of our times, so be advised not to judge them too harshly. I wish you to learn all you can, and perhaps one day you will know how to choose your associates more wisely and prevent misfortunes such as you are having presently from occurring, every now and then … Court is adjourned!"

The First Court Attendant sounded the adjournment chimes again.

"All Rise and Bow before the Honorable Mediator! Court is adjourned!"

Outside Stoner limped gingerly down the steps that led to where the air cars were docking. Just as he came to the local and commercial docks he thought he heard someone behind him calling his name. He turned to find it was Olivia hailing him and prancing his way.

"Stoner! You weren't planning on leaving without saying goodbye, were you?'

"Sorry, I didn't see you around."

"That's no kind of compliment to me."

"Miss Strombold, you were a beautiful and lovely study partner. I wish you every degree of Higher Learning."

"That's more like it. Now no public displays of affection."

"Perish the thought," Stoner MacKay chuckled.

The wind played through Olivia's brunette tresses as she parted her lips.

"No, that thought doesn't have to die, Stoner. Just file it. For later."

Stoner put out his hand.

"Thanks for everything, Miss Strombold. Take it from a criminal and a sex pervert, it was heaven being your study partner. Bye now."

"Take care of yourself. Stoner."

Stoner thrust his hands in his pockets and descended wincing to the next available air car awaiting him.

Olivia sighed and said goodbye to Stoner's back.

She returned to the courtroom to meet with one of the Deans from the Institute of Encyclopedic Studies and a few of the instructors to find out what would be her next assignment. But when she got back there past all the stray reporters still somehow milling around, everyone she knew was gone and the courtroom was left deserted.

She turned on her heel to go when she spotted a duffle bag sitting half open on one of the chairs along the aisle. Going over to it she immediately recognized the welding torch sitting on top of a pair work boots inside.

"Oh hello!" A court attendant peeked inside. "We're closing up now, Miss."

"Yes, I know." Olivia hefted the duffle bag. "Could you help me take this to my car?"

"Sure thing, Miss. Where are you parked?"

"Just the other side of the East Wing?"

"Alright then, come on…"

The court attendant took up the bag and they proceeded.

"Stoner…" Olivia slowly shook her head and whispered as she took the steps down to her air car. "Really, Stoner…"

Solving For 'X'

"Why do you have a Blackboard in your bedroom?"

She looked at him solicitously as she stood there naked. She folded her arms over her ballooning breasts and the swelling and the stiffening of her nipples in the chill breeze. He gazed at her soberly and tried to collect his thoughts, but the sight of her only made his throbbing erection all the more rigid. She was not unaware of the passion she inspired in him.

"Sometimes ideas come to me in the middle of the night. I like to write them down."

"Oh, I see."

She sat demurely at the head of his bed against the pillows and picked up a stray piece of chalk threatening to roll off the nightstand. She watched him mark off the last remaining integers of a test question for his night class. He looked back at her with relief. He set his stick of chalk back onto the stand.

"There! All done now."

"This was one of those moments, huh?"

"Right. Hope you won't hold it against me."

"Come here. I've got a few ideas about what I want to hold."

"Right. Here I come."

Stephanie would stay after class mulling over his story problems. Even she could not tell you where her emotional block to Algebra sprang from in the beginning. She would complain to her teacher, Mister Landon, that she just did not see where all this figuring with numbers and letters was leading. But the more she fell behind, the more desperate she became to master this subject. When she saw the flyer on the Student Board offering free tutoring sessions she eagerly signed up.

She made appointments with Landon to discuss her difficulties. But no matter how her instructor attempted to explain the subject to her, somewhere between the simpler operations and the ones building upon these to the more complex, her mind would slip a gear and fall into the abyss of non-comprehension. There were blank spaces in her understanding that made her squint into the same computational blind spot over and over again.

Stephanie even latched onto a fellow classmate, Marion Purvis, who was always volunteering answers and obviously doing really well in the class. She appealed to him with her charms and started dating him between course sessions. Between going out to the Star Theater after class and attending Comic Book Conventions with Marion, she discovered much to her astonishment that she was a tactile learner.

This discovery came to her sometime after she and Marion returned to his apartment from the Computer Exhibit at the Art Museum. After the obligatory French kissing, he led her to his bedroom and she was startled to find the entire wall behind his bed was some kind of blackboard covered with chalk equations, conic sections and geometric figures.

There was a stack of books at the head of the bed next to the nightstand. Above it was a reading light hanging from a cord. The carpet was grey and blended in well with the black back wall.

"What do you think?" asked Marion as he fumbled over her breasts in worshipful awe.

"Impressive…" Stephanie murmured as Marion unzipped his pants, "– some of this is Algebra right?"

"That and assorted formulae," he sighed into her ear while nibbling her lobes.

"This over here looks something like the assignment we have to turn in for Mister Landon next Wednesday," Stephanie remarked as Marion unbuckled her jeans.

"Something very similar, I'm sure," Mario agreed as he slid her panties down around her ankles. "Glory! You are really beautiful, Stephanie!"

"Thank you. Uh!" Stephanie exclaimed as Marion found his way between her legs with his tongue. "God! Explain all this to me some time, promise?"

"Find a way in and find a way out," Marion declared on his knees as he teased Stephanie again after catching his breath. "– then after all that, you can create a new pattern. Don't worry, Marion shall make it plain to you, honey."

"Thank you, Mario. Wee! Put me down! Ah! That's nice! Your tongue feels really good against my clit! Now put me down! You've got a blowjob comin', buster!"

Stephanie knelt over Marion as he backed into a seated position on the bed half out of his drawers. She took his throbbing erection into her mouth and began to suck for extra credit. Stephanie unlaced his shoes as he began moaning and raised his legs.

She sat cross-legged on the wooden dining table in her bare shoulders and black shorts, tapping the soles of her soapstone sandal clogs. The Sun came through the window and caught highlights in Stephanie's honey yellow hair as it spilled over her shoulders and down to the generous cleavage she was displaying for Marion. The rhinestone pattern just underneath on her black halter blouse glittered under the overhead lights.

"Mister Landon sent me some homework by Email, Marion," Stephanie began diffidently.

"Let's see it," Marion said as he brought out two large bowls of salad, "Hey! What are you doing sitting on the table?"

"I thought we were going out someplace tonight, Marion…"

"We shall see, we shall see," Marion playfully retorted as he carefully set their meals down. "What were some of the problems he sent you in the Email?"

"I don't know. Just more of the same stuff we've been studying in his class, I imagine."

"Like what? Give me a 'for example'."

Stephanie sighed and looked towards the window.

"You really want to hear all that now?"

"C'mon, Lady Bug. You know Math is my thing."

Stephanie sighed and looked up at the ceiling and then began to read what was written there in the invisible ink of her mind.

$$\text{"Uh} - \text{'p x 5 / (1-p) x 6} = \text{p x ? / (1-p) x 1}$$
$$(1\text{-p}) \text{ x 5} = \text{p x 2}$$
$$5 = \text{p x 7}$$
$$\text{p} = 5/7 = 0.714'\text{…"}$$

Marion sat down at the table with a question mark on his face. He gave Stephanie a searching look, but she simply shrugged again.

"I don't know… That's what it said in the Email…"

Marion looked away drumming his fingers on the table.

"That's algebra, right?" Stephanie asked with an innocent expression.

Marion looked her way and chuckled.

"Yeah, that's algebra, Lady Bug. Come on, let's go back into the bedroom, okay?"

"Oh no! Not that crazy blackboard again!"

"C'mon, c'mon! Get your bare legs off the table and let's go check this out."

"Do we have to? I thought we were going out tonight –"

"C'mon, you've got the wheels in my head spinning. This will only take a minute. We've got plenty of time to catch a movie."

He took her by the hand and led her into the bedroom to do some brainstorming.

Stephanie sat on the bed and watched Marion wipe the chalk marks off the black wall behind the mattress with a damp cloth.

"Let's have that problem again, Stephanie –" Marion requested as he took an unused piece of chalk off the nightstand.

"Oh, Marion, do we really have to do this now?"

"Better now while it's still fresh in your mind, honey chile."

"I thought we were going out some place tonight. Can't we do all this once we've come back from the movies?"

"Come on – come on –" Marion gestured her way with the stick of chalk, "Give me the problem again."

Stephanie sighed and her palms began to sweat as her breathing became labored.

She bowed her head and muttered to the floor with a sense of growing mortification.

When she raised her eyes, she saw the entire problem committed on the wall in chalk dust. Marion turned to her with amused regard.

"Is that it, Lady Bug?"

"Yes, Marion," Stephanie uttered in a tone barely above a whisper.

"Better check Mister Landon's Email to make sure we haven't missed anything."

"Alright, Marion," Stephanie said with an air of resignation, "— alright if I use your computer over there?"

She kicked off her sandal clogs with barely concealed resentment and padded barefoot over to the Dell computer against the black wall.

"Be my guest. You know you can have anything I got, Stephanie." Marion told her as he began to break the problem down.

Stephanie copied and pasted Mister Landon's Email onto a document and printed it out on the Fax machine. She snatched the sheet out of the tray and moved wearily over to Marion's side. She looked around for a piece of chalk and Marion snapped his in half and handed her a piece. She looked up into Marion's dark brown eyes ruefully and at the ready with her stick of chalk poised between her fingertips.

"Here —" Marion began as Stephanie undid the clasp behind her neck to her halter. "I'll start over here and you just mark what I tell you over there. Okay?"

"Alright, Marion —"

Stephanie let the halter fall around her hips while her bare breasts fell free to Marion's eyes. She was thinking she might be able to get him to stop by undressing while he worked to solve this problem. Carefully she unbuckled the thin silver and black belt at her waist and let her flared black shorts descend around her ankles.

"I write '— **p x 5 (1 – p) x 6 —**'." Marion looked over and caught her challenging gaze, "— and you write '- **= p x 7 + (1 – p) x 1 —**'. Okay? Think you can do that?"

"Okay. What was that? Run that by me again." Stephanie asked, standing only in her panties.

"That's '— **p x 7 —**',"

"Right. '— **p x 7 —**',"

"— '+ **(1 – p) x 1 —**'. Got it?"

"Yeah, I got it."

Stephanie let her panties fall to her feet as she continued the first line of the equation. She stepped out of them and finished marking on the black wall.

"Stephanie," Marion looked askance at her as he started the second line of the equation, "– what are you doing?"

"What?" Stephanie protested as she showed him her palms. "It's more comfortable for me this way."

"Yeah, I'll bet it is."

"Look, I can always put my clothes back on, if you want."

"Hmnnn, that's okay."

She reached down and tossed her panties off the floor onto the bed. Stephanie knew how much he enjoyed looking at her. After solving this problem, he would want some kind of reward for this exercise of brilliance. Stephanie realized that with her trim pinup girl figure, she was just enough eye candy to induce Marion to help her with all her Math.

"Alright." Marion nodded at the blackboard and licked his lips at her. "Now let's go further in simplifying the expression. I write '– **p x 5 + (1+ -p) x 6 –**' and you write '– '**= p x 7 + (1+ -p) x 1 –**'. Right?"

Stephanie furrowed her brow and frowned as she marked down the integers on the second line. She rubbed the sole of her foot on a bare shin. It seemed unlikely they would be taking in a movie tonight. She stood on one toe and looked over to him.

"Is that how you wanted it?"

"Yah – baby. Now let's take it on down. Here – '**– p x 5 + 6(1+ -p) –**'" Marion marked down quickly on the board, "– and you write '**- = p x 7 + 1(1+ -p) –**' We straight?"

"Hold on – hold on –" Stephanie whispered the last of the integers and symbols to herself. "There!" She cradled her breasts in her arms and cast a coy look his way. "What's next?"

"We continue to simplify the problem, honey bunch. Now I write, '**– 5p + 6 + -6p –**', and you write '**- = 7p + 1 + -p –**'."

Stephanie could feel his eyes roaming her body. The sight of her was mixing in with all those calculations in his head.

"Is this what you said?"

"That's it. Now write this down after I write – let's see –" He marked the chalk stick rapidly down the board, "– let's see – '– **5p + -6p + 6 –**', and you write '– = **7p + -p + 1**'. Do you see where we're doing the canceling now?" Stephanie put her stick of chalk to the corner of her mouth. She narrowed her eyes at the board before her and then regarded Marion with a wry smile.

"I guess – I mean, sort of – kind of –"

"That's alright, Stephanie. Just work with me here. We'll go over all this again once we're done."

"Promise?"

"Scout's honor. Now. I write, '– **-p + 6 –**', and you put down this; '– = **6p + 1 –**'

Okay?"

"This is getting easier, Marion –"

Stephanie felt like when she was a little girl. That was when her Father would put her feet on top of his own while he walked her to bed for the night. She would be moving, but he would be taking all the steps.

"That's because of the canceling. Alright, underneath all this, I put '– **-p + 6 + -1 –**' and you put '– = **6p + 1 + -1 –**' Do you follow me?"

Stephanie moved over to Marion's side and quickly scanned both sides of the equation.

"Wait a minute. Wait a minute. Now – now – this becomes, '– **-p +5 = 6p –**' Is that right, Marion?"

"There you go. What did you just do?"

"Uh – well, on the left side I subtracted…"

"Uh huh. And on the right?"

"I think on the right side I canceled to get '– **6p –**'. Right?"

"Starting to get the method a little?"

"I think so, a little…"

"Now, let's try this; $p + -p + 5 = 6p + p$ … see where this is going?"

Stephanie checked Marion's expression as she tentatively pressed her piece of chalk against the blackboard.

"Is this right, Marion? $5 = 7p$?"

"What did you just do, Stephanie?"

"I think – I think – I cancelled with $-p$ one side and added with a positive p on the other side."

"Now what comes next?"

"Divide both sides by 7? Or should we divide both sides by 5?"

"Well, we're multiplying p by 7. Let's try dividing both sides by 7 first, okay?"

"Okay."

Marion's dark brown eyes glinted with a new insight. He scratched the symbols across the board with renewed fervor.

"Actually… we could do this… $1/7 \times 5 = 7p \times 1/7$…"

"Cancel out the 7 on both sides?" Stephanie asked with narrowing eyes.

Marion and Stephanie regarded each other for several moments evenly.

"What does that leave us with after that?" Marion asked her quietly with a searching gaze.

Stephanie returned to marking against the board cupping her breasts in her hand.

"$5/7 = p$?" Stephanie uttered as she placed her chalk stick upon the nightstand and covered her crotch with her other hand. "That's the answer, isn't it?"

Marion drank in the sight of her and then returned to view the expressions scrawled before both of them. He turned back to Stephanie with amusement.

"Is that what you think?" Marion asked her. "Yes, it is."

"What would happen if we divided 5 by 7?" "I have no idea."

"Why don't we find out, Lady Bug?" Marion approached the board once more, marking it with his stick of chalk. "What do you say you finish this for me, baby?"

Marion handed his piece of chalk to her.

"Alright," Stephanie marked out a decimal point, "I'll just put this behind the **5** and add a bunch a zeroes..."

"Okay," Marion nodded, "now what?"

"Divide **7** into **5.0**, of course, smarty pants." Stephanie furrowed her brow in concentration. "– then **7** into **10**, and finally **28** into **30** which leaves you with **0.714** and a remainder of two sevenths."

Stephanie looked at Marion over her bare shoulder.

"That's right, isn't it?"

"So what?" Marion shrugged indifferently. "What has all this got to do with anything?"

"Well, I would suppose it means **p = 5/7 = 0.714** when it's rounded off?" Stephanie turned and crossed her arms over her breasts.

"Right?"

"Well, how about this, Stephanie. Let's say you have **5/7 = p = 0.714**. Is that the same expression?"

"I don't understand your question, Marion. What has changed by you switching the terms between the equal signs?"

Marion sat at the foot of the bed, making the mattress bounce.

"So you would say this expression is essentially the same as the previous one?"

"I don't understand. Don't these equal signs determine the relationship between the – the..."

"The terms?" Marion interjected.

"Yeah, that's right. That's it. The terms..."

"Hmmnn," Marion began as he undid his shoelaces, "why don't you write this down, Lady Bug, **0.714 = 5/7 = p**?"

"Marion! Why are you playing with me like this?"

"Go on," Marion insisted as he removed his shoes and then his socks to her relief.

"Alright Marion," Stephanie sighed, knowing as Marion undressed that this 'skull session' would all soon be over.

She dutifully marked down this third version of the expression and turned with a questioning glance to note his nod of approval.

"But how does this change anything?" Stephanie insisted as she placed the stick of chalk on the ledge beneath the blackboard. "We just said the exact same thing three different ways, that's all."

"Really?" Marion observed thoughtfully as he unbuttoned his shirt. "Do you think we've exhausted all the possible ways we can say the exact same thing?"

"I don't know. Can't we talk about it later?"

"We certainly can, Stephanie." Marion concluded as he finished undressing.

Before the last shoe dropped to the carpet, it seemed to Stephanie that Marion was inside her once more plying the labor of love into their mutual calculations. Somehow all those marks on the blackboard found their way into her mind between every chance she took to catch her breath blanketed as she was beneath Marion's sweat. She felt the muscles bunch between his shoulder blades and pinched the skin on his back with her fingertips as he strained to arrive at some place within her where all her wildness would come sweetly rushing out.

Somehow the darnedest things would come to her while she was making love to Marion. What occurred to her now was that there couldn't be more than three places where you could put the **p**; couldn't be more than three places where you could put the **5/7**; and finally couldn't be more than three places where you could place **0.714**. She cried out as this little epiphany mixed itself in with her swelling orgasm while Marion drove himself to moaning and beached himself upon her breasts with the pink nipples going erect as Stephanie was mired and swirled inside their cascading sighs.

The glare of the overhead light bulb hanging from the cord was mirrored in Stephanie's blue eyes as she lay on her back. She seemed to be looking at a thought on the ceiling that somehow captured her attention. A thought crawling like that spider she saw between the panels above her and into molding where the edges of the room joined together. A notion that somehow remained suspended glowing above Marion and his frenzied rhythmic thrusting into her with blind wild joy.

When he was done and finally sleeping in the crook of her arm, she very gently disengaged herself from his embrace. Stephanie padded barefoot over to the wall and the blackboard, her naked form swaddled in the bed sheet while she picked up a piece of chalk and began marking out figures. She could hear Marion as his breathing slowed down into the languid rhythms of slumber. Stephanie shrugged to herself reflecting upon his comment about exhausting all possible ways to say the same thing. What could it possibly matter?

Nevertheless…

She marked down all the different ways the answer could be stated differently.

ALL POSSIBLE STATEMENTS OF 'P'

1) $p = 5/7 = 0.714$
2) $p = 0.714 = 5/7$
3) $5/7 = p = 0.714$
4) $5/7 = 0.714 = p$
5) $0.714 = p = 5/7$
6) $0.714 = 5/7 = p$

"There!" Stephanie said to herself with relief as she made the last mark on the board. "That should make a nice surprise for him."

She returned to bed trailing the bed sheet behind her.

When Stephanie woke up the next day, she reached over for Marion and found he was not there. As she fully opened her eyes, she found him completely dressed and holding his briefcase at his side. He was standing at the board and humming a little tune to himself.

"Combinatorics. Yep, that should be the next step…" Marion said nodding.

"Good morning, Marion," Stephanie began drowsily, "what was that?"

"Oh! Good morning. I have to make sure I'm not late for my first lecture. There's breakfast for you in the kitchen."

"Okay…" Stephanie rubbed an eye.

"When you get a chance," Marion said casually as he headed for the door, "check out the difference between a combination and a permutation. You can Google it if you want."

"Marion is tutoring you?" Stephanie's girlfriend Shirley exclaimed with surprise.

"Sure he is. What's wrong with that?" Stephanie bristled defensively. "He's doing a very good job and I'm learning a lot."

"What is he charging you for a fee?" Shirley asked with an arched eyebrow.

"It's not like that, Shirley," Stephanie insisted, "we help each other out, that's all."

"Oh. So now you're going to tell me the two of you are exchanging your tutoring duties?"

"Something like that."

"So if he's tutoring you in Math, what pray tell are you tutoring him about?"

"You wouldn't understand."

Shirley lowered her head reluctant to speak.

"Go on," Stephanie sighed, "say what you were going to say."

Shirley turned away, waving Stephanie off.

"No, I'm through with it. You go do what you gotta do."

"I appreciate your concern, Shirley."

"Just watch yourself, girl. Marion's known as a goofball among all the tutors around here. Be sure to check your figures when he adds everything up. He's been a digit off here and there from time to time."

"I'll be sure to take your advice to heart."

"I hope you do, honey. I just hope you do."

"I don't think you understand about us, Shirley. Marion and I make sense together."

"Don't tell me that's all the two of you are making these days."

"Marion knows an awful lot about algebra. I read somewhere it leads to an understanding of all other branches of mathematics."

"Uh huh. I suppose you're going to say that's all you've been studying with Marion."

"Now Shirley. That really is none of your business."

"Uh huh. You better hope he doesn't start surfing the Internet about you. He's bound to get an eyeful he never expected that way."

Stephanie gave Shirley a guarded look of apprehension. The two of them stirred their coffee somberly in the small café.

She stood with her bare feet on the ledge of the bookcase. Stephanie leaned and swayed on the shelves bracketed into the black wall. She wondered what Marion would reach for first; her naked form gleaming in the sunlight or these Math books she was looking over in the glaring shadows. She fingered the spine of one of the smaller textbooks and wondered what Marion found in mathematics that made him fall in love with the subject.

Stephanie opened the hardcover book and started to idly thumb through its pages. There were the usual underlined passages and scribbled notes in the margins where Marion turned over a notion or something. Lots of definitions for principles or objects such as **area** and **circumference** and **diameter** and **perimeter** and **radius**; and things like **cone** and **cube** and **cylinder** and **pyramid** and **sphere**. She tossed the book onto the mattress, making a mental note to ask Marion about some of the things he chose to underline that she did not understand.

She stood on her tiptoes and reached high for one of the books in a three-volume set. The dust jacket was covered with mathematical symbols and the only one she really recognized was the symbol for **pi**. Stephanie remembered Marion telling her how **pi** was the fractional equivalent of **3 and 1/7** or rounded off to the hundredths **3.14**. This volume she held in her hands was evidently edited by mathematicians with Russian surnames she could barely pronounce. Here again she could see where Marion underlined things and she yawned and shrugged her shoulders. She glanced behind her as the book bounced on the mattress with the other one.

Stephanie knew she would have to start simply and build her knowledge from there. She stepped down off the bookcase with catlike grace and flopped heavily onto the bed. There was no need to pretend. She knew what **pi** was, but not how to put it to any good use in her own life. There were formulae involving **pi**; like the one for the circumference of a circle, **C = pi times diameter**, and the one for calculating the area of a circle, **A = pi times radius squared**. But all that stuff seemed vague and esoteric and somehow divorced from the tangible needs of real life. Maybe she was missing the whole point and just needed enough examples of the uses of **pi** to make the concept vivid in her memory and imagination.

That seemed to be the trouble with all these professors. They were all cloistered in their big words and high sounding phrases, but were hard put to match all of their pet indoctrinated ideas to the real lives of the students under their care. Stephanie often wondered what made Marion fall in love with all this chalk on the wall. That was the curious thing about it all. She would see these people here and there enthusiastically in love with some thing or someone and all it did was make her wonder how they got there. She couldn't help but feel she was missing out somehow on what Life was all about. The simple truth that kept staring her in the face was that she could not imagine herself falling or being in love with anyone or anything. This inner realization was something she was reluctant to confess. Besides, who really cared? All the guys she ever met were so into how her body looked it was hard to discuss serious matters with their fingers up her panties.

She heard her cell phone ring on the nightstand and irritably clasped it to her ear.

"Hello?" The sound of the voice on the other end made her heart freeze into her throat as the frown on her face tightened. "This is she…"

"Hi baby," she heard the voice coo glibly, "how's my Star?"

Silence. Stephanie moved her lips in a curse, but made no sound.

Stephanie quickly glanced around her to see whether or not Marion was home yet.

"What do you want?" She whispered harshly into the palm of her hand. "How did you get this number?"

"Oh, you know me, sugar, I have my ways…"

"What do you want now, Johnny?"

"What does Johnny Money ever want, darling? I thought I might offer you an opportunity to see a little cash come your way. How 'bout it?"

"I don't do that stuff anymore. You know that, Johnny."

"Seems to me there are certain obligations you have yet to fulfill, darling. I would have brought it up with you but for you leavin' all of a sudden the way you did."

"I told you when I had enough saved up for school I was out of there."

"The least you could have done was say goodbye to ol' Johnny before you took it upon yourself to blow town."

"I thought it was best to break clean without causing any drama. You knew I was going to college to study to be a teacher. I never left you in the dark about that."

"You left a big hole in the operation when you left, sugar. A young thing with all your assets isn't easy to replace."

"I'm sure you'll manage somehow."

"Why don't we meet somewhere and discuss this? There are a few loose ends I could use your help in nailin' down."

"Look, I've got to go now, Johnny. I would appreciate you not calling this number anymore."

"The way I see it, you've still got unfinished business to settle with me, darling."

"Oh? How do you figure that, Johnny?"

"I figure it at about six months more of movie work and exclusive photo shoots, sugar."

"I told you I was through with all that stuff, Johnny."

"Sorry darling, you don't get to make that call. I do."

"I told you I was going to college by the end of summer."

"That doesn't release you from your obligations to me, doll."

"I told you I was willing to forfeit the rest of my salary."

"I thought about that. We still have work to do, you and I."

"Oh? What makes you say that, Johnny?"

"Looking at this release form you signed makes me speak my peace this way, doll."

"I paid all my modeling fees. You've got no more hold on me."

"Hold on you? You gotta be kiddin' me. I own your little white ass, sugar. When I say stay, you stay. When I say go, you go. That's the name of that tune, darling."

Stephanie fingered her cell phone in a dread filled silence. "Excuse me, Johnny. I'm going to hang up now."

"Really would be a shame, baby girl."

"What!"

"Oh, you know. Your new boyfriend might get wind of your more glamorous past on the Internet. I hear he's real smart, Stephanie. Some kind of Math whiz, right?"

"THAT is none of your affair."

"Just sayin', just sayin'…" Johnny Money chuckled to himself. "He might not take too kindly to seeing you spread-eagled all over the Internet celebrating what Nature gave to you. Isn't Marion his name?"

"The name of my boyfriend hasn't got anything to do with you."

"I'm just looking out for your interests, sugar. Be a shame to see him dump you over a bunch of so-called 'dirty pictures' you consented to pose for when you were going hungry with the rent coming due."

"That's all behind me now. I paid good money to have my files trashed and deleted."

"I should have told you I suppose."

"Told me what?"

"I keep backups of all my work. Just sound business practice, you know."

"You do whatever you want on your website, Johnny. Just leave me out of it from now on, that's all."

"I'm afraid that's not in the cards, baby. We've been kicking it around and have decided to plan a comeback for you."

"Sorry to disappoint you, Johnny. I'm not coming back to anything. I'm going forward and getting my degree."

"Oh yeah? What kind of degree is that? A Bachelor of Science in Sluttiness? Come on, Stephanie, stop fooling around with all this College Life stuff and get back to where you belong with us. There will be a lot less of the midnight oil to burn over books and useless classes and the payoff a great deal better and more immediate that what you will get writing up lesson plans for a room full of howlin' kids."

"I like writing up lesson plans. I happen to enjoy being around kids."

"I can introduce you to a bunch of kids who'll take to you right off."

"I bet you could. Look, Johnny, I've got to go now."

"Right. Meet me at the Cooked Goose Café tomorrow around seven in the evening. Don't stand me up unless you want your boyfriend to get a load of how you were in your more notorious days.

He could always be sent a package of exclusive photos signed, sealed and delivered to his address with your autograph."

Stephanie shuddered and gave her cell phone the evil eye. She stifled a quick impulse to throw it against the wall. She shrugged to herself, sighing with resignation.

"Cooked Goose Café?"

"That's right, my little candy ass. My treat. Wear something casual and revealing."

"Alright."

"Trust you to do the right thing, darling. Until then, give my regards to your boyfriend, Marion."

Stephanie heard Johnny's cell phone click off and go dead.

"What's the matter?" Marion asked as he marked off the formula exercises on the board. "You seem to be someplace else, Stephanie…" Marion peered across at her as the chalk broke in her hand. "Stephanie?"

"What?" Stephanie reached down to pick up the broken piece of chalk.

"Oh! It's nothing. Don't bother to concern yourself, really…"

"Alright then," Marion began again in a more professorial tenor. "What is the circumference of a circle equal to?"

"Uhhh…"

"Write it down on the board – write it down on the board…"

"Lemme see, **C = pi times diameter**. Right?"

"Good, good. What is the area of a square equal to?"

"The area of a square?" Stephanie marked **A = (s) squared** on the blackboard. "Right? 'The area of a square is equal to the square of its side'. Right?"

"That's right. How about the volume of a prism?"

"That's equal to the product of its base **(B)** by its height **(h)**. Am I right?"

"Uh huh. Now you've got a rectangular kitchen floor you want to cover with tile. It is 15 feet by 11 feet. What formula do you use to determine the number of square yards needed?"

"This one –" Stephanie marked down **A = l x w**. "That's right. Isn't it?"

"To begin with. Don't forget to calculate the area of a square yard into the equation."

"I wouldn't forget that."

"When letters stand for numbers in a formula what are they called?"

"Uh – **literal numbers** – look, I need to be some place by seven. Could I leave early tonight?"

Marion cast a curious gaze upon her.

"I suppose the Math Lab can manage without you for one day." Marion mused idly as he finished marking out an equation on the board. "What's the matter?"

Stephanie looked askance at Marion with a start as she reached for her coat off a desk chair.

"The matter? Nothing is the matter. I just have a little business I have to attend to, that's all."

"You'll be back tomorrow, won't you?"

"Of course."

"Good. The male students all love being tutored by a pretty girl…"

"Oh, go on… I'll call you when I get back, okay?"

Marion nodded while Stephanie buttoned her coat and slung her purse over her shoulder departing.

Stephanie came to the dinner table as Johnny waved her over through the hustle and bustle of diners and waiters scurrying back and forth from the kitchen. She placed her purse on the lace-embroidered tablecloth and regarded Johnny with simmering contempt. He shrugged his shoulders as he chewed on a toothpick. He beckoned to her with open palms to be seated before him.

"You're on time, my dear. That's a first. What can I get you?"

"I just came here to find out what you want, Johnny."

"Fair enough. Sit down and I'll tell you exactly what I want."

Stephanie was beginning to sit down as Johnny rushed over and pulled back her chair.

"You don't have to do that…" She whispered lightly in protest.

"I just want you to be comfortable. What harm is there in that? I also want to say welcome back, Stephanie."

"Welcome back to what?"

"Why to your true calling, of course. But here, let me refresh your memory…"

He reached into his suit pocket and pulled out his tablet computer. He tapped to the picture file on Stephanie and put it on 'slide show'. He reached around eagerly and pointed to Stephanie in all her glory.

"Remember now? Those were the days, baby. Nobody could work that 'girl next door' stuff like you, Stephanie…"

Stephanie looked up at him with a chilly expression.

"I don't know about all that, anymore," Stephanie said with lowered eyelashes, "I've moved on with my life, Johnny. I suggest you do the same."

"Awww now, don't be like that, sugar. You could still make a lot of money for us with the right marketing. We could even work this 'College Girl' thing you're into these days and milk it for all it's worth."

Stephanie muttered something silently to herself as she rubbed her bare shoulders.

Johnny placed the tablet on the table in front as he paced back to his seat across from her. Stephanie tapped the 'slide show' off as she clasped her hands together.

"Here." Johnny said as he opened up one of the menus, "I'll order us something while we nail down the details and the particulars."

"Look, I've got a little money saved up," Stephanie began in a whisper while she looked around anxiously, "what would I have to pay you for the backups you have of me and the work we did together?"

"Face it, little girl, that stuff is priceless. It's not for the trash bin at any price. You were a star, Stephanie, and ol' Johnny Money knows a cash cow when he sees one."

Stephanie pushed the tablet computer back across to Johnny Money with a surly pout and a frown.

"I'll tell you what; you do me this little favor and we'll call it even, alright?" John told her as he perused the laminated menu in his hands.

Stephanie crossed her arms over her bosom and gave him a resentful nod.

"What kind of little favor is that, Johnny?"

"We got these new girls coming in from overseas. You know, no real experience to speak of and that sort of thing. You remember how green you were when you first started. You just come back and help these new girls learn the ropes and there will be a big bonus in negotiation for you. Huh? What do you say?"

Stephanie lowered her head as all the images of the times past her eighteenth birthday swirled around her in an accelerated whirlwind of racy abandon. Back then, the ripeness of her face and figure was just coming into bloom. She was as new as a mint green dollar bill, Johnny Money kept cooing to her, ready for change. He did everything he could to cash in on her girl next door looks and before long was cutting checks for her to the tune of thousands of dollars. It all seemed such a casual and easy way to earn a living in the beginning. Johnny and his crew would set up their cameras and lights. All she was required to do was stand where they told her to and smile, or look serious when she parted her lips. Sometimes she kept all her clothes on, but the less she wore the more she earned for Johnny and herself.

Stephanie's face broke with a bitter chuckle. Perhaps a somewhat bizarre version of the Law of Diminishing Returns that. She found the idea intriguing she was worth more au naturel than sporting or representing any kind of fashion. But, of course, she must be worth more than the approved flavor of her flesh in season. She felt compelled to explore what that might mean for her, but knew this was not a subject to explain to the likes of Johnny.

"How 'bout it, snowflake? Enough of this helping the little ones and the needy for chump change. You're not a social worker or a miracle worker. Come back with me and let me help you make some real money putting your best assets to good use."

Stephanie's mind was seized with the image of her bent over a young boy puzzling with a math problem.

"Is that how you do it?" The youth looked up at her hopefully.

"Let me see, Reuben…yeah, this looks about right…"

"See? I multiplied that base there like you showed me."

"Uh huh, that part looks good…"

Stephanie recited the formula for finding a triangle to herself. **Area equals base times height.** She looked over Reuben's work again and tapped his paper with her finger.

"Now you got to find the volume, Reuben. Just make sure you check your arithmetic afterwards, okay?"

"I will."

"Raise your hand and I'll come back and check your work."

"Okay, I will…"

Stephanie blinked and glared at Johnny through narrowed eyes.

"What's on your mind, snowflake?" Johnny mused as he observed her coming out of her reverie. "I know you'll probably want more money this time…"

"No, it's not that."

"What is it then?"

"I was just wondering. That's all."

"Wondering? About what?"

"About how it is you know so much about what my best assets are."

Johnny shrugged again showing her his open palms.

"Now is that any way to talk to the man who showed you how to make a living? You were a star on the Internet, a regular cyber-sensation. Those little movies we did were just the beginning, Stephanie…"

The young student flashed into her mind again. Reuben was looking up at her, his eyes shining with understanding.

"Is that right?" Reuben asked her.

"What do you think? Did you check your work?"

"Yeah, right here…"

Stephanie reviewed the formula for finding the volume of a prism in her mind. **Volume equals area times height.** She nodded to herself as she scanned over the figures on Reuben's paper. There was something satisfying about having the right answer and being able to share it with someone else.

"Look," Johnny began again, "this time you can spend more time behind the camera and show some of the new girls what to do."

"Learn modeling and movie-making from both sides of the coin, eh?"

"That would be something to look forward to, wouldn't it?"

"I think there may be more growth for me in the education game, Johnny."

"Is that the kind of future you want, Stephanie? To be underpaid and overworked for all your life? Kind of late in the game to take the suckers road, isn't it?"

"There's more respect in the community for teaching, Johnny."

"Oh, wow, I cant' believe what I'm hearing. All that nigger talk about 'respect' and 'prestige'. A lot of groceries and mansions that stuff will get you."

Stephanie regarded Johnny with knowing distain.

"I don't know, Johnny," she began dryly, "I think I'll take that 'nigger talk' about respect and prestige any day. I just want to have something you can't get your hands on."

Johnny chewed thoughtfully on his toothpick.

"That's not going to happen. Face it, snowflake, I own your ass. The main thing I hope you'll learn from our little chat today is that I can still pull the strings on you any time I want."

The silence gathered about them as their gazes locked upon each other only to be punctuated by the clink of knives and forks. A young waitress appeared at their table.

Johnny unfroze and handed her the menu.

"Are we ready to order yet?" The young lady inquired as she held the menu to her breast. "We have a special on beef brisket tonight."

"Yes we are–" Johnny beckoned to her with a crooked finger.

The waitress bent over as he whispered something in her ear. Adroitly, he slipped a fifty dollar bill inside her blouse. She quickly rose up again laughing, sharing with him a confidential smile. Gaily she scribbled his order onto her note pad.

"Bring us a bottle of your best wine, now that I think about it," Johnny added with a flourishing gesture.

"Can I get you anything else? Something special for the lady, sir?"

Stephanie opened her mouth to demur, but was cut off by Johnny interjecting.

"I want to give her time to think about it. Ask us again after dessert."

"Very good, sir. I'll be back with your order."

"Take your time," Johnny assured her, "we're not going anywhere."

Johnny clucked his tongue at Stephanie with renewed sense of proprietary interest.

"What was all that about?" Stephanie snidely commented. "You working up a new recruit?"

"You never can tell, snowflake. I can use all the help I can get."

Stephanie squirmed uncomfortably in her seat and stole a glance at the wall clock.

"You might as well face it, doll, you've got a reputation now in certain parts. What you can do is cash in on that reputation with the rest of us. We're going to do it anyway, so if I were you, I would be sure to get my cut."

"I don't want any cut, Johnny. Can't you understand that? All I want to do is turn the page and get on with my life."

"You can do that a lot better when your purse is lined with cash, doll."

"There's more to Life than turning tits and ass into a pot of gold, Johnny."

"Especially when it's your tits and ass all over the Internet, huh, sugar? Well, this 'more to Life' that you've been dreaming about would be easier to get to without your past coming back to bite you in your behind, wouldn't you say?"

"What's that supposed to mean? Are you threatening me or something?"

"No, not really. I just think your fame on the Internet doesn't have to spill out into the newspapers or onto any college campuses or universities. Leaking that kind of information about your past might have a deleterious effect on your educational opportunities or potential advances in your new chosen career. Who knows? It might even spell disaster for your love life. Now we wouldn't want that, would we?"

The waitress and the bus boys returned with trays of food while Stephanie boiled red and seethed in her newfound hatred for Johnny.

"Ah! Here's the wine!" Johnny took the bottle and began to unscrew the cork. "We can have some now or save it for later. What do you say?"

Stephanie took a deep breath and spoke down into the tablecloth in a defeated whisper.

"I'll take my wine now," she requested with a flickering look of resentment.

"Coming right up, sugar…" Johnny filled her cocktail glass up to the brim. "Here you go!"

Johnny shoved the glass across to her.

"Thank you," Stephanie said as she took the glass in her trembling hand and rose to her feet. "Here's shit in your eye!"

Stephanie threw the wine into Johnny's face and set her cocktail glass back carefully onto the table. She reached for her purse and turning on her heel departed from the Cooked Goose Café. The waitress and the busboys watched with anxious, surly surprise as her shapely form strode resolutely back through the entrance. They watched as her startled dinner companion reached gasping for his handkerchief and wondered whether or not they would still receive their tip.

Stephanie sat back on Marion's bed between two open suitcases that belonged to her. There was nothing for it now but to blow town. She was of two minds whether to leave Marion a parting note in chalk on the wall behind her that served her pedantic boyfriend as a blackboard or simply to get while the getting was good. Nervously she clicked the remote for the flat screen television on the wall before her and watching it for a few minutes would just as nervously click it off.

She lay back on the bed and looked up at the ceiling. There was no doubt in her mind what Johnny would do now. Soon Marion would see the videos of her and the pictures and no amount of hard work and study would salvage the damage done to her reputation and attempts to establish a good name here. She couldn't bear to make her way amongst the students on campus bracing herself against the catcalls and jeering that was sure to come.

Even now she couldn't seem to reach Marion on her cell phone and she dreaded going back down to the Math Lab. There was no need to wait until the other shoe dropped for drop it most certainly would in due time. She could take a Greyhound Bus or book a flight on Delta Airlines back home. No matter how you sliced or diced it, her plunge from apprenticing educator to pin-up girl and former Maiden of Sleaze was no further away than nanoseconds.

She could easily envision how Johnny would spin this and was sure he would leave nothing to the imagination. Stephanie glanced over at the closet where her dresses and professional attire were racked. She turned over on her side to stifle a sob as she swore softly under her breath. The killing thing, she thought cursing Johnny to herself, was how she would have made a good teacher in the end. Now nobody would ever know what kind of positive difference she might have been able to make.

Stephanie heard her cell phone go off on the blanket beside her and picked it up.

"Hello? Marion?"

"Yeah, Steph. I just wanted you to know I been charging up my cell phone in case you tried to reach me."

"Where are you, baby?"

"Down at the Math Lab still. Grading papers and the usual boring stuff. Did you take care of your business?" Marion listened for her answer and heard none. "What's the matter?"

Stephanie took a deep breath before she spoke again.

"How long are you going to be down there?"

"The Lab will be open until midnight. You know that."

"I'll tell you all about it when I get there."

"Sure, lady bug. Hey, could you –"

But before Marion could request she bring him the textbook he needed, the cell phone clicked off. He started to redial when a student called him over.

"Mister Purvis?"

"I'll be right there, Claudia."

"Show me how to do this…"

"I'll be right there. Better yet; why don't you come up to the board and write it down?"

Claudia gave Marion an irritated frown.

"Aw, Mister Purvis. You mean you want me to write the whole story on the blackboard?"

"That's what I mean, Claudia. That way the whole Study Group can see how we solved it."

Claudia looked around anxiously as the dozen or so other students snickered from behind the computers at their desks.

"Y'all need to quit. I ain't goin' up there."

"C'mon, Claudia," Marion urged her, "let's show 'em how it's done. I'll help you."

"I don't know how to do this mess. How I'm gonna show somebody?"

"I'll help you Claudia. We'll go through it together; step by step."

Claudia looked around at her jeering classmates with a helpless shrug.

She gave up a halfhearted attempt to shield her face from their taunts. Soon she was making her way to the blackboard with a weary, forlorn shrug and reaching for the stick of chalk Marion held between his fingertips. She cast a gaze in Marion's direction before she began marking on the board with his nodding approval. Slowly, according to the staccato cadence of her marks she spelled out The Story Problem in its entirety...

THE STORY

THE KANGEROO HAS A NUMBER OF TIGERS IN HIS DEEP FREEZE. THE NUMBER OF TIGERS PLUS EIGHT ELEPHANTS IS EQUAL FOUR LESS THAN FOUR TIMES THE NUMBER OF TIGERS. HOW MANY TIGERS DOES THE KANGEROO HAVE?

"Is that right, Mister Purvis?" Claudia asked as she flitted a glance at the paper in her hand. "I didn't miss anything, did I?"

"No, that's fine, Claudia," Marion assured her as he took her seat in the lab, " just keep in mind you're solving for '**X**'. Right, Claudia?"

"Yes, Mister Purvis…"

"– and '**X**' is what, Claudia?"

"The number of Tigers, Mister Purvis?"

"That's right, Claudia. Now can you take it from there?"

Claudia furrowed her brow in concentration. She kept in mind what Marion had taught her and that she was solving for '**X**'. Underneath the lines on the board she began to strip away the imagery and took the frightening plunge into abstract thought. She realized dimly as she set up the form of the problem and its elements, that the form was the problem and the elements could be any countless number of things.

The elements could change into an infinite variety of things as Marion would explain later to the students in the Math Lab eliciting varying degrees of comprehension. The form was changeless although the elements could change into anything. Marion watched in amusement as Claudia worked out this exercise in Change and Changelessness for herself.

THE ABSTRACTION

$$X + ? = ?X{-}?$$
$$8 = ?X{-}?$$
$$? = ?X$$
$$? = X$$
$$? + 8 = 16{-}?$$

Stephanie burst suddenly into the Math Lab and sat in the back, exciting an additional buzz from the rubbernecking students. Claudia looked her way and exchanged a sympathetic glance with her. Marion was too absorbed in the problem on the board to notice much her entrance.

"Now you noticed we substituted the '**X's** for the animals to begin with, right, Claudia?

"Yes, Mister Purvis, I already did that."

"Now what happens next?"

"We put the numbers where they belong. I guess."

"That's right. Now where do they belong?"

"Let's see…"

Claudia took the eraser and erased the question marks. Slowly she marked in a number for every question mark she erased.

Now the problem appeared this way:

$$X + 8 = 4X - 4$$
$$8 = 3X - 4$$
$$12 = 3X$$

Claudia looked over haltingly at Marion before she committed herself to the last step.

"Go ahead, Claudia." Marion said with a nod.

"Okay…" She whispered to herself and the blackboard.

Claudia marked in the rest and looked over to Marion for confirmation.

$$4 = X$$
$$4 + 8 = 16 - 4$$

"So what is '**X**', Claudia?" Marion asked.

"Uh, **4** is **X**. **X** is **4**. I mean–it's both!"

More titters and snickers from the rest of the students in the Math Lab.

"Everybody got that?"

Explosions of laughter come from an out of the way corner in the room.

"Oooo – lemme see that!"

Stephanie's attention jerked their way.

"Reuben! Darius! Settle down and pay attention!" Marion warned a couple of his students. "I see you playing around with that I-Pad again, it's mine!"

"Aw, Mister Purvis. Don't be like that."

"Put it away then. Your eyes should be up here, not surfing the Internet."

Stephanie moved over and extended a trembling hand to the young boys.

"Here, give me that. You can have it back at the end of this session."

Reuben and Darius regarded Stephanie with expressions of defiant challenge.

"You heard me." Stephanie repeated. "Give it to me."

"Why? We don't have to give you our stuff. What you need with it anyway?" Darius asserted with unexpected boldness.

Stephanie blanched at his insolent tone.

"I – I don't need to have anything to do with your 'stuff'. But you came here to improve your Math skills, not distract the other students from doing so."

Reuben and Darius sat there considering this. Finally, Darius slid the I-Pad across the table towards Stephanie with some reluctance.

"Thank you." Stephanie said as she took the I-Pad over to Marion's desk.

"Next time we'll just call your parents," Marion warned as he checked over Claudia's work on the board.

"Aw, Mister Purvis," said Darius protesting.

"Why you got to do us like that, man?" Reuben complained petulantly.

"Because Stephanie is right. You can check out all that girlie stuff someplace else, dudes. The Math Lab is the place where you learn MATH?" Marion took the I-Pad from Stephanie, tapped it and held it up for Reuben and Darius to get a last look at the nude girl they had been ogling.

"Am I right?"

Claudia and Marion looked over at them while Stephanie put a hand to her mouth and blushed beet red.

"Aw man, why you got to put our business out there like that?" Darius exclaimed with a kind of grinning mock outrage.

"Because you're not here to entertain yourselves. You're here to learn. Am I right?"

Marion turned again and fully regarded them.

"Am I right? Thanks Claudia. You can return to your seat now."

Marion waved the I-Pad over his head with the image of the young, voluptuous girl still flickering on the monitor.

"Am I right?"

Stephanie half-heartedly attempted to reach for the I-Pad and at length sat down at Marion's desk. She crossed her legs and looked away, hiding her face with her hand.

"Alright, you done made your point, man." Reuben wearily conceded with a sigh of exasperation.

"I hope so. I don't want to have to deal with this again. The next time you bring this stuff into the Math Lab we'll just have to have a conference with your parents, understood?"

"We understand, Mister Purvis. We won't do it no more." Darius promised as Reuben nodded in agreement.

Claudia resumed her seat giving them both a haughty look of vindication.

"That's more like it. Now. Here Stephanie, shove this porn down in the bottom drawer where it belongs. Come on up, dudes, the water's fine. Time for you to wade in the water of problem solving."

Stephanie took one last glimpse at herself on the I-Pad before tapping off the image and sticking it under a pile of files in the last drawer. She swallowed with mortification as a little girl named Kimberly appeared at the entrance to the Math Lab. The young student gestured to speak to someone.

"Yes Kimberly?" Stephanie's voice quavered as she addressed her. "Is there something I can help you with?"

"Somebody's here to see Mister Purvis..." Kimberly said shyly with downcast eyes.

Marion let out an exasperated grunt. He irritably placed his stick of chalk on the ledge beneath the blackboard. Reuben and Darius were arriving next to him casting around brazen, quizzical glances.

"Take over, Stephanie. I'll be back. Just follow my notes for the next problem, right?"

"Alright," Stephanie nodded as she shuffled through his papers on the desk, "Let's g-go, Reuben. You mark down the story. Darius? Darius! Look over here at me. That's better. Do you remember how to set up the problem?"

Darius smirked and shook his head. Stephanie rolled her eyes as she sighted Marion exiting with Kimberly. He mouthed silently to her he would be back.

"See? That's what happens when you don't do your homework. Oh, no you don't! Stay right here."

"I don't know it!" Darius said petulantly. "Besides –"

"Besides what?"

Stephanie and Darius regarded each other confrontationally. A sharp feeling of dread ran slicing through Stephanie like an icy dagger. There was somehow no sign from him that he recognized her as the woman on their I-Pad. She picked up Marion's piece of chalk from the ledge without taking her eyes off Darius.

"Here," she said, as she took a deep breath, "I'll help you..."

Darius reluctantly took the piece of chalk from between her fingertips. "What wrong with you?" Darius looked askance at her querulously as he began marking on the board. "Why you lookin' at me like that?"

How could he not have recognized her? Did she really look that different now? Marion, who ought to know every square inch of her at this point, seemed oblivious to the fact. How could he not know that just a few moments ago he was holding over his head and waving around a nude photograph of his girlfriend straight off the Internet? Reuben paid her no mind as he carefully marked out the story problem.

THE STORY

A VULTURE CAN SNATCH A CERTAIN NUMBER OF PIGLETS, THREE TIMES THE SUM OF THE NUMBER OF OKLAHOMA PIGLETS PLUS TWO SLAUGHTERHOUSE PIGLETS IS EQUAL TO THREE TIMES THE SUM OF EIGHT SLAUGHTERHOUSE PIGLETS MINUS THAT CERTAIN NUMBER OF OKLAHOMA PIGLETS. HOW MANY OKLAHOMA PIGLETS CAN A VULTURE SNATCH?

Reuben looked over at her, still turning his piece of chalk over and over between his fingers.

"That's right, ain't it? Did I leave somethin' out?"

Stephanie stifled a shrug and moved over coolly to check what Reuben had marked on the board against Marion's notes.

"No, that looks like all of it. Good."

She warily looked around at the rest of the students idly tapping behind the monitors of their computers at their desks. Some made a stray glance out the window. A few others in baggy pants and tattoos unnerved her by returning her gaze with mysterious smirks. But she sensed nothing different in the emotional atmosphere of the room. How could that be? It did not seem to her that her hair was that much shorter and did she really look all that much different fully clothed?

Stephanie started as she noticed Reuben shifting uncomfortably from one foot to another.

"Oh. You can sit down now, Reuben." She told him as he bounded and strutted back to his desk.

Stephanie looked over her shoulder after peering again at Marion's notes. She caught Reuben whispering something to one of the cute female students at the side. He stopped when their eyes met and with a sly look picked up the booklet from his desk and opened it.

"Is this how it go?" Darius asked her in the middle of marking down the equation.

"Let's see…" She leafed over a page of Marion's notes. "Yeah, you've got it so far…"

Stephanie quickly reviewed the way in which the problem was set up.

THE ABSTRACTION

$$3 (? + 2) = 3 (8–?)$$
$$3X + ? = ?? – 3X$$
$$?X + ? = 2?$$

Darius looked over to her like a driver not sure of what Exit to take. "Uh huh, keep going now…"

$$6? =$$

Darius eyed her again and Stephanie could not tell whether his expression was accusatory or simply filled with student uncertainty.

"Go ahead," she reassured him, "don't stop now."

Darius turned to the board once more and resumed resolving the equation.

$$6? = ?8$$
$$X = ?$$

Darius closed his eyes and turned his mind into a calculator.

"Do you think you have the rest of it, Darius?"

"Think so," he whispered, "think so…"

"Okay then, check your answer."

He went back to marking on the board, more slowly this time.

$$3 \ (? + 2) = 3 \ (8 - ?)$$
$$? + 6 = ?? - 9$$
$$?? = ??$$

"Are you ready to fill in the question marks, Darius?"

"Yeah, I think so. Yeah. I think so…"

Darius began again this time more confidently.

THE EQUATION

$$3 \ (X + 2) = 3 \ (8 - X)$$
$$3X + 6 = 24 - 3X$$
$$6X + 6 = 24$$
$$6X = 18$$
$$X = 3$$

Darius looked over at Stephanie with an embarrassed smile of dawning comprehension.

"That's right, ain't it?"

"'Isn't it,'…" Stephanie corrected him. "'That's right, isn't it,'…"

"Yeah, that's what I said. Isn't it?"

"Want to put the '**3**' where all the '**X**'s are? Check your answer maybe?"

Darius looked around at all the other students and shrugged.

"Yeah, I guess so…"

THE EQUATION

$$3 \ (3 + 2) = 3 \ (8 - 3)$$
$$3x3 + 6 = 24 - 3x3$$
$$6x3 + 6 = 24$$
$$6x3 = 18$$
$$3 = 3$$

"Do you see a simpler way to put it, Darius? Maybe?"

Darius scratched his chin in deliberation.

"Yeah, I could – I guess I could do this…"

Darius began again scratching chalk onto the board.

"Yeah, we could break it down this way…" Darius said as he narrowed his eyes.

$$3 (3 + 2) = 3 (8 - 3)$$
$$9 + 6 = 24 - 9$$
$$15 = 15$$

"Yeah, '**X**' is '**3**'," Darius pointed at the board, "but THAT there is the answer."

"Are you sure about that, Darius?"

"Yeah. I would bet money on it."

Stephanie took the piece of chalk out of Darius' hand and looking at him ruefully stifled a snicker. She gestured for him to return to his seat.

"I bet you would. That's all right. You can sit down now. This is a Math Lab, not a Casino."

Darius hitched up his pants and pointing at Stephanie with his index fingers coolly returned to his desk.

Stephanie turned around and surveyed the class for a new student to come up and set up the next problem.

"Alright. We've got one more problem for demonstration purposes. Who wants to try it?"

She looked around the room at the young girls in their pigtails, buns and ponytails. The young men rapidly scribbled down what was on the board when they were not chatting and flirting with these females next to them. Stephanie waited for someone to raise a hand in the silence.

"Anyone?"

Now Stephanie reviewed the acned faces of the teenagers before her. She divined no clue from any of them that they knew about her glamorous and notorious career on the Internet. She hesitantly sighed with relief as she turned back to the board. Since nobody was at this point airing the dirty linen in her past, she decided she would focus on the present as long as she could.

"Let's see how you do with this one…" Stephanie said as she began marking on the board.

THE STORY

THE IRISH DRAGONS WERE SITTING AROUND IN THE SAUNA AFTER A GOOD WORKOUT. THEY WERE SHOOTING THE BREEZE ABOUT WHO AMONG THEM ROASTED THE PEASANTS BEST WITH THEIR FIERY BREATHS. THIS IRKED THE EGYPTIAN CROCODILE WHO DID NOT DINE ON PEASANT MEAT MUCH AND USUALLY SATISFIED HIS HUNGER WITH CLUMPS OF ROOTS AND HERBS.

AFTER LISTENING TO THEM GO ON FOREVER ABOUT THIS, THE EGYPTIAN CROCODILE DETERMINED TO SHUT THEIR YAPS AND GIVE THEM A TOUGHER PROBLEM TO CONSUME USING THE INFO HE GATHERED FROM THEIR CONVERSATION. (BESIDES, HOW BRIGHT COULD A BUNCH OF FIRE-BREATHING DRAGONS BE ANYWAY?)

THE PROBLEM TO BE SOLVED ALL CAME DOWN TO THIS: THE NUMBER OF SMALL HAIRY PEASANTS THE WHITE DRAGON COULD DEVOUR LESS THE ONE HORSE FLY THE BLACK DRAGON COULD GULP DOWN, ALL DIVIDED BY THE THREE DINOSAUR EGGS THE RED DRAGON COULD EAT WAS EQUAL TO THAT SAME NUMBER OF SMALL HAIRY PEASANTS MINUS THE TWO GARGOYLES THE BLUE DRAGON COULD

MANAGE, ALL DIVIDED BY THE EGYPTIAN CROCODILE'S TWO CLUMPS OF ROOTS AND HERBS.

Stephanie glanced around to see who among the students were following the problem and writing it down. When her eyes lighted upon the police officer and Marion standing inside the entrance to the Math Lab her lips parted in surprise.

Out of the corner of her eye she could see Marion motioning to her to come over.

"Just a moment..." she nodded as she marked down the last statement in the problem.

HOW MANY HAIRY PEASANTS COULD THE WHITE DRAGON DEVOUR?

Stephanie paced over to them wiping the chalk dust from her fingertips onto her skirt. She could feel the thump of her heart with each step she took.

"Yes?"

Stephanie shifted her eyes uncomfortably between their somber faces.

Marion reached out and squeezed her shoulder.

"Officer Shelby would like to speak to you for a moment," Marion began, "I'll take over from here, Stephanie. You can use my office, sir."

"This way, Miss..." The grizzled officer said as he took Stephanie by the arm.

Officer Shelby fingered his red mustache as he watched Stephanie hold the photo in her quivering hands.

"Do you know this man?" Officer Shelby muttered behind his fingers.

"Yes." Stephanie swallowed, looking down shamefaced. "I used to work for him. Has something happened, Officer?"

Officer Shelby removed a notebook from his breast pocket and clicked his ballpoint pen.

"He's dead, Miss."

"Dead?!"

"Yes, I'm afraid so. Are you sure you wouldn't like to have a lawyer present?"

Stephanie bowed her head.

"No, I mean – I don't know…"

"You were seen having an altercation with him at the Cooked Goose Café. Is there anything you would like to say about that? Or would you rather have a lawyer present?"

"I don't need any lawyer. I haven't done anything. He wanted me to come back to work for him. I said no."

"The deceased worked in Adult Entertainment, didn't he?"

Stephanie scowled at Officer Shelby defensively.

"That's right."

"You need to decide right now whether you want a lawyer present, Miss. I have questions to ask you and I have to get your statement."

"Ask your questions. I don't need any lawyer."

Officer Shelby flipped open his notebook.

"Alright then. Let's get started."

Stephanie returned from the Police Station and started packing again. What was she thinking? She should never have gone down to that Math Lab. She snapped the latches on one of her suitcases and started folding her clothes to throw into the other.

The flat screen television set mounted on the wall seemed to blare out news about Johnny Money every half hour and she fished under the sheets for the remote.

" …JOHN TODD MONROE AKA JOHNNY MONEY WAS FOUND SHOT DEAD IN A DETROIT BARBER SHOP ON THE WEST SIDE TODAY WHILE RECEIVING A HAIRCUT AND A SHAVE. WITNESSES REPORT A YOUNG WOMAN WAS SITTING IN THE SHOP AGAINST ONE WALL WHEN SHE PULLED OUT A THIRTYEIGHT HANDGUN FROM HER PURSE. SHE ANGRILY CONFRONTED THE ENTREPRENEUR KNOWN FOR HIS SUCCESS IN ADULT ENTERTAINMENT. AFTER DISPUTING WITH HIM OVER UNPAID WAGES, SHE SHOT HIM SEVERAL TIMES WHILE HE SAT IN THE BARBER'S CHAIR. THE YOUNG LADY WAS TAKEN INTO CUSTODY AND IS NOW RESIDING IN THE COUNTY…"

Stephanie angrily pressed the button on the remote and clicked off the television set. The cell phone rang and she looked at it bitterly as she snapped closed the latch on the second suitcase now that it was all packed. She knew she could just make her Delta flight, but she would have to leave now.

She watched the cell phone ring on the bed as it lit up each time. Somehow she knew it must be Marion. She went over with a weary sigh to where it was nestled on a pillow and picked it up.

"Hello?"

"Steph? This is Marion."

"Yes? What?"

"I want you to do me a favor."

"What?"

"Go over to the blackboard behind the bed and find this equation for me – **'X minus one over three equals X minus two over two'**. Do you see it?"

"Just a second." Stephanie went over to the chalk marks behind the bed. "Yeah–I see it…"

"That's good. Now underneath is there a six in parentheses?"

"Uhhhh, yeah, I think so…"

"Okay then. Read back the rest to me."

"Marion?"

"What is it?"

Stephanie looked at her suitcases and the digital clock on the bureau. She held the cell phone in her hand pensively.

"There's something I have to tell you."

"Sure. I'll be home soon. Read the rest of the answer back to me."

Stephanie swore softly to herself and knelt down over the bed.

"Is this it? '**Six in parentheses times X minus one over three equals six in parentheses times X minus two over two…**"

"That's it. Go on…"

"I think you struck out the six and the three and the six and the two to begin simplifying terms…"

"That sounds right. And then removed the parentheses?"

"Uh huh."

"Okay. I think I can get the rest. Thank you."

"Don't you want the part where you check the answer?"

"No, I can check the answer. See you soon."

Stephanie heard the phone click off on Marion's end.

She sat on the bed and turned the phone over and over in her hand.

Spiritual Signature

When the box arrived around Christmas time, I was hard put to know what to make of it. There was a substantial heft and weight to the thing when I lifted it up. The weighty contents did not rumble or rattle when I shook it. The name above the return address was recognizable and presented no mystery to me. I traced my fingertips over the big letters scrawled with a red Sharpie over the brown cardboard. I felt elation while a strange sense of foreboding crept over me. I was stealing a glance around as I stood on the snow-covered stoop to my apartment building. I warily took the box inside the vestibule and set it on the stand.

The rays of the morning light broke through the faceted glass above the door and I knew I would have to be going. When I looked down upon the box again, that same strange mixture of emotions I felt when I first came upon it once more unsettled me. I frowned apprehensively, and underneath that felt a smile of satisfaction gathering inside my heart. That curious sense of satisfaction swelled within me much as a glowing ember swells with its heat of flame. There was still a vague dread layered over all this, stabbing through like the streaks of light now scrawling and scratching their way across the face of my package.

Later, when I came home from work, I asked myself what I was going to do with this thing that now awaited my inspection. The box sat obstinately on my dining room table, making its own wrinkles in the green tablecloth. I fingered the button on my utility knife pensively. Anyone watching me would have concluded I was attempting to extract the contents of some kind of bomb. I gingerly pressed the blade forward and after several false starts, found the best way to go about getting to the contents. I sliced along the edges and the sides of the wide swaths of scotch tape and at length got the flaps up and the box opened.

The truth was I barely knew this guy and now the final drafts of his first two books were in my possession and sitting on my dining room table. There was something in a plastic bag that I took off the top before I could get at the typed scripts. I opened it up and pulled out a black T-shirt. There was an illustration of a slumbering, voluptuous, female nude emblazoned across the front of the thing. The naked figure was reclining on a vivid red blanket. I laid it aside on the arm of the sofa and took out the first pack of typewritten pages. I carefully smoothed over the loose bed of popcorn styrofoam in the box that nestled these literary products. Scanning over the title, I placed the stack on the dresser bureau. I headed for the bathroom, deciding I would do my reading after a nice shower.

The drenching scent from my wet body rose with the hot steam the showerhead. At the same time, so did my anticipation for the discovering more about the box left at my doorstep. I must admit I came out of the shower so quickly, I did not even stop to put on my shower robe. I wiped myself off with a towel and after patting some baby powder on my underarms, went to the Refrigerator and got me a yogurt. My hair was still slick and wet down my back so I hotfooted my way again into the bathroom. I wrung out my hair over the washbasin and wrapped a towel about my head.

I sat up in bed crossing my legs with my yogurt and a spoon. I spread out the pages across my bedspread. I was curious to see what kind of writing he did more than anything else. I pored over page after page with growing intrigue. The more I read, the more I thought of my own novel now starting to gather dust in the closet.

Now I could recall how Ernest Randall came lumbering through the door on the last day of class. I'll never forget that smug smile plastered all over his face. He was showing up early which surprised me in and of itself. Oftentimes he would show up ten or fifteen minutes late. Sometimes he would burst in grave and thoughtful, and I would muse to myself as to where he was burying the bodies. At other times he would enter our class with great ceremony and a flash of a roguish grin. I figured disposal of the corpse must have gone without a hitch on those occasions.

We were all anxiously grinding away in hopes of a good grade for ourselves. You could definitely count me in on that account. I took copious notes and was keeping my head above water, so to speak. Everyone was collecting wisdom from our instructor like manna from heaven and dutifully inscribing it. All of us except our good Mister Randall. More than once, I would catch him in the back of the room, gleefully sketching some pretty girl who was catching his eye. I knew eventually he would get around to me.

That's why when I came to class I would usually sit on the other side of someone else. This way I could block Ernest's view of my wonderfully inspiring profile and my gorgeous hunk of long hair. Let him pay the lab fee for an art class where models are hired to pose for that kind of stuff. Hopefully, he has the bread for that, but no matter to me. Let him have cheesecake somewhere else.

Do you know what that Ernest did just after class one day? He walked right up to one of my classmates and asked her to autograph the sketch he did of her. Phyllis signed the thing just to be nice, but can you believe the nerve of that guy? She told him had she known what he was doing, she would have covered her head with her hood. He simply told her that was one of the reasons he taught himself to draw so fast. The nerve of that Ernest! Anyway, we were sitting there the only two people in the whole classroom. We were preparing for the last exam of the course and I was bored out of my skull. I was tired of studying and I decided I would finish the last few pages of the novel I brought with me. I was just about done with it when Ernest asked me what I was reading.

"'Dragonflight'? By Anne McCaffrey?" I glanced at him nervously, because this was the first time we were ever close enough to speak to each other. "Have you read it?"

"Oh yeah," he said absentmindedly, reaching deep into his book bag for that last sheet of notes. "-that's the one where the Dragon Riders fly in and out of time battling some kind of outer space menace, isn't it?"

"Close enough. Did you like it?"

"Sure. Great sweep, tight plotting. Would've made a great movie." Ernest tossed a wad of paper at the waste receptacle near the door. He winced when he missed it. "Did you ever read 'Starship Troopers'? by Robert Heinlein? There was a movie made out of that one."

"No. You say a movie was made out of it?"

"Oh yeah." Ernest moved over to the waste container and retrieved his wad of trash before tossing it. "Simple enough theme when you get right down to it. 'War is Good for Society and Brings Out the Best in People'-"

"Nooo," I waved my hand at him.

"Oh yeah. It takes a great writer to get away with that one."

"Really? Is that what you think?"

"Oh yeah. That's what I know."

"What makes you so sure of yourself?"

"Just trust me. These things I know."

"Really? You're in the business somehow?" I smile ruefully with my pen poised aloft. "Let me write down the title of your latest book. After class I'll run down and get it."

"Whoa. Slow down, sister. I'm still up and coming."

"Aren't we all?" I cracked at him and turned back to my novel. "Don't tell me you're a writer too?"

A part of me said just ignore him, he couldn't possibly care about my writing. I was making up my mind not to pay him any more attention, when I looked across at him before I could catch myself.

I will never forget the expression on his face. I felt like he was reading something that was tattooed across my forehead. I determined to resume my reading, but I could feel him waiting me out for some reason. He was just sitting there waiting with that smug smile on his face. I felt like I was in a confessional or something.

"Yeah, I've written something." I whispered to myself. "What? A short story? A play? A novel?"

"I wrote a novel."

"Pleased to meet you," Ernest reached over and shook my hand. "I don't run into many of us these days. We novelists have got to stick together. Otherwise we might become an endangered species. What's the title of your book?"

"'Self Inflicted Tendencies'?"

"'By'?"

"'By Amelia Dougherty', I guess."

"What? Don't you know?"

"Yeah, I know. Sure I know."

"Are you sure?"

"Sure I'm sure." I hid the smile that was peeking between my fingers. "I mean, have you been working on something?"

"I've got a few irons in the fire."

"Anything with a title to it?"

"Yeah, it's your standard Action and Adventure fare. I'll tell you what, I'll trade you one of my books for one of yours."

"You want to read my novel?"

"Oh yeah. Before I have to pay twenty five dollars for it at Borders. You give me an autographed copy fresh out of the typewriter, and I'll give you a professional critique free of charge."

"I don't really need a critique all that much. What I really need is an agent. The problem is I can't afford one."

"We should become a conspiracy of two. Who knows how many books we might manage to get published when we put our two heads together."

Now there was a line if I ever heard one. But there was something refreshing about a guy trying to impress me by feigning interest in my writing. Chances were all he really wanted was to get me in the sack somehow some way with all this talk about my writing, but precious few guys I met at the car wash or at college started out for first base with me using anywhere near that kind of approach. I decided I would skate the ice with him for a little bit of it.

"What kind of stuff do you write?" I asked him with piqued interest.

"I've been working on mastering the Science Fiction genre, but this next time out I think I'm going to try something a bit more contemporary."

"Oh? That sounds interesting. Have you ever sent anything to be published?"

"The last two books I send to about a dozen publishers and a literary agent. I think I was close to seeing myself in print between hard covers, but coming up this time I want to be right on the money."

"Don't we all?" I said, a tentative smile catching at the corners of my mouth.

How many times did I fantasize about rolling around in the folds of green bed sheets embroidered in crisp, fresh, thousand dollar bills?

Even now I could see myself having pillow fights with one of my boyfriends. We're whacking each other over the head and pounding each other in the sides with bags of dough bursting through the seams of overflowing pillowcases. Soon I'm hot footing it naked through a river of moolah exploding out of a quaking mattress through the very springs and stuffing and every which way while it rains dollar bills upon me through the ceiling. The walls of my bedroom release buds of flourishing green lettuce like clouds of spores. I open my window just in time to barrel through and hang ten on a humungous wave of green. I surf my sea of prosperity into the front yard of my opulent mansion. I find to my amazement that now I am suddenly garbed in a revealing gown of glittering jewels and dancing the minuet with Bill Gates in a powdered wig!

"Amelia?"

"Hmp?"

"Have you ever thought that maybe the journey might turn out to be more exciting than the destination?"

The glowing reddish brown orb of Ernest Randall's face suffused with the sunlight behind us brought me out of my reverie.

"Nooo," I murmured the way I used to when my mother would wake me up for school and I still wanted to sleep some more. "No way!" An embarrassed laugh escaped my lips. "I've heard that one before. I think that's a fractured logic myself. Just going can't be an end unto itself. It's only natural to want to arrive someplace."

"I didn't actually mean-"

"That would be like someone running a marathon in winning time and never crossing the finish line! I know it's 'how you play the game' and all that jazz, but as for me, give me the cash and prizes and the trip to Bermuda and the red Saturn Ion 2, Pat."

"I didn't mean there shouldn't be a destination-"

I nodded at him with a flickering rueful smile.

"Oh, I've got an idea what you mean, all right. I just don't believe in riding off towards the horizon in search of the Holy Grail beyond the vanishing point. I'm no philosophy major."

"What is your major, Amelia?"

"English. How 'bout you, Ernest?"

"I'm doing my Master's in Art Education. The truth be told, that is, the real deal is I'm doing everything I can to put myself in an environment that's mentally stimulating enough to make it possible for me to write and publish my novels."

"I wish I could say that. I've always wanted be a writer too, but right now I'll be satisfied to just be an English teacher and draw a paycheck. I just don't want to drive cars through the P's and Q's Car Wash all my life."

"I think I've heard of that place. Over on the east side, isn't it?"

"Yeah, it's out there by Harper Woods."

"Yeah, I know. I used to live out that way."

"Since I've been going to school, I've been able to adjust my schedule around my classes. My boss has been real good about that."

"What times do you work there?"

"Usually in the afternoon, but the times can vary."

"What do you do? Do you work the cash register or direct the cars through the rollers?"

"We have our customers leave their keys in the car and we drive them up onto the ramp and click them into the washing platform and send them through. I have worked the cash register and handling the money, but I like driving the cars and locking them into the washing platform the best."

"I should stop by and see you in action. Have you ever written about what you do on your job?"

"Nooo," I gave him a wincing, mocking glance. "Do you think I should?"

"What can it hurt? You would definitely be writing about something you know."

"Yeah, I see what you mean by that. Yeah, I guess you just might have something there."

"I'll tell you what-"

"What?"

"I'll show you mine if you'll show me yours."

"What do you mean by that?"

I was a little miffed by his choice of words.

"Send me your novel and I'll send you mine."

"Oh, I don't know, you really think you would be interested?"

"You never know. It just might make the both of us better writers at the very least. What harm would there be in that?"

Ernest seemed so sure of himself and his reasoning, on the surface, seemed impeccable and above reproach. However, there was still this feeling on my part that he might be hankering after something a little more emotionally engrossing than a literary alliance.

"I'll tell you what, Ernest;" I heard myself saying in spite of myself, "why don't I give you my address and you give me your own? We might as well give each other a thirty day free trial offer."

"My sentiments exactly. Now that we're talking turkey, let me show you some of the poetry I worked on with a few high school students I was teaching." He handed me stapled sheets of paper with typing on them. "Oh, here's my address-"

I scribbled mine on a scrap of loose-leaf paper and took his information and put it in my purse. We talked a little more while a couple more students came into the classroom. Ernest joked that I shouldn't be surprised when he showed up at the P's and Q's to get his car washed and asked for me. He asked me for a business card, but I didn't have one on me. A clean-shaven middle-aged man wearing glasses told Ernest where the exact cross streets were located, but I don't like it when my male friends show up asking for me at work.

I read a few of the poems Ernest had given me and we talked a little more about getting ready for this final exam we were going to take. That was when the teacher walked into the room. I handed Ernest back his poetry,

"The first one I read was very powerful," I whispered to him as I started to put my notes under my desk, "who wrote that one?"

"Thanks. I did." Ernest nodded at me. "Talk to you later."

That actually was the long and the short of it. Ernest wanted to talk to me after we were finished with the final exam, but there were two more classes for me to study for before I went to work. We did not speak to each other again for quite some time after that. Now I am sitting here in my nightgown with my novel in my lap. I cannot stop wondering whether to wipe the dust off of it and send the thing to him, or just turn around and put it back on the shelf above my clothes in the closet. Fellow authors should encourage and support one another. That is right, isn't it? That is the way whole literary movements begin, through writers coming together to offer each other mutual aid and help when needed. Ernest and I might start out as a movement of two and end up a wide-ranging, far-reaching world cultural influence. This could be the genesis of such a thing. That is the way such things have occurred in the past.

What doesn't quite sit right with me in the pit of my stomach is this palpable sense of risk. I don't know why I feel I'm taking such a chance sending my work to a near total stranger. Oh, he seemed nice enough in class, but after all, you never really can tell. There is a foreboding in all this for reasons I can't quite put my finger upon. The tangible apprehension I attempt to stifle has nothing to do with thoughts that he might be an axe murderer or a serial rapist. No, my troubled thoughts have a vaguer hue to them. I cannot disabuse myself of the conviction that once I send this story of mine to this young man my life will be changed forever. There is a cosmic gravity to all this that seems to come from nowhere and everywhere all at the same time. I just want for another person beside myself to read my novel and like it the way I do. Love it even if I am capable of arousing such a depth and height of emotional response.

Why do I feel that sending this novel to Ernest Randall is tantamount to signing some kind of contract with destiny?

That is what bothers me to no end.

While I wrestle with this momentous decision, I snatch some tissue out of the box on the night stand and blow my nose. Oh, I might as well wipe this layer of dust off my novel, I think to myself. No use getting it all over my nightgown. I drum my fingers idly on the cover sheet of my little literary effort. I know what, I decided, I'll sleep on it and talk to somebody about it later.

"What's an Ernest Randall?" Howie Manchester asks me, wiping his glasses with an incredulous expression while we walk to class. "No, I never heard of the guy. But look, Amelia, what can it hurt to meet the guy in some public place where lots of people are around and he can't grab you? There are plenty of libraries on campus. Send him a printout of your book and set up a time and a place for a meeting. Be really professional about it. That's the equitable way to go about it. After all, he showed you his, now it's time for you to show him yours."

"Hmmm, I don't like the sound of that." I said as Howie opens the door for me as we enter the Cohn Building. "Your choice of words does not become you, Howie."

"Look, from what you've told me the fellow has been pretty straightforward." Howie swilled his soda and tossed it into a garbage can. "Besides, don't you writers like to bare your hearts and souls to each other, anyway? The thing of it is, you don't have to send him your entire script either. Just in case you're worried he'll run off with your trade secrets, just send him samples."

"Samples, Howie?"

"Yeah, samples; certain select chapters that represent the flavor of the work. That's what you were doing when you sent your novel to the publishers, yeah?"

"Yeah, but this is different-"

"What's different about it? Look, I know what you're thinking, Amelia. He's just another of an endless parade of guys that want to talk you up because you're a good-looking girl. You don't have to tell me that isn't part of the equation." Howie pushed his glasses back onto the bridge of his bulbous nose. "He must not be that cute, Amelia. Otherwise we wouldn't be having this conversation."

"No, it isn't that. He's okay, I guess. He's sort of charming in a funny sort of way."

"There you go. Now you've got to admit he gave you more than a line. Here-" Howie gave me back my notes. "From what you've told me, two books worth. That deserves at least a chat and a cup of coffee. By that I mean, you give him the chat and he provides the coffee."

"Or tea, maybe."

"There you go. You want me to come with you, Amelia, when you meet with this fellow, just say the word. Okay?"

We came to our Russian Literature class and Howie fitted his gawky frame into one of the desk chairs. I sat in another chair against the wall. We were studying Dostoevsky and I hastily reviewed my notes. Now that we were finished discussing 'Crime And Punishment', I would have to buckle down and finish the last two hundred pages of 'The Possessed'.

Howie leaned over to me just as Phyllis entered the room. She pulled up a seat next to us and asked me to let her check her notes against mine. That was okay with me, so I handed Phyllis everything that I wrote down.

"Did you finish that novel., Amelia?" Howie whispered to me.

"Don't make me laugh. I was up until nearly two in the morning with a dictionary! How about you, Phyllis?"

"Yeah," She nodded, flipping through my notes. "I couldn't put it down. I haven't been that emotionally engrossed since I finished 'Valley of the Dolls' in one sitting."

Phyllis is this tall, striking blonde and I've heard people tell her when she's waitressing how much she reminds them of Gwyneth Paltrow. She certainly knows how to handle the men folk whenever they try to hit on her. I sit next to her a lot when we have classes together, hoping a little bit of her own self confidence will rub off on me.

"You didn't find Dostoevsky a little longwinded?" I asked just as Mr. Scaley our teacher entered the room. "He really wrings the towel out, if you ask me."

"I don't know if I would call it longwinded." Phyllis started writing stuff down from my notes as Mr. Scaley approached the lectern. "There's something…oh–I don't know, 'operatic' about the way he writes. I think that's the best way to describe it."

"Longwinded and full blown," Howie muttered to me under his breath. "My buddy took this class before me. He said the one thing about our boy Dostoevsky was his mania for twisting his characters into emotional pretzels.

"That's pretty apt," Phyllis nodded agreeably.

"Where were you anyway last week, Phyllis?" Howie almost started not to ask.

"Didn't I tell you, Howie? Phyllis went and got herself married last week!

"That right," Phyllis beamed at us as she put a ring finger to her lips. "Shhhh–he's starting-"

"Since when?" I could not believe I was standing here arguing with this fellow. "Since always! Since forever! That's our policy, sir. Look, I promise I won't hurt your vehicle. You take my word for it. Just give me your keys and I'll drive it up onto the ramp so we can send it through the blowers and the rollers. Your car is safe with me, I promise."

This bearded fellow stands there in his Cossack cap and his red plaid jacket towering over me. He explains so much to me about his black 2003 Ford F350 Super Cab that I feel like I'm in a showroom or something. The wind whips around us and I feel like telling him that he can decide either to give me the keys or go to that Car Wash up the street. This has never happened to me before. The people in Harper Woods are pretty friendly as a rule, and I can't understand why he's making such a fuss about this.

"Look, if it's all the same to you, I would rather drive her up." He tells me for what must be the umpteenth time. "These off road vehicles can take some handling and I'm carrying some stuff on the bed I don't want anything to happen to in any way. I would just feel more comfortable driving her up the ramp myself."

This is getting too involved for me and there would be no point in my repeating myself.

"I'll tell you what," I say, blowing my warm breath through my hands. "I'll go get the manager. If it's okay with him, then it's okay with me, all right?"

I give the customer a nervous wave, but he just glowers at me impassively. I can see Davey Carter at the cash register inside, but what I cannot see until I come through the entrance is how his stocky frame is handcuffed to the guardrail next to the service counter. There is a thin, reedy man wearing a red and black padded wind breaker standing next to him. He is holding some kind of weapon you feed clips of bullets into. I never was any good at identifying guns or what have you, and when I come in flashing a startled look, he determinedly nods me over while he gestures to Davey to open the cash register.

Ding! The cash register drawer pops open. Quick as lightning this wiry fellow who looks like he just darted out of an Al Capp comic strip is over at the till. He motions me over, and even though I glance around wildly, I somehow manage to stifle a scream. "C'mon, little missy, time you gave a customer a cash refund, I say-" He keeps waving that gun at my head and I go into panic mode. "C'mon on now, scoop the proceeds into here-"

He grabs me by the hair and leads me over like a sleepwalker to the cash drawer. I feel something hard press my hair against the back of my skull. Davey is a feverish red and hyper- ventilating like crazy. The terror in his eyes gives me a visceral chill, which I match with my own expression of questioning desperation.

"C'mon girl, scoop it in-scoop it in-" This fellow hurriedly tells me as he motions me to the leather pouch open on the counter.

"Daaa-vvvey," I hear myself utter in a frightful sing-song, "where's Mister Jacobs, Davey?"

"I don't know, Amelia, I don't know-"

I clutch handfuls of coins and dollar bills out of the register and release them from my trembling fingertips into the leather pouch with its slack drawstring.

"Shut up! The both of you. I don't recall giving either of yous permission to open your yap!" Davey keeps glancing at the Janitor's closet behind me, and taking a cue from him, I sneak a quick look behind me. Now I can see the soles of Mr. Jacobs brogues splayed out of the door to the closet. The bulk of his body is nestled against a black garbage bag, a mop head and a dustpan leaning inside the closet against a rusty metal bucket.

"AlrIght! Thanks for the contribution, little missy." This unshaven little twerp tells me as he pushes me against my back over to where Davey is handcuffed. "Where did I put them things?"

I watched him pat the back of his soiled jeans and the pockets to his windbreaker. "Oh! Here we go, little missy! A pair of bracelets for your very own."

I find myself handcuffed by the wrist despite my fretting protestations. I'm locked with Davey to the guardrail. We watch with a queasy, sinking despondency as the black Ford Super Cab comes swiftly swinging into view with a lurching stop. A raspy voice calls to us from outside.

"Ho!" I can hear even through the glass door. "How we doin' in there? Any problems?"

"None to speak of." I see coins splatter against the gritty floor as this spidery fellow chirps back his reply. "Ain't that right, little missy?" He takes me by the waist and grabs at my breast, but I twist away, reflexively raising a hand to slap his away and spitting at him. "Ain't no need for that, little missy-"

The grungy fellow raises the muzzle of his loaded gun, and I quail back with a gasp and a shiver of fear.

"Here I come! You guys stay put, you hear me?" He combs back my hair with his gun. "I especially mean that for you, little miss sweet ass-HERE I COME—-"

The stranger scurries out of the office to our car wash with the sack of cash. He hops into the passenger side of the Ford Super Cab and Davey and I watch the vehicle like a great big black beast turn screeching out of our driveway and down Warren.

"Mister Jacobs!" Davey and I take turns calling out to him. "Are you all right?! Mister Jacobs!"

"He's not moving," Davey wheezes at me. "Do you think he had a heart attack or something, Amelia?"

"I swear to God, I hope not! We gotta get help, Davey. Where is everybody else, for Christ's sake? Don't you have your cell phone on you?'

"Whoever robbed us lifted it from me when he knocked the phone out the wall."

"We gotta get help for Mister Jacobs. Do you see anybody coming, Davey?"

"No, I don't think so-"

"Wait a minute! I think I hear somebody coming–HELP! We're over here! HELP -"

"Yeah, see? Here comes Lorenzo! And I think that's Kasem! HEY! OVER HERE!"

We both kept on shouting to the top of our lungs.

Phyllis and Howie listened to my tale of ill fortune with rapt interest alternating at times with outrage and sympathy. Howie offered me a Salem Light when he saw my hand was still shaking and I very nearly took it. I clutched my bottled water to me, relieved to be back on campus safe and sound and all in one piece.

"Ready to chuck the Car Wash business, Amelia?" Phyllis sat back smugly, 'I told you so' written all over her face. "We can always use another waitress where I work." She twisted her wedding ring around her finger. "At least I doubt you'll run into anymore thugs like you have at 'P's And Q's'."

"You sound like my mother."

"I can't help it. I said from the beginning that 'P's And Q's' was no place for a girl."

"What about that Mister Jacobs?" Howie interjected with sober concern. "Sounds like he got the worst of it of anyone. Is he still in the hospital?"

"He'll be out soon. I know for a fact he sustained a pretty bad concussion when those guys conked him. He's getting up there, and he was lucky not to have a heart attack or a stroke or something. So far all the tests the doctors have been running on him are coming back negative."

"That's good," Phyllis said, letting out a sigh. "-he could easily have ended up a homicide statistic."

"You watch too much 'Law And Order', Phyllis." Howie scoffed at her.

"Yeah Phyllis," I teased, taking up Howie's part, "in case you haven't noticed, we're dealing with real life here."

"You mean real life as you know it, Amelia." Phyllis gravely corrected me.

"Have the cops caught the creeps who did it yet?" Howie asked, holding his cigarette.

"Oh yeah. Once we went in the ambulance with Mister Jacobs to the hospital, a bunch of us went down to the precinct to file a police report. Lorenzo, myself, Davey, Kasem; a few others too. One of our surveillance cameras caught everything, despite them having knocked a couple off their moorings. Their mugs ended up on the evening news and it wasn't long before employees from the 'P's and Q's ', myself included, were called down to pick them out of a lineup."

"Who were those guys, Amelia?"

"I remember one was an unemployed auto worker for the Rouge plant or something like that. The other fellow, believe it or not, was a laid off security guard!"

"Takes all kinds," Howie said, shaking his head. "At least you can't say you have nothing to write about now, Amelia."

We chuckled to ourselves a little. I watched the crisp brown leaves skip across the sidewalk of the Plaza. The wind feathered fingers of air through the trees and whipped past the hedges and the statues standing, kneeling and reclining in the splendor of their green patina on pedestals of jagged granite. We watched the students, some older and some younger, strolling back and forth and milling about between the Student Union and College of Education buildings as light faded into evening. I could feel the sequestered ease of campus life settle about my shoulders, and I found myself snuggling in it like a warm blanket.

"Amelia?"

"Um?"

"What did you ever do about that guy who wanted to read your novel?"

"Oh," I frowned at Howie with a flip of my hand, "I haven't got time for that now. A few of us are going down later to see how Mister Jacobs is doing. You wanna come?"

Howie pulled out a handkerchief and blew his nose.

"Better wait until I get over this first," Howie replaced his handkerchief in his pocket, "The way I feel, whatever moral support I have to offer might finish him!"

When I went to see Mister Jacobs that evening, the nurse was pulling the plastic partition back across the track in the ceiling. She met me at the entrance, cradling the blue plastic bed pan carefully held between us. I took Mister Jacobs' hand into my own and gave him a sympathetic smile. I sat down in the cushioned chair next to his bed and wondered whose voice that was coming from behind the curtain. There was a wan expression on Mr. Jacobs' round, florid face. The slurred way he spoke to me as I bring him up to date as to what's happening at the Car Wash, was everything that told me he's fighting off the effects of the medication they're giving him. There's one whole side of his scalp shaved clean and I saw the stitches holding together an angry strip of flesh just a little above his temple.

"How are your studies going, Amelia?" Mr. Jacobs asked, placing his Car Buyer's magazine over the rising crest of his stomach.

"You know how it is, Mister Jacobs. It's a lot of reading, but I'm keeping my head above water."

"No, I don't know how it is-" Mr. Jacobs shrugged his shoulders to sit up in the bed a little bit more, "I never went to no college. Never could afford to; came straight out of high school into the service. I got my mechanic's license and certification in the Army, and when I came out, took out a couple of loans and opened up my own place. Goin' on twenty years and I never had nothing like this happen before."

"I know, Mister Jacobs, I know-"

"Sign of the friggin' times, if you ask me-"

"I know, Mister Jacobs, but at least they collared the fellows who robbed you."

Mr. Jacobs shrugged churlishly.

"I suppose that's something. Me and my wife used to sit over the kitchen table when she was expecting and I was workin' on cars for Sears & Roebuck." He scratched his red curly locks tinged with a shock of gray on the side that was not shaven. "I always told her I would never start no business unless it was in a nice neighborhood. Some place decent where you didn't have to look over your shoulder all the time. A place where the neighbors still looked out for each other and your kids could be safe." Mr. Jacobs made an effort to thumb through his magazine again and finally set it aside in exasperation. "Now this happens. I tell you, this keeps up there won't be no place where you can walk the streets that's safe."

"Oh—you're just getting beside yourself because you're cooped up in here, Mister Jacobs," I said, in an attempt to soothe him, "once you're out and about again, it'll be a different tune. Besides, where would the rest of us be without you keeping us honest?"

Mr. Jacobs looked at me with a disgruntled frown while I handed him his ice water with a straw. He was mulling over something when Davey peeked a look around the doorjamb. Mr. Jacobs archly folded his arms around his breadbasket and gave Davey a grudging nod. "What have we here?" Mr. Jacobs said, peering critically at Davey. "Aren't you supposed to be at the Car Wash about now?"

"That's right, Mister Jacobs, but I had to come and see how you were doing. I switched shifts with Lorenzo to come down here."

"Hmph. What happened to me is no excuse to take off from work," Mr. Jacobs gave Davey a look of warning while he scratched his chaffed elbows, "I've got family and relatives to see about yours truly."

"I didn't take off from work, Mister Jacobs. I just switched shifts with Lorenzo like I told ya." Davey settled his portly bulk in a chair next to me. "The gang down at the P's and Q's all wanted to know how you were doin'. Here, I brought you the paper-"

"Thanks," Mr. Jacobs started fishing for something under the covers, "put it over there by the flowers."

"Don't you wanna see how the Spartans are ranked since Sunday?"

"I can find that out on ESPN -" Mr. Jacobs muttered, still fumbling under that blue blanket.

"What are you looking for, Mr. Jacobs?" I asked, rising from my seat.

"The remote, Amelia, the remote–I could have sworn-"

I cast glances about and became aware of that voice on the other side of the plastic curtain again.

"There it is. Next to you, Davey."

"What?" He spotted it on the stand next to our chairs. "Oh Yeah." He picked it up and looked at Mr. Jacobs with a solicitous expression. "Was there something you wanted to see?"

"The nurse must have moved it-" Mr. Jacobs resolved with another mutter. "Here, lemme see that. There was a good movie on the other day. Let me see if I can't find another one."

"Careful, Mr. Jacobs," I cautioned, as he reached out jangling the I.V. cords atttached to his wrists, "-why don't you let me do it?"

"Naw, I can manage, Amelia–" he assured me as I took the remote console from Davey and handed it to him.

"I think it's too early for a prime time movie, Mister Jacobs-" Davey remarked as he sat back down. He tossed his head at the voice on the other side of the curtain. "From what I can hear, the Game Shows have just started."

"Yeah," Mr. Jacobs clicked the overhead set on, "it must be around seven by now. But I can still get Cable on this one-"

"Get the Games Channel, Mister Jacobs-" Davey blurts out impulsively and is checked by Mr, Jacobs' scowl, "- oops! I was thinkin' 'WHO WANTS TO BE A MILLIONAIRE' might be on about now, sir -"

Mr. Jacobs just grunted and casually looked my way.

"What about you, Amelia? Was there something you wanted to see?"

"Anything is fine with me, Mr. Jacobs, you just go ahead. I normally just watch 'ANIMAL PLANET' or 'E' or something." I hear a loud smack of a clap from behind the curtain. "Someone is certainly having a good time! Who's your neighbor, Mr. Jacobs?"

"Oh, some black fella retired from the Department of Transportation, I think he told me," Mr. Jacobs kept clicking through the channels until he got to 'ROMANCE NETWORK', "this looks like a pretty good love story here, Amelia. You wanna watch it? Here -"

Mr. Jacobs scratched at a bald spot islanded in the nest of his curly red hair and reached out to me with the remote. Davey looked at me with a wry smile and folded his arms, shifting uneasily in his chair.

"Anything is fine with us, Mr. Jacobs. We came to visit with you."

"Sound like my daughter up in Boston-" Mr. Jacobs muttered as he picked up his magazine again and started fiddling with it.

We can hear this rinky-dink music swelling with the volume from the other side of the blue curtain.

"Sounds like the 'FAMILY FEUD', Mr. Jacobs," Davey cheerfully volunteered as we arose to take a tentative peek behind the curtain.

When we caught sight of Ernest Randall sitting genially bedside with this wizen-faced old reedy black man, I couldn't keep a look of startled surprise from registering on my face. The venerable old gentleman with the cottony gray mane was fingering through the channels with the remote, while Ernest idly patted his knees among the gardenias and the potted fuchsia shelving the windows. He regarded me with an even thoughtfulness while the nurse returned to check the old man's charts.

"Ernest! Is that you?"

"That you Amelia?" Ernest squinted at me, blinking in the suddenness of wide-eyed recognition. "What are you doing here?"

"That's what I was about to ask you!"

"Hey, Mister Jacobs," Davey craned his neck to the other side of the curtain, "they can jolly well get cable over here, too."

Ernest stood up, while the nurse bustled about and rearranged the pillows under the elderly fellow's back and neck. We moved around and out of the way as Ernest stepped forward. "That's all right, I'll only be a minute," the waspish nurse casually tossed to us, reaching up to check the saline solution, "you two know each other?"

"Yeah, we do; from a class in graduate school. What are you doing here, Ernest?" I caught the gaze of the old man decorously clearing his throat. "Oh, I'm sorry! I'm Amelia Dougherty, I-"

"- and how are you, young lady?"

"This is my grandfather, Amelia, Talmadge Randall," Ernest led me over by the fingers to the old man's bedside, "-this is Amelia, grandpa, she's a classmate of mine."

When I took the gnarled hand into mine, a twinkle flashed in those coal eyes embedded in a network of fine lines and deep wrinkles. The long face of Ernest's grandfather was like those carved wooden masks you find posted against the walls in the museum. The laugh lines that fanned out from the corners of his eyes twitched like tiers of smiles while the rest of his face remained somberly immobile. Davey nodded at the aged fellow over my shoulder, mumbling a self-effacing greeting and introduction.

"My grandson," the elder Randall coughed into his hand, "cain't make up his mind whether he wants 'FEAR FACTOR', 'AMERICAN IDOL', 'JEOPARDY' or 'WHO WANTS TO BE A MILLIONAIRE'!"

"I don't know," Davey stole a glance at me, "from what we could hear over the way, it seemed to us like you guys were havin' a pretty good time."

"Aaaa," Grandpa Talmadge raised his hand at Davey scoffing, "see I told you, Ernest. Turn that bunch a foolishness down some. Probably kin hear it clear 'cross the hallway."

"I was just tryin' to help you out, Grandpa," Ernest protested with a chagrined expression, "so you could hear it a little better."

Ernest pointed the remote at the overhead screen and commenced to dim down the sound. "That Jacobs must have been fixin' to jump out of his skin," Grandpa Talmadge stopped to catch himself, sucked in a breath and went on, "-the way we was carryin' on watchin' that there 'FAMILY FEUD'." Ernest's grandfather raised himself up in his bed a little bit more. "Hey there, JACOBS! How you doin' over there?"

"Better than you, buddy," the retort came from behind the blue curtain.

"Yeah? We'll see about that-"

Grandpa Talmadge smiled to himself with a smug chuckle, before catching at his next snort of a breath and sucking it in feverishly.

"Y'all want some chairs?" The old man inquired with a peevish expression.

"No, we just-" Davey pointed back towards where Mr. Jacobs awaited us.

"I gotcha. You just wanted to know where all the noise was comin' from. That it?" The old man sat back again with a shuddering sigh. "You wasn't plannin' on visiting, just thought you'd check things out-" Ernest's grandfather paused for a sharp intake of air. "Right. Just to see what was goin' on."

"- it did seem to us that maybe you were having just a wee bit too much fun, Mr. Talmadge, sir-" I kidded, measuring the air between my thumb and index finger.

"That figures," Ernest muttered as he plopped in a chair next to the window, "there's only so much time you can spend reading the Bible and consultin' your Dream Book for a hot Lottery number."

"Speak for your own self, son," Old man Talmadge coughed out into his hand again. "You know that Psalms and Proverbs don't never make me weary."

"Oh?" Ernest looked askance at his grandfather. "Next thing, you'll be tellin' me it was my idea to turn to the 'FAMILY FEUD' marathon."

"Well naw," Mr. Talmadge's body began shaking with racking coughs, "I'll admit I likes my 'FAMILY FEUD' every now and then,"

The coughing was getting worse.

"We better be getting back to Mister Jacobs, Amelia-" Davey tugged at my jacket.

"Y'all ain't gotta go just yet-" Mr. Talmadge insisted as he snatched gasping for a napkin,

"I tole Ernie he could come here and study his lesson when he wanted to some time. I'd like to hear what it is you be studyin' up at that university some time -"

"Why don't we come back one day and we can tell you all about it, Mister Talmadge," I suggested, "we just came to check on Mister Jacobs today."

Ernest looked up at me with a worried flicker of a smile. We watched as his grandfather began to wheeze and he nodded that it was okay for us to go. I hung my fingers on the edge of the curtain and involuntarily gave a backward glance.

"You want me to get the nurse, grandpa?" Ernest asked as he drew the covers to the old man's throat. "I'll go get her if you want."

"Naw son, just let me rest here for awhile. It should pass after a spell. You wanna read to me some?"

"Ernest? Is there anything I can do?"

When Ernest looked up at me with that distracted expression, you would have thought I was somebody's ghost.

"Huh? Naw, Amelia, naw, we're good."

"Alright, Ernest. See you later in class, okay?"

"I'll be there. Take care, Amelia."

Davey stumbled back behind the blue curtain and I followed him. We sat with Mr. Jacobs for a little more, chatting about bits of trivia and answering pointed questions from him about what was going on at the 'P's and Q's'. Davey made a few off-color quips when Mr. Jacobs asked him about his girlfriend, and it wasn't long after that before we were being dismissed so that he could get some sleep. We left to the sound of Ernest's grandfather wheezing and coughing from behind the curtain.

Davey and I mumbled our goodbyes in the parking structure and were about to part ways when we heard the shuffling footsteps and low voices coming out of the darkness around the curve. I barely had my car keys slipped over my fingers when a towering obese blob shrouded in shadow emerges into the lights of the parking structure. He approaches, his brow framed in a beige beret and his considerable girth harnessed in blue jean overalls. There was a gangly, stick of a youth in a T-shirt and basketball shoes strolling next to him, stoking the fires of a raging argument. I gasped as my footsteps echoed on the pavement.

I grasped Davey by the wrist.

"Davey, let's-" I began to exclaim as the two figures whirled us between them. "I think we better-"

There were scraps of invective hurled over us that I barely caught. The usual stuff and nonsense about 'dissing' and 'being dissed'. The more they traded insults, the louder they became. We did our best to try and walk around them, but Davey and I kept getting cut off between their waving arms and shifting bodies.

"Where you think y'all going, huh?" The obese fellow in the beige beret said as he swayed unsteadily. He pulled out a shiny black weapon and asked me in outrage, "I wanna know what you think about Mister Big Stuff dissin' me that way?"

I looked to Davey and squeezed his arm until he could feel my fingernails digging into his sleeve. I have to say one thing for Davey; I could feel him trembling beside me, but that didn't stop him from doing what he could to protect us. He stepped forward and pressed the palm of his hand against the looming silhouette of the bulk before us.

"Look, guy, I don't know what your problem is, but-"

Before we even saw him, the tall, skinny fellow was between us. Davey painfully drew back his arm after having it whacked with the barrel end of a nine-millimeter. The next thing he knew, he was being drawn up by his lapels and lectured to by this walking stick.

"Hey! Whoa-whoa-whoa! I think mah man just asked you a question, bro. Now you gon' be polite an' answer him, or what?"

The hardest thing to explain to people is how the oddest thought will occur to you while you are being accosted and robbed. Just before Davey puckered up to spit in his assailant's eye, I thought I detected just a hint of a Mexican accent. I screamed when our NBA version of Sancho Panza back handed Davey and slung him down against a concrete pillar. I ran over in helpless anguish and tossed out my pocket book, spilling credit cards onto the sloping pavement.

"Leave him alone! Don't hurt him! Here! Here, I said!" I kept stabbing a finger at my pocket book. "Take it! Just take it! Isn't that what you wanted?"

I am pleading to the hulking mound of fat swaying headless in the cloaking blackness of shadow. The nine-millimeter appears magically out of the darkness with a belching hiccup. I kneel down to shield Davey with my body, fighting back and stifling every impulse to cower before the flickering Buddha-like visage that looms over me.

"Whatchu say, man? Should we shoot 'em?"

We heard the faint, hollow sound of footsteps behind us.

"Naw man, let 'em go."

When I whirled in the direction where the voice was coming from, I was startled to find that Ernest was standing there in his green parka, idly pulling on the fingers of his winter gloves.

"What makes you think we would do some shit like that?" The mountain in the beige beret asks with a scornful laugh.

"Yeah," says the Walking Stick as he pulls out his weapon and racks it, "what planet you come from, bro? Why would we do some mess like that?"

"People can hear you all through this parking lot, for one thing," Ernest took a step forward towards us, "- the other thing is you're drunk, and I don't believe you've thought this all the way through."

The Walking Stick and the Buddha in the Beret looked at each other before erupting into a contemptuous laughter.

"What have we got here, Pedro?" Buddha winked at his comrade in arms, wiping sweat away from his sideburns. "I do believe we got us here uh – uh–what they call that thang?"

"Eh, bro," nodded Pedro with a gleeful smile, "- what we got us at this particular time here is a 'hostage knee-gotiator'-"

"Yeah! That's what I'm talkin' about!" Buddha said, chuckling until his shoulders shook. "Whatchu think this is, bro? You think this is some kind of movie or somethin'?" Pedro boldly approached Ernest with his weapon raised. "Why don't I bust a cap in yo' ass so you can fade to black? You like that?"

"Naw," Ernest's eyes flitted over to Davey and I crouched against the concrete pillar, "I ain't down with that. But since you got the guns, I guess you call the shots. I just thought you was smarter than this; to get caught up in a sucker's play."

I could taste my stomach in my mouth when Ernest said this. Davey groaned as I cast a furtive glance at him in dismay. We looked up at Ernest with a pang of resentment. He was going to run his mouth and end up getting us all killed.

"Ernest! Please don't say anything more!" I pleaded with a desperate gesture. "Just – just–leave! Run! Get out of here! Now!"

Ernest stood on the sloping drive of the parking structure. He didn't move a muscle. I cringed inside when I saw him shrug at our assailants and then continued to shoot the breeze.

"Ain't no place to go." Ernest turned to the Walking Stick. "Ain't that right? Shoot–I done seen your faces now. I'm a witness." Ernest shrugged again as he turned to the Buddha in the Beige Beret. "Ain't that right? I mean—were the situation reversed and I was in your shoes,

I sure couldn't afford to let you get away alive and rat to fuzz while I copped some bitch's bread. I mean—I already heard you call my man Pedro. You got kids, man?"

Pedro strode resolutely forward and clicked the safety back from his weapon.

"That's 'Big Man' to you, bro-"

"Right. 'Big Man'! Right. You won't get no argument out of me. How 'bout you, Pedro? I mean—is it all right for me to call you Pedro?"

"That's my name, ain't it?"

"Right. How 'bout it, Pedro?"

"How about what?"

"Kids, man, kids. You got any?"

Pedro looked at 'Big Man' in consternation as he replaced his feet over and over to adjust his stance before shooting Ernest down. The Buddha man folded his meaty arms before fingering his broad lips to barely suppress a drunken giggle.

"Answer 'em, Pedro."

"What?"

"Answer the man! You deef? He wanted to know about yo' kids, man!"

"I don't see how that's any of your stinkin' bizness, bro-"

The way Pedro glared at Ernest and narrowed his eyes, I swear to God I thought he was going to shoot him right then and there.

"Noooo!" I screamed and Davey and me held on to each other.

"Don't! We gave you our money! You don't have to kill anybody! Please! Don't!"

Buddha regarded us impassively for long unbearable seconds before he cocked his head at Pedro and then gave Ernest a chuckle.

"Yo' bitch got a loud mouth on her-"

"Yeah, I'm sorry about that," Ernest began apologetically, "And I'm in the wrong place at the wrong time. I know that. But I think the moment's come and gone for you to rob 'em now. You let too much time pass to do that, plus you can hear people gettin' in their cars now. You know what I think?"

Pedro's eyes widen as he glances at the Buddha for the O.K. sign to shut Ernest up for good. I watch his lips quiver as the incredulous expression on his face becomes more and more pained. "Billy! Why you listenin' to this fucker, bro? We can leave him in this lot and let the cops take out the garbage."

"Hold tight, Pedro, hold tight." Billy the Buddha fingers his chin meditatively. "We runnin' this shit. Home boy here knows that. We might as well let the niggah sing before we start pluckin' feathers and wringin' necks. Come on with it, good sir, what in your humble opinion are the options open before us?"

"This is what I think, Big Man. I mean–it's okay to call you Big Man, right?"

Billy the Buddha nodded gravely like a judge in high court.

"Okay. I think you an' Pedro just got drunk and went a little too far. I mean-if you felt like raisin' some hell, you done definitely achieved that goal tonight! But if I had kids, I wouldn't want them to read in the newspapers how they Daddy was brought up on murder charges for stealin' some money and some charge cards that would barely pay a car note and one month's rent. That is too high a markup just to be terrorizin' some whiteys, don't you think?"

Billy the Buddha looked over at me and Davey, now shivering against the concrete pillar. I could smell the scent of gas fumes mixed with the cold, dank air. I looked up at Ernest, not knowing whether to curse him or to thank him. We heard the squeal of a car coming down from the upper levels, and Ernest walked over and started to gather up my credit cards and money.

"Look, no harm–no foul," Ernest hastily explained from a kneeling position as he scooped up my valuables, "you showed us where it was at and we gave you your props. I mean–look at my man here and look at girlfriend; the one is about to shit in his pants and the other is fixin' to pee in her panties. I say it's enough you got our attention and our respect. Nobody should have to die and go to jail on top of all that–"

The pea green Mazda Tribute lurched down the sloping driveway with glaring headlights and red flashing turn signal and by the time it passed us, our assailants had buried their weapons back inside their coats. Ernest stuffed my possessions back into my coat pockets. He lifted me, and then Davey back up from the pillar. He patted the dust off my shoulders and backside before glancing with a nod of reassurance at the Buddha and the Walking Stick.

"We straight, man?" Ernest asked as he took me by the shoulder.

I flashed our assailants a flaming look of hatred in spite of myself.

Billy the Buddha with folded arms scratched the side of his jaw and regarded us. Pedro darted a look at his partner and then at us. You would have thought we were getting away with something.

"Naw! Hell naw!" Pedro exclaimed with wild hip-hop gesticulations. "This ain't hardly about it!" He whirled on Ernest with a ferocious glare. "What you think this is, bro?" He paced in front of us furiously. "What? You think this is a comic book or something? I will waste yo' ass right here and not even blink!"

He stabbed his finger in Ernest's face.

"That would earn you a degree from the University of Murder. Pull back the curtain and take a look at your future, my man, and then tell me if the costs add up to a profit margin you can leave your kids."

Davey gives Ernest an incredulous look before tugging on my shoulder. "C'mon, Amelia, let's go -" Davey whispers in my ear.

We all stand there shivering in the night breeze awaiting the next move from somebody. A car alarm went off and Billy the Buddha started chuckling again.

"Niggah, you sound like a commercial from the United Negro College Fund," the almost bass voice of Billy the Buddha breaks the crisp evening silence, "- you full of all kinds of bullshit. C'mon, Pedro-" Billy belches and makes a tittering turn as he shows us his shoulder. "I'll give you one thing, bitch, you sho' can rap when you beggin' for your life. You oughta stop hangin' round them whiteys so much. I said, c'mon-Pedro! Uncock and throw 'em back."

Pedro eyed Billy with protest before shrugging with resignation. He paced towards Ernest and roughly patted him on the cheek. There was a faint satisfaction on his face as Ernest flinched away with a frown.

"Know what I would do if I were you, bro? I would say mucho gracias to Our Blessed Lady of Guadalupe. Straight up–she must have intervened on your behalf, amigo. I'm just telling you, were it my call, we wouldn't be standin' here talkin'. Yo' ass would be ready for the grass!"

"Pedro!" Billy the Buddha jerked his head for Pedro to heel. "C'mon man," He glared at us as he struggled to steady his stance. "Case dismissed."

Billy the Buddha lumbered back into the shadows with Pedro in tow, vehemently berating him for not dealing us some more tangible mayhem. We collectively heaved a sigh of relief and heard one last snatch of conversation spear at us from out of the darkness.

"- now you got that bitch thinkin' he's 'El Asombroso Hombre Arana' or some weird shit like that!"

"Whut? You cain't talk English–shut the fuck up!" Billy's big voice boomed in an echo back at us.

When I got home, I wearily lay on my back in the bedroom. I stared uneasily at the ceiling. I was thinking to myself about how everything went haywire that night, just like before at the Car Wash. None of it really made any sense no matter how I turned it over. The first twenty three and a half years of my life were pretty uneventful by anyone's standards. Oh, there were the usual tiffs with my sisters and the times I would fall out with my mother about breaking curfew when I went out on dates, but nothing ever verging on any kind of disastrous tragedy. So why all of a sudden were these things happening to me now? Poor Davey! He must think I'm some sort of bad luck charm by now.

More than ever, I am all mixed up about Ernest. I don't know whether I should be grateful to him or angry at him for nearly getting us wasted. I pleaded with him to just run, but he would not listen to me. At least he can say he didn't desert us, but I'm not sure I appreciate the way he gambled with our lives.

What did he do anyway? We were both trying to keep the situation from escalating into a more violent confrontation, but I can't make up my mind whether he was instrumental in saving our lives or nearly got us killed when we might have only been robbed. Besides, he was awfully chummy with those thugs; and on the far side of the moon I even wonder whether or not he knew them from his old Detroit neighborhood or something. Did he manage to talk us out of something that might have really spawned lasting, tragic consequences, or did he nearly talk us into something that would have left us unable to walk away? I'm trying to look at the incident from all sides, but all I can figure is that everything must have worked out okay. After all, I can still count all my fingers and all my toes.

When I went to register for new classes, I ran into Ernest again. We were standing in line to get assigned a computer when he recognized me. He could see I was still somewhat shaken about what happened. So what does he do? He starts bugging me again about when I'm going to send him a copy of my novel.

That's another thing, now that I think of it. Davey and I told him we were going down to the police station to file a report and he told us to forget it. He kept insisting that the guys were drunk and that since nobody was hurt and nothing got taken, we should just forget about it and go on with our lives. That's the thing that kept bothering me. How he was almost defending them because they were black. I didn't care for the way he kept trying to explain things and smooth it all over while he brushed the dirt from my coat.

"Thanks Ernest," I said to him nearly on the verge of tears and just about ready to bawl against his chest, "that's all right, you don't have to do that."

"You all right, Amelia? How about you, my man?"

"We're good," muttered Davey, checking his arm and the side of his head for bruises, "we're good-Whew! That was close, huh, Amelia?"

"It certainly was!"

Davey did bruise up later on his arm and I noticed it when we went to file the report. But in a few days, even that bit of physical evidence was nearly gone. While we were calling up our classes on the computers, I asked Ernest again why he didn't come with us to file the report. I told him we gave the officers a good physical description of both our assailants.

"What good will that do?" Ernest asked, squinting at the screen. "When those dudes come down from the high they were on, they'll barely remember us. Besides, do you really think they would 'fess up about what they did? Nobody sustained any real physical injury and from what you told me they didn't get away with anything of value. Why should those thugs confess to what almost but in fact didn't happen when there's no physical evidence, as it stands, to support anybody's word either way? I mean, look -"

The grim expression on my face seemed to take Ernest aback.

"You seem pretty smug about all this." I utter contemptuously between clenched teeth.

"No, I wouldn't say that. I wouldn't even say something like that. Look," Ernest stops again when I raise my eyebrows skeptically, "those dudes were just playing 'Gangsta For a Night' is all. Whatever they were drinkin' or smokin' loosened the old social inhibitions just enough to cause them to act out. Once they got to flyin' high and above it all and feelin' the power, you know what? The first thing they wanted to do is run into somebody they could oppress and exploit."

"Oh, spare me the philosophy!" I scrolled to one of the classes I wanted to take, only to find it was already filled. "Like that gives them the right to hold up two innocent people at gunpoint—"

"Why not? They learned it from y'all —" Ernest mumbled to his screen.

"That's just fine and dandy! Show the oppressed and exploited all the love and compassion they need, and excuse and forgive all their crimes. That right, Ernest? After all, they're only modeling their behavior after their white oppressors, right?"

I looked over at Ernest's screen and saw he was taking the same class I was clicking on in my own schedule. He nodded as he scrolled it down.

"Now you feel me."

"You taking that class, too?"

"Yeah."

"Ernest, that's the most hokey thing I ever heard anybody say!"

"Look, it's over, Amelia. Like the Big Man said; 'Case Dismissed.'"

"That's rich. You've already taken their side in the matter. I guess you might as well quote their words of wisdom on top of that."

Ernest glared at me glinting anger and a hint of rancor.

"I'm through with it, Amelia. See you in class,"

He got up and went over to the printer. When his class schedule came out, he snatched it out of the bin and left the Registration room. Ernest didn't cast so much as a backward glance my way. I know because I was looking. I shrugged my shoulder and went on scanning for classes to fill out my class schedule.

I thought it was nothing, but after a few minutes, I started having this unsettled feeling. The next thing I knew I was vaguely uneasy and feeling vulnerable. Before I knew it, I don't know; you could say something akin to remorse started to settle about my shoulders and work its way down inside me. Which struck me as strange, since I really didn't have anything to be remorseful about.

When Ernest didn't show up for class the second time, I became concerned. I found myself looking towards the door the way I did when I was in the Registration room. The teacher called his name now that he was handing out the syllabuses.

"'Ernest Randall'?" He looked around to see who would raise their hand. "Anybody know what happened to Ernest Randall?" The teacher tapped his lectern and tossed the syllabus onto a separate pile. "Does anybody know how to get in contact with him?"

When I saw that nobody was going to speak up, I decided to raise my hand.

"Are you going to see him before we meet for class next time?"

"There's a chance I will. I—I have his address?"

"That's fine." The teacher barely looked up from his notes at me. "Why don't you see that he gets this syllabus; uh, Miss Dougherty, isn't it? Maybe you can see what he's planning to do."

"I will, sir."

"Good. 'Howard Kitchner'–?"

What I realized after thumbing through the scripts Ernest sent me was that I did have his address, but I never got his telephone number from him. I know I should have my head examined for going back down to that hospital all by my lonesome, but in my defense, I went in broad daylight and parked in a well-lighted parking area out in the open; not in that darn parking structure. I resolved not to stay until it was dark this time.

"Hi, Mister Randall," I said, as I cradled my package in my arms. "- have you seen Ernest by any chance?"

The elderly gentleman appeared to be all but completely withered away. There was this energy pouring out of him in much the same way that a green plant releases carbon dioxide. The only thing was he did not seem to be getting back much in the exchange. He was more like some kind of kind of vapor escaping its husk for the final exhalation of release.

"Ho! Who's that there?" The old man asked in a scratchy, sibilant tone. "That you, Ernest? That you?"

I saw his hand rise up out of his bed and I took the wrinkled and knotted knuckles into my own.

"No, Mr. Randall. This is his friend. I'm Amelia Dougherty. I came by to see you. I thought you might know where Randall is."

"That you, Ernest? Why you take so long gettin' here? I thought you were going to read to me some. You still gon' read to me, aren't ya?"

"No, I—"

"You don't have to read me Proverbs this time. Read me something from one of them books you call yo'self writin' alla time."

"No, Mister Randall, I'm not —"

"Yeah, read me something. Read me something you wrote. I wanna see how good it is. Read it to me, son."

"You want to hear something I wrote?"

"Why, that's what I been countin' on. You keep braggin' on it so much."

"Well, it's not so much, really—"

"Let me be the judge of that. C'mon man, hold my hand and read me some. That's not too much to ask, is it?"

The old man's grip on my fingers tightened.

"I think I need to sit down, Mister Randall—"

"There's a chair over there somewheres. Now read to me some."

I drew my chair up to his bed and pulled out the first chapter of my novel. I started to read and I think he liked it. I could kind of tell because of the way a smile settled on his face. We sat there for awhile and I read to him, expecting Ernest to show up at any moment.